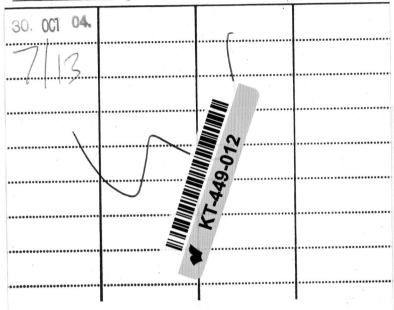

PRIVATE PAPERS

Margaret Forster

Chatto & Windus

LONDON

Published in 1986 by
Chatto & Windus Ltd
40 William IV Street
London WC2N 4DF

British Library Cataloguing in Publication Data

Forster, Margaret
Private papers.
I. Title
823'.914[F]   PR6056.0695
ISBN 0—7011—2987—5

Typeset at The Spartan Press Ltd
Lymington, Hants
Printed in Great Britain by
Redwood Burn Ltd
Trowbridge, Wiltshire

for my mother-in-law
MARION BRECHIN DAVIES
to whom family
has always been all

What *is* this?

*

— and lies about the past are so safe, so very unlikely to be exposed. I have been frightened by their distortions. Listening to them, all three of them, I have found it impossible to believe that *they* can believe what they are saying about their own lives. None of them seems to have any recollection of choices being made, decisions taken, paths chosen. I am given to understand that either everything that happened was in some way my fault or that it was random. How extraordinarily convenient. I have three daughters who have apparently wiped from their memories the part they played in their own lives. They need me, it seems, to bear witness. And I shall, I shall tell you, and if —

*

Who *is* she talking to, writing for? Is this a diary or a letter?

*

— and if what I write seems confusing you must be tolerant. Life does seem confusing and those who seek to impose a pattern upon it cannot expect to find it easy. I have to imagine a stranger as I write, I have to create a stern, judge-like figure to whom I must address myself, or, otherwise, this will disintegrate into a rambling, incoherent sequence of memories. Memories there will be, I have no evidence without them, but this is not a memoir, not in any way an autobiography, though it will be inevitable that, in the process of setting the record straight, a great deal of my own life must be gone over. It is relevant, for a start, to say something about my own birth. I was born —

*

Oh, Christ. Now I begin to see it. If I don't stop now, put this pencil down – and how very conveniently placed it happens to be, sitting so provocatively on top of this neat pile of virgin paper – she'll have me hooked. I should walk out, now.

*

— born on, or around, December 26th 1915. I was found on the morning of December 31st on the steps of a Children's Home, near Oxford, on the Abingdon road. I was securely and warmly wrapped against the intense cold in four shawls and lay in a small wickerwork basket of the type commonly used for putting wood in. To the top shawl was pinned a note saying my name was Penelope and would someone please take care of me. Nothing else. No other evidence of maternal care or tenderness. I weighed only five and a half pounds but was in good health. It was quickly established that I was no more than four or five days old and that I was probably born prematurely (there were little flecks of a creamy-like substance in the folds of my skin, a sure sign). The cord was still attached to my navel, two inches of that rapidly withering tissue which had held me to my mother, but it had been expertly cut and tied, suggesting that the services of a midwife or other medical person had been employed.

In those days, it was difficult to trace the mother of an abandoned baby. Nobody took my photograph and printed it in a newspaper. The local hospitals were not subjected to close scrutiny nor were doctors and district nurses closely questioned about recent confinements in the area. Some forty years later, when I set about trying to trace my birth I found no written record of any enquiries at all, and, naturally, neither the shawls nor the basket nor, more importantly, the note survived. I had been told about those but nobody had thought fit to keep them. The shawls, I expect, were washed and used many times until they were torn up to provide rags with which to wash the floors. The basket would be filled and emptied until the straw split and frayed. But the note should have been filed away, surely. Probably it is as well that it was not. I would have become obsessed with it. The handwriting, the very composition of the words, the colour of the ink (was it ink or pencil?) and the texture of the paper would have had a terrible fascination for me. I would have fingered that note, held it against my cheek, smelled it, even. I would have examined it more ferociously than the most zealous of forensic scientists. It was, I believe, kept for some years and then 'lost' when the Home closed down. No one could ever appreciate what it would have meant to me.

But I had a name. The note may have been consigned to bureaucratic oblivion, if not actually torn up and destroyed (the thought of this vandalism causes me pain), but the name written upon it was at once transcribed onto several documents. I was Penelope, the name my mother had chosen and cared enough about to pass on to those to whom she was surrendering me. This was of tremendous importance to me – not only that my mysterious mother had bothered to name me, but also the name itself. Shakespeare cannot have been an abandoned baby to wonder what was in a name. Everything, I could tell him. For me my name was invested with a holy significance. It seemed, among other things, a clear message. Why call me Penelope if the legend was not meant to be meaningful? I learned at school about the wife of Ulysses, who had waited ten long years for his return, resisting all those suitors who tried to persuade her he was dead. I thrilled to the triumphant end of the story, when Ulysses returned safe and well to the faithful Penelope. I, too, would be faithful. I would believe that somewhere my mother, like Ulysses, was fighting some war, was undertaking her own personal Odyssey, and would one day return to claim me. I would be there, as patient and enduring as the wife of Ulysses.

Well, I was ten years old before I read the story in *Myths and Legends of Ancient Greece*. By the time I was fifteen I had faced what seemed to be the facts: my mother, unlike Ulysses, was not going to return nor, in our modern world, was she going to avail herself of the opportunity to telephone or write. But my name still seemed significant. I began to think about it in a different but equally romantic way. Nobody else in the Home was called Penelope, nor was anyone in the school I attended. When people in authority, meeting me for the first time, asked me for my Christian name, they were always surprised. They would raise their eyebrows, and sometimes smile and look at me again more sharply. Penelope was a rather grand, even pretentious, name for a child from a Home to have. I saw it gained me some small consideration, some status, which I would not otherwise have immediately rated. And so I began to think my mother must have been an educated person. This was a great relief to me at that stage, as I was becoming aware of the kind of woman or girl who usually abandoned babies. My great fear that this mother of mine had been 'a loose woman', a term I hardly understood but certainly heard, was soothed by the thought of my name. Later, I fantasized further. My mother, I decided, might have been at the University (of my father I never then thought). My birth would have wrecked her career and she would have had no option but to abandon me. This theory gave me such comfort that, even as an adult, I was reluctant to admit its inherent absurdity, although I had by then certainly appreciated how very few women could go to University at the time I was born.

At one stage in my young life I used to walk the streets of Oxford with pounding heart, waiting to be recognized. I had spent many, many hours, as adolescents do, examining my face and body in mirrors, wondering about all those ancestors of mine whose genes were my inheritance. My complexion, I felt, must be a very strong family trait. When I was young I had wonderful colouring, brown (but not olive skinned) in all weathers and bright pink cheeks. Somewhere there were grandparents and great aunts and second cousins once removed, who would take one look at me and declare *how* Penelope has the family look! Then there was my hair, extremely black, extremely thick. It gave me, with my complexion, a gypsy look (that, of course, was another fantasy, for I also learned that according to old Welsh tales gypsies used the name Penelope, in the form Peneli, for fairies). I was sure my mother must look the same, that she too walked around with the same startling colouring. The connexion between us would be unmistakable. Our eyes would meet as we passed in the High Street and her heart would thump too. She would cry out my name and we would embrace and then she would take me home, to my family . . . I wanted that family as much as I wanted a mother. No child in a Home ever underestimates the overriding importance of having a family. It meant more than simply having brothers and sisters, aunts and uncles. It was so much more extensive, stretching wide and deep, a complicated network of hidden strength. Family meant support, it meant belonging, it meant confidence, it meant claims. Even when the pull of family was cursed it was acknowledged as undeniable. My idea of happiness was to have a family, with all its onerous ties and responsibilities, to which to belong. Even an adoptive or foster family would have sufficed. Throughout those years children from the Home were regularly adopted or fostered out and my longing to be one of the chosen was desperate. But I never was. I remember once —

Oh *shit* – it's obvious I'm going to carry on reading this, I can't control my own curiosity. And this pencil is doing a St Vitus Dance in my hand with the need to put my own comments down. But I can't stand reading it all, so I'll just have to skip when it gets too much. I'm not going to read this next bit, for example. I know it all, I was reared on it, I know exactly what is coming. It always made me furious, her tale of being inspected by a couple who came looking for a 'nice little girl' and being rejected and crying for a week and thinking she must be ugly or that she stank and all that tedious rubbish. Furious with her, not the couple. Furious that she told the pathetic story at all, furious at the expression on her face – tremulous, solemn, sickly. She wanted us to fling our arms around her and cry and say poor, poor Mummy. All I ever wanted to do was shout at her. This evidence of how vulnerable she was as a child disgusted me. The point of regaling us with this stuff was always so apparent. *We* had not been abandoned, *we* were wanted and loved, *we* had a family. We, in short, were much, much better off than she had been and she wasn't going to let us forget it. Everything was meant to flow from this wonderfully privileged start. As if it mattered, basically: as if whether you've got a secure family background really makes a shred of difference in the end. Well, that's silly. There are millions of reports saying it does. But Mother didn't have to make it into a religion, thrusting our advantage down our throats all the time. She might have known we would sick it up in the end. Look what a fool she made of herself over my father's family – we'll be on to that in a page or so, doubtless.

*

— would even have welcomed what Florence Nightingale called 'the *tyranny* of a good English family'. I do not want to describe my life in the Home nor touch upon my circumstances more than I have already done. It will be obvious, to all but the most unaware and insensitive, that I suffered severe emotional deprivation quite apart from the sort of hardship common to children brought up in Homes in the inter-war years. It does not bear going into, not here. By the time I was eighteen and free of the Home's guardianship, I had stopped looking back and was instead looking forward, greedily, for my missing family. I was in training to be a nurse. Again, I lived in a Home, straight from one into the other, and it was hardly more congenial than the first. Again, life was hard and, again, I lacked affection and emotional security. There were rules and regulations governing our entire lives, most of them relics from the nineteenth century. I stood the discipline better than any of the other student nurses – it was nothing to me to have to work hard, to be vigilantly supervised or to lack privacy. I was used to such a regime. In fact, life without dragooning of one sort or another might have been difficult for me to accept. So I thrived where others wilted. It was an asset not to have Mummy or Daddy to whom to return home. When my training was complete I still lived, by choice, in the Nurses' Home, having neither the courage nor the money to set up on my own. Yet I dreamed of my own place all the time. Yes, it was a cottage and, yes, there were roses round the door. And inside was a husband with his slippers by the fire, and upstairs babies, my babies, in their beds. One day my prince would come and, when he did, he would not only create a family with me, but he would take me home to his family and I would be absorbed into the fabric of their corporate existence. It was a terrible, crushing disappointment to me that when I did fall in love, and was married, it was to a man with virtually no family.

Oliver was always fond of telling people that I had almost turned him down because he only had a mother. He said my eyes filled with tears when he told me and my arms dropped from round his neck to hang despondently at my sides. All he had was a mother for whom he had little feeling, someone to whom he rarely wrote and whom he saw perhaps twice a year. She, Mrs Butler, was a widow, and (as Oliver was) an only child of only children. Moreover she had been born in India and had few connections with England even though she chose, unwisely, to return here after the death of her husband. Oliver's father had been the last of his own particular family. Somewhere in Scotland and, it was rumoured, Australia, there may have been some extremely distant cousins but, if so, Oliver had never known them – they were vague names, perhaps mentioned once or twice in his hearing as living in Fife, or Melbourne, but never established as real people. No, there was no getting away from it: I, who had craved multitudes of in-laws, had married into the smallest family unit possible. Nor could I for very long cling to the comforting thought that at least I was to have a mother-in-law. Once I had met Mrs Butler (she never allowed me to call her by her Christian name and was appalled at my timid suggestion that I might refer to her as Mother) it was clear that there would be little joy in that relationship.

Once the children were born, I gave Mrs Butler, or Grandmother Butler as she insisted on being addressed, a position of great reverence in our lives. To Oliver's bewilderment, since he was the least filial of sons, I inaugurated a regime of dutiful visits which must have puzzled her. Since Oliver was her only child I don't think even in her most suspicious moments that she thought I was after her money (she was quite wealthy). She knew I knew Oliver would get everything, no question of that. But considering we never got on, and that she was quite openly contemptuous of me as a wife for her son, I should imagine she was rather startled at my refusal to be put off visiting. We went to Brighton, where she lived, at least every two weeks. Sometimes we drove down for the day – oh what a lovely drive it was in those days – but more often we stayed at The Old Ship for the weekend. In the early years we stayed only once with Grandmother Butler, just before Rosemary was born: she made it plain that visitors were 'not convenient'. She did not like us actually to sleep in her house, extraordinary though that is to believe. Oliver did not care. For his part, he hated staying there. He only went along with my desire to visit, because he happened to be fond of Brighton itself. If his mother had lived in Macclesfield or Manchester, I doubt very much whether I would have been able to get him to agree.

I loved Grandmother Butler's house. It was in Bedford Square, one of those beautiful Regency squares of which Brighton is full, just across the road from the West Pier. It was four storeyed, with an elegant balcony on the first floor curving round a long bow window. Later, when we lived there, we had the two top floors, and our sitting room was the one above the balcony. It was an enormous room, also with a bow window facing south west, with the pier dominating the view. I used to lie for hours on the window seat looking out over the channel, quite hypnotized by the tides. From the attics above, where we slept, our view over the rooftops was superb, more of the sea and, to the left, a glimpse of the Downs. I never grew tired of this view. Nor did I mind the endless toiling up and down the many narrow stairs. The kitchen of course was in a rather dark, narrow basement. There was no garden, but with the beach literally a hundred yards away we had no need of one. It seemed to me the perfect family house. Several rooms were big enough to hold a large number of people in comfort and it was so arranged that, if necessary, everyone could get away from everyone else. I thought, when first I went there, of children playing violins at the top of the house and of Oliver studying at the back, while I sewed in the quiet rooms below: all of us separate but together. I thought of family meals round the great oak table in the dining room and family parties spilling onto the gracious balcony. I thought of all those stairs pounded by hundreds of busy feet and the basement area full of prams and bikes. I thought of babies being born there and the perfection of having that healthy sea air to hand. Every Sunday, as we sat in state with Grandmother Butler and her companion, four people lost in the brocaded sofas and rich carpets (brought from India), I thought of the same room filled with family life. I longed to live there.

Where we actually lived, when we first visited Bedford Square, was in a small cramped flat not far from University College Hospital, where Oliver was a houseman. Our nearest tube was Mornington Crescent but we were close enough to walk to the hospital where I also worked, as a nurse in the Children's Ward. We had married on April 11th 1934, as soon as Oliver completed his clinical studies at the Radcliffe Infirmary in Oxford. We could have afforded somewhere more salubrious, since Oliver had some money of his own, but we were saving to buy our own house as soon as he qualified – we had a three year plan. Yet, strangely, it was no part of our plan to prevent the birth of children. We chose not to. Other people, in particular Grandmother Butler, might think it folly for us to have a child at that stage, but we did not. We wanted to start our family immediately. We hated that 'wait-until' attitude – wait until Oliver is qualified, wait until you have a nice flat or house, wait until you've been married a while, wait until you're older. No wait-untils, thank you. Rosemary, our first child, was born a year to the day after our marriage and nobody could have been happier than I was. We named her Rosemary for remembrance, remembrance for all time of our intense happiness. All was brilliantly radiant around me —

*

Jesus Christ. Who wants to be a remembrance of someone else's happiness? Especially as I cannot remember this so-called divine bliss.

8

I was only nine when the love's-young-dream act ended. It's all legend, Mother's legend. Another saga we were told and re-told, and hurt her by groaning and not wanting to hear *yet* again. How perfect it had been – The First Meeting, The Engagement, The Wedding, The Honeymoon, etc., etc. A hospital romance, smouldering eyes over gauze masks and heavy breathing under the starched white gowns. Young Doctor Butler and young Nurse Penelope. Oh la. Whirlwind courtship but no slap-and-tickle – wasn't nice, not part of the package. 'All was brilliantly radiant around me,' she boasts. Oh yeah, as Emily used to say when she was little, oh yeah? Who says so? Apart from her? What has *she* wiped from her memory? One rather important thing for a start. My father was married before. Spoils the scenario a bit, I think. She never told us and of course he never had a chance to. I wonder if he ever would have done, and how? Grandmother Butler told me, with malice and definite forethought. What an evil old bitch she was. She told me about six months after my father was killed, when Mother was ill after having Emily, and Celia, Jess and I were packed off to Brighton with Linda, the girl who helped to look after us. We went to stay with Grandmother Butler in this Bedford Square place Mother drools about – horrible dump – for a week. By that time it stank. Grandmother Butler still had plenty of money but she couldn't keep servants, not even a cleaning lady, so the house was filthy and neglected. How on earth Mother persuaded her to have us, I cannot imagine, because she made it clear from our arrival that she resented our very presence. I remember we all huddled together in one bed and cried. Jess wet the bed in the middle of the night and we cried even harder because we were too frightened to get up and go and find Linda in the dark. We lay awake the rest of the night, Celia and I, worrying about what Grandmother Butler would say if she found out about the sodden sheets. (Ironic, really, when she was probably just into wetting her own sheets and pretending she hadn't.) Linda washed them next day in the sea and we spread them out in a secluded spot on the beach, anchored with stones, and nobody ever knew. We sat and giggled at how mortified Grandmother Butler would be if she knew where her sheets were on display and why – 'mortified' was one of her favourite words.

The weather was brilliant, surprisingly hot and sunny, and we lived on that beach from seven in the morning until dark. Linda was marvellous. She may have been only sixteen and no intellectual giant (her grammatical errors certainly 'mortified' Grandmother Butler when we innocently copied them) but she was loving and she was fun. She knew, of course, that our father was by that time 'previously reported missing believed killed in action now presumed killed in action'. She knew we hadn't been told, because Mother went on hoping and never gave away, by the smallest hint, that every sensible person believed him dead. When Grandmother Butler wept and wailed and sighed over us, which she did daily, and when she called us poor fatherless little girls, Linda helped us ignore her. When I asked her what Grandma meant, Linda said, at her most placid and phlegmatic, that she just meant Father wasn't with us. Beautifully simple. How different from the convoluted answers Mother gave.

So we had a good week. We swam in the icy water, got sunburned, and quarrelled a great deal less than normal. If it hadn't been for wanting to see Mother and the new baby again, we wouldn't have wanted to go home, in spite of being frightened of Grandmother. I think I was more frightened than Celia or Jess but I pretended not to be. It was expected by them, by everyone, that being the eldest I should be the bravest. I tried hard to live up to that expectation. And I must have succeeded, because Grandmother Butler made me her favourite. She said I was exactly like my father (and also, inevitably, what a pity it was I had not been a boy). The former claim at least was totally untrue. I was exactly like my mother to look at and, as for temperament or personality, Grandmother Butler could hardly claim to be an expert on my father, even though he was her son. So far as I can make out, she hardly knew him. He was sent back to England, to prep school, at seven, and even before that he'd been looked after by amahs. But the point was that Grandmother Butler wanted me to be a Butler so she simply decided I was one. Butlers were brave, outspoken, independent, proud, clever, honest and possessed of all the other dreary Victorian virtues. The biggest compliment was to be told one was *pure* Butler, untainted by whatever genes came through my mother's side. That, of course, was a source of great trouble. Grandmother Butler never left off, not for a single minute if the subject came up, never stopped muttering darkly about Mother's 'doubtful origins'. She despised her for not having a family and made her suffer acutely. Considering Mother herself feels exactly about family as Grandmother did, it was all rather painfully unnecessary. But Grandmother simply had to find a way of letting me know that, not only was my mother tainted by not belonging to a family, she was also a mere substitute for someone who had, in this respect, met with her approval.

One evening, just before we went back to London, Grandmother Butler took me into what she called her boudoir. This was a foul little over-decorated room leading off her utterly repulsive bedroom. It was difficult to move about anywhere in that house since it was so stuffed with furniture, but in the boudoir it was quite impossible. Everything in that tiny cupboard of a room was purple – carpet, curtains, cloth on the round little table, chair-cover. Dark purple, stifling. Grandmother manoeuvred her bulk round the table and into the chair and patted the arm of the chair for me to perch on (there was no space for another chair, not even a stool). I don't remember exactly what she said, though I remember the gist, but I do remember most vividly her expressions and the general atmosphere. I knew I was nervous, wary, on my guard. I didn't want to be there alone with my grandmother. Physically, she was repulsive. She was small and squat with a great shelf-like bosom that seemed to collect foodstains, however carefully she ate. Her hair was a dirty grey, cropped into an ugly square shape round her ears – almost geometric, like a clipped privet hedge. She wore heavy, long earrings made of jade or jet, set in antique silver casings. They were much too large for her fat face and made her look absurd. Her eyes were black and piggy, lost in the podginess above her cheeks. When she smiled, which was never with conviction, they disappeared entirely. But it was her arms and legs I hated most. They appeared to be solid, straight blocks of muscle without any of the normal indents for knees or elbows. One looked in horror at Grandmother Butler's limbs and wondered if they could bend. Maybe I am being cruel, maybe her arthritis made it difficult to bend them and that was why she held her arms and legs so rigid and stiff, seeming to work them from some swivel at the top. She looked like a badly made, over-stuffed guy on a bonfire, one you knew would burn beautifully with all that straw in it.

On her lap was an album with a slightly soiled, white velvet cover. With her arms hanging over the sides of the chair, the only position in which they ever seemed to be comfortable, she indicated by a nod of her head that I was to open the album. I did so fearfully, wondering what dreadful thing I should see, wondering how soon I could get away from the sour smell that seemed to envelop the entire room. As I opened the album, Grandmother said something about seeing photographs my mother had never seen and it must be my secret, as Mother might be upset and we didn't want that, did we. Even at nine I swear I sensed the hypocrisy. I knew Grandmother Butler lived for upsetting my mother. But I opened the album and there was nothing in the least nasty in it. On the contrary. I stared at a lovely photograph of a handsome young man. I stared at it for some time, knowing the face seemed familiar but not quite sure why, until Grandmother murmured that it was my father when he was very young, wasn't he splendid. I turned the page and there was another photograph of a girl I was quite sure I had never known. She was slight, pretty, with frothy blonde curls all round her face. I remember her teeth were slightly prominent. But I still didn't twig why I was being shown this album, until I turned the next page and there was my father and this girl together and in different clothes. Wedding clothes. My father was in topper and tails, the girl clinging to his arm almost lost in the cascading lace of her white dress and veil. Grandmother Butler said, 'Aren't they beautiful, quite perfect, but then it was a perfect day, perfect wedding. She was a Dacre-Dunnett you know, very old family and of course they know how to do these things, terribly grand. Poor child. Poor Oliver.' I didn't speak. I didn't ask any of the questions a normal, inquisitive nine year old would have been expected to. But Grandmother Butler wasn't put off. She talked and talked in her special pretend-sad way that I hated. I had to keep turning the pages and looking at more and more photographs of wedding cakes and flowers and endless groups of over-dressed people. Grandmother told me who they all were but I didn't take any of it in. Why should I have done – it meant nothing to me. I was upset, without knowing why, but determined not to let her see. She went on and on about them – the bridal pair – being poor, poor loves and far too young to marry, only twenty and eighteen, but it was what they wanted and who could stand in their way. I still didn't say a word. When I had got to the end of the book, I got down from the arm of the chair and walked off. I don't remember Grandmother trying to stop me. Her job was done, I suppose. The amazing thing was that I didn't tell a soul and I have never to this day told my mother. It sounds ridiculous, all these years later, but it is the truth. At the time, though, I thought about nothing else for weeks and even now, if something triggers my memory, I can spend hours speculating about my father's first secret marriage – secret from us, I mean. I assume the child bride died. There could not have been any children – my mother would never have allowed any of my father's children to be excluded from his life. I suppose I could quite easily find out, if I wanted to, but that has always been the trouble – I'm not sure I do want to. I've always felt it would be indecent while Mother is still alive. Reading this is indecent, too, I suppose. Mother is in the next door room, chatting to Celia. 'There are boxes and boxes of photographs, darling,' she said, 'you take your pick.' All I did was to look for them, and found this. Yet I feel furtive. And I feel as if I'm doing something dangerous. Why am I so agitated? Oh, for Christ's sake – I'll have to go back to them in a minute anyway.

*

— all was brilliantly radiant around me, though in the greater world outside our own happiness everything was becoming very dark and ominous indeed. Oliver read *The Times* assiduously every day and worried about the future. He was sure there was going to be a war even when *The Times* thought there would not be. I didn't like him to talk about it. It annoyed me that he should make himself deliberately unhappy, just when he ought to be the opposite. He had qualified, he loved his work, we had moved to a lovely flat in Primrose Hill, we had a darling baby – why must he fret about things that had nothing to do with us? I am ashamed now.

The girls say their childhoods were ruined by the war. That is untrue. They do not seem to appreciate how many years of complete happiness they were privileged to have before the war ever happened, and those years cannot be discounted because of what came afterwards. Their childhoods, particularly Rosemary's, were happy, I insist. Even Emily, born fatherless, had a happy childhood. I know. I was there and saw. My memory stretches back to those years effortlessly and I am *quite sure*. I don't want to go into humdrum detail or drag out my old diaries to substantiate my case. I have, in my head, clear and vivid pictures of three laughing, normal, happy children and that is enough to —

*

Wrong, as ever. She doesn't bloody see how she falsifies things. How arrogant; she has this sloppy inner picture show of us 'happy' and that is pronounced 'enough'. QED. If it wasn't so irritating, it would be funny. Mother doesn't even realize when she is suppressing things. And she makes what people call Freudian slips. She says 'three' laughing, normal, etc. children, but there were four of us. Surely she isn't going to leave Jess out? I hardly think so, not if this is about putting some kind of record straight so that she can confront us with these choices we made, whatever they were. Jess was her choice and a bad one. Disastrous. But she can't be forgotten just because she spoils the symmetry of Mother's mental pictures. I wish she'd get on to Jess. Quickly, before she loses all credibility. I'm tired already of this foolish pretence that she's addressing some boring old fart of a judge and not me. All this is for me. I know it is, I'm sure of it. So what should I do about it? March out, clutching it, saying what the hell have you been playing at, Mother? Yet all my instincts are to keep quiet, to be as secretive as Mother herself.

*

— to make me state with assurance that the war 'ruined' their childhood is a lie. It changed it, but it did not ruin it. Celia, Jess and Emily were all war babies and Rosemary was only four when war was declared, but their experience of war, or of suffering the effects of it, was slight. Everything went on in their little lives more or less as it had always done. Even Oliver's absence was not the traumatic thing it might have been, because they saw so little of him anyway. He worked long hours and spent most of his time at the hospital. I was the major feature in their lives and I was always there. I am not denying that the war *affected* us. Of course it did. But I think people forget how life for many women and children appeared to go on much the same. Once Oliver had gone off to the war, our lives closed in. It was Rosemary, Celia and me against the world. And Jessica. Quite secure in our home, whether in London or Brighton. Every day the same reassuring routine: Rosemary trotting off to school, Celia playing contentedly in the garden while I got on with the usual jobs mothers do, perhaps more harassed than most because of the state of the house. And because of Jessica, because having Jessica was really too much.

I cannot accuse my daughters of not facing up to what they have done to their own lives, while bewailing accidents of fate, if I do not acknowledge my own mistakes. Deliberate ones. Times when I made major decisions which had a direct bearing upon their future. But what

14

words will serve to relate something so delicate? Whatever I say will shock – shock me apart from anyone else. I can only tell the truth as it happened and hope it makes its own sense. Oliver came home one night from the hospital very cast down and despondent. It was the spring of 1940 and he had not then joined up, but I know now that he thought of little else. He had become silent and withdrawn, totally obsessed with the progress of the war, constantly debating with himself the moral niceties of doing what he was doing. The hospital had prepared itself for action, sandbags had been installed everywhere and wards cleared for expected casualties. But of course, to some extent, normal hospital life also continued. Babies were born there, even though the maternity unit was officially evacuated. People were operated upon, the usual emergencies took place. Oliver worked harder and harder, mostly sleeping in the basement of the hospital at night. I was lucky if I had him at home one night a week.

Celia had been born on New Year's Day and we had moved into our house the following month. It was a large, flat-fronted Victorian villa in Primrose Hill, just one street away from the park. We moved in the worst possible conditions and found our house in an appalling state. It was not that we had not known it would be, but the actual extent of the damp, the bulging ceilings, the non-functioning plumbing was so much worse than remembered. Everything seemed too much. When I wept at the filth everywhere, Oliver would remind me that outside there was a war going on: what were my problems compared to that?

On this particular night, Oliver was even more morose than usual and I was even more exhausted. All that we had to say to each other, it seemed, was that we were so tired. Then Oliver began to talk about his day. A young girl, not more than eighteen, had been admitted the night before and he had been detailed to attend to her. She had come to the Salvation Army Hostel near King's Cross, where she had collapsed. They sent for an ambulance and she was brought into UCH. She was heavily pregnant and very ill – not with the pregnancy but for all sorts of other reasons. Oliver had quickly established that she was suffering from a number of serious conditions, all of which had been aggravated by becoming pregnant. She refused to give her name or age or to say where she was from or what had happened. She appeared absolutely passive, accepting whatever was done to her, neither resisting nor helping. Yet she obviously exerted some kind of fascination, or Oliver would not have bothered telling me about her. He quickly regretted doing so, for of course I identified immediately with this girl. My old fantasies about my unknown mother returned to plague me. I imagined her, like this poor girl, ill and distressed, lying friendless in some ward, disapproved of by everyone, too miserable and weak to defend herself. Every day after that I made it my business to find out about Mrs Victoria as she was known – every expectant mother was Mrs in those days, married or not, and the Victoria part was taken from the name of the ward. Oliver reported that she was holding her own. Her main problem was that she only had one kidney and that the other was infected. For such a young girl, she was a ruin. And yet, as some strength returned to her, she began to win over everyone who looked after her. She still did not talk much, but she smiled and was grateful, and all the staff were impressed by her stoicism and by her determination to keep her baby. About that she was adamant.

I would like to have visited her. I wanted to be her friend, to help her, but Oliver would not allow it. He said if I visited I might be starting a relationship I could not maintain, and I would do his patient more harm than good. And he said my desire to go to see her was not healthy. I was not prompted by genuinely altruistic motives but by morbid ones. We quarrelled and I became upset, but he would not relent. I suppose I suspected he was right. I never did see her. Oliver himself delivered her baby by Caesarean section on June 21st 1940. It was a girl, a fine healthy girl weighing seven pounds two ounces. Mrs Victoria died three days later. She had seemed to stand the delivery so well, but then her one defective kidney packed up and there was very little they could do. The hospital staff were sad, inured though they were to such tragedies. But I was distraught with grief. What would happen to the baby? Oliver was impatient with my anxiety. The child would be well looked after. By whom, by whom, I demanded? He did not know, he said it was not his job to know, by some orphanage he supposed, and at that word I burst into tears. I wanted Mrs Victoria's baby, passionately. I begged and pleaded with Oliver to adopt her straight away, to bring her home at once. My passion scared him. He tried to calm me, suggested we should discuss it rationally like the two sensible adults we were but I was incapable of logical reasoning. I did not feel in the least sensible. There was a baby, its mother dead, nobody else wanting it and I wanted it: that was the only argument I could understand. Oliver made the fatal mistake of saying we knew nothing about Mrs Victoria, we could not know what we were taking on, we did not even know if others had a claim on this child. I said he knew nothing about me, it was exactly the same and yet he had taken me for myself alone. He said that was different: I was a mature person and – oh, it went on and on. Oliver grew weary of my persistence. He said he was worn out, too drained to battle with me. He added bitterly that it seemed as if I cared more for this child of a girl I had never known, than I did for my own children. What kind of state did I think I would be in if I took on yet another baby? As it was, I could hardly cope with the house, it was the worst time in our lives to be thinking of increasing our problems, I must be mad to contemplate adopting Mrs Victoria's baby even if we could. And he said it would be unethical, which started off another dispute.

I won in the end. Oliver was never convinced, but he gave in. Perhaps he had himself been more moved by the child he had delivered than he cared to admit. He said it was against his better judgement, but he would make enquiries. Maybe it would be our little extra war effort, he said. Duty swung Oliver over, but it had no part in my decision. I *craved* for that baby, for Jess. Jess came to us at two weeks, straight from the hospital, and I was indescribably moved by the sight of her. She was exquisite. Next to Celia, who was by then a plump six months, Jess looked fragile and delicate, though in fact she was exceptionally robust. She was fair skinned, with downy blonde fuzz all over her head and funny little wisps of longer hair growing on the nape of her neck. Her head was beautifully shaped, small and neat, and her features tiny. Naming her had been a solemn business. Oliver suggested Victoria but I did not like the idea of naming her after a public ward. If only we had known her mother's name, but we did not. When I went to collect Jess I talked to the two young nurses who had had most to do with Mrs Victoria and asked them if she had ever mentioned names for her baby. They said no, but that, when she heard one of their names was Jessica, she had said how pretty it was and that her grandmother had been called that. So we called her Jessica, after her great-grandmother, and I was consoled by this connection. Jessica would be told she had a *family* name.

One of the things I made sure of was that everything that had belonged to Mrs Victoria came home with Jess. Everything, every last rag and her things were mostly rags. I carefully washed and ironed them and put them away in a box. There was a brown dress, a red cardigan, a pair of thick fawn woollen stockings, a black cape and a Paisley-patterned fringed shawl. The shoes, broken down at the heel and with holes in the soles, I did throw out as too dreadful to keep. There was also a cheap, black plastic handbag containing a lace-bordered handkerchief embroidered with the initial M – perhaps her name was Mary? – and a tin of sweets, boiled sweets. The hospital gave me, in an envelope, the gold chain that had been round Mrs Victoria's neck and a ring, a gaudy thing, bright blue stones in a cluster with a 'diamond' in the centre. When Jess was old enough I would have some tangible proof that her mother had existed. I would show her the clothes —

*

Those ghastly clothes. That was so awful for Jess. I wasn't there when Mother produced them but Jess described it all so clearly that I could touch her pain. We weren't poor, that was the point, never had been except perhaps for a brief interval I was too young to remember. As far back as I can remember, we were always comfortable, and that was at a time when a lot of people round us were not. So what shocked poor Jess was the poverty those clothes symbolized. It wouldn't be the same today – even Vanessa, Emily's daughter, went through a phase of wearing rags all the time, deliberately, smelling and stinking, all holes, straight from the jumble. But young girls didn't, then, not on purpose. I saw them myself later and saw what Jess had meant. The dress was the worst, an old woman's dress, horrible, scratchy sort of material, absolutely shapeless but then, as she was pregnant, Jess's mother I mean, that was useful. It was the ugliest dress in the world. It had a square neck with rows of black ric-rac round it and two *bobbles* hanging from the button at the top. You would've thought at least she could've cut the bobbles off. It was patched under the arms, presumably to cover up the place the previous owner had worn away with sweating. You couldn't imagine any young, beautiful girl putting it on. None of the other things were as upsetting, except the tawdry jewellery. Mother had kept the chain and ring carefully, but they'd both gone black, not being real gold. They looked worse than Christmas cracker rubbish. Jess wouldn't touch them, of course. She said she wanted everything burned, they gave her the creeps. Mother made a little speech about how *she* had always wished she had had something, anything, of her mother's and that was why she had kept them.

That was always the trouble – Mother always expected Jess to identify with her. Always. That one fact, that they were both orphans from birth, was supposed to bind them together automatically. And it didn't. It wasn't even the same, Jess once said to me, not really the same. *She* had not been given away, her mother had died but if she had not died she would have kept her. She resented my mother equating their circumstances. And she had been chosen, by us, by a family. Mother never had, she knew nothing about what it was like living in a family yet not being really of it. Jess hated the family. We all did, all four of us, but Jess hated it the most. Mother's hunger to have her revolted her. She would rather have been someone's special adopted child, someone who had no children of her own. She thought Mother had been greedy and that there was something suspicious about her desire to take on another child.

And she wasn't beautiful. Perhaps she was as a baby. I only know the photographs and it seems to me you can make all babies look beautiful, if you try hard enough. But by the time she was four, which was when my father died and all my memories suddenly become very sharp, she certainly wasn't beautiful. The much lauded ash-blonde hair and the fair skin made her look as colourless as an albino and, as she grew up, she became distinctly whey-faced and scrawny. Being miserable most of the time didn't help, of course. Poor Jess – the most common remark made to her was always 'whatever is the matter with you?' There was never anything specific the matter, just everything. I think the root of it all was that she wasn't clever. We were, all of us, not necessarily academically clever but intelligent. Mother was clever too. Jess was slow. Then there was the overwhelming proximity of Celia. As my mother says, Celia was about six months older than Jess, and she was an amazingly 'good' baby. Celia's also the cleverest of all of us, and the most talented – she plays the piano and oboe and was brilliant at sports. Jess was naturally shoved up against Celia all the time. People assumed they were twins, because of their ages, though they looked nothing like each other.

Mother couldn't have known how things would turn out – she couldn't have looked into the future and seen how Celia would outshine Jess at every turn – but she ought to have seen how bloody stupid it was to take a baby into the family, when you've already got one. I don't know how she did it, technically, I mean. Perhaps it was because of the war, perhaps the adoption procedure was slacker or perhaps my father's position had something to do with it. But I do know something Mother doesn't mention which is that Jess could have gone to several other homes. My godfather told me. He was Dad's closest friend, Simon Birch, also a doctor, an anaesthetist. He was in the same team as Dad and had been the anaesthetist for Jess's delivery. Once, when Jess was in real trouble, he took me to the theatre for a birthday treat and I blurted out all about Jess and what she had been doing and so on. He said maybe it was unfortunate she hadn't been adopted by any of the other people anxious to have her. I was too young to press him on this, but it was a pity he didn't offer more information. I suppose he remembered I was only fourteen and he ought to be discreet. This was the first time I queried my mother's version of events. I had always believed she rescued Jess from a terrible fate. Frequently I'd envisaged Jess in some dreadful Dickensian institution, down on her knees scrubbing stone floors and crying into her metal bucket. I'd never thought of her cosily installed in some other loving home, actually better off.

So my mother was a fool. She ought never to have adopted Jess. It was not an act of mercy and kindness, it was an act of self-indulgent folly. Especially, since there was a war on and everything was in a state of turmoil. I'm surprised at my father allowing it. Why did he? Was he weak, always persuaded by my much more forceful mother? It doesn't sound like it from everything else I know about him, but then what I do know is all from her. Was *she* going to bring us up on a diet of hearing our father was a vacillating, pliable character? Was she hell. He was a War Hero and war heroes, once dead, were Brave and Strong and Masterful. Where, one wonders, are *his* private papers? Those are the ones I'd like to find. I don't think they ever existed – he wasn't a writing man. What a relief. Mother would probably have framed his Letters from the Front to his Darling Children and hung them on the walls as texts. Instead, all I am left with is a memory of him as big and blond and slow. Slow moving, I mean. He was a calming presence, I think. And shy.

My father never died as far as my mother was concerned. Unfortunately. She had a mother she wouldn't allow *not* to exist for her, and she then added a husband she could never admit was dead. Throughout our childhood he was 'missing', just missing. She expected him to re-appear at any minute and I suppose, on the one hand, that was her strength and, on the other, her undoing. It meant she endured those early post-war years better than most, endlessly buoyed up by hope, but also prevented by it from starting again. When my father was killed – sorry, posted eternally missing – my mother was not quite twenty-nine. At twenty-eight she was much too young to withdraw herself from other men. But that is what she did. Other men were anathema to her. She was determined to bury herself even more securely within her precious family. She tried to be a father as well as a mother to us, and to fulfil both roles perfectly. Her family was to be enough. But it doesn't matter what she is going to go on to say: a family is *not* enough. She committed a kind of emotional suicide, for which I blame her severely. It's irrelevant whether she owns up to 'wrong choices' like Jess. What she ought to be owning up to is the strangling of her own ambitions.

I can hear her in the kitchen, clatter of the metal coffee machine she bought specially to make the kind of coffee I like. She hates coffee, likes delicate teas herself, rose-hip and lemon and camomile. But now she's making that strong Black Stuff Rosemary Likes (but-I-am-sure-is-bad-for-her). Celia has gone, I heard the door shut, heard her shout goodbye to me. Soon the coffee will hiss and bubble and Mother will call me. There will be a piece of Celia's famous chocolate cake. Every time I say I like it, Celia offers me the recipe and tells me the secret of her cake's success is using ground almonds instead of flour – as if I'd mess around baking any kind of cake. Mother, all excited at my promising to do this painting of us all, will say, 'Did you find what you wanted, dear?' And I will say – what will I say? Yes, thanks, and a lot more besides? *Look* what was in the bottom drawer, behind the last box of photographs? No, I won't. I need to think. I might want to read on, without her knowing. If I decide not to, no harm is done. 'Keep your options open, children,' Mother used to say, at her most hatefully prim. There we are, the summons. Deep breath. Out I shall go, carrying only a few snaps. I'll say I got side-tracked looking at the ones that were useless. I'll say I need to look again. Then I shall drink the coffee, scoff the cake, listen to her telling me the latest Good Deed Celia has done, and leave.

January 1st 1984

Wasn't going to keep a diary this year, not when I'm trying to write this – whatever this other thing is, whatever it is I am trying to set down, sort out. But I can't survive without a diary too, it's a habit, maybe a bad one, but a lifetime's habit. I need it. *Can't* survive without it. It is for me, not them. No need to imagine the judge-like figure, no need to fret over the fairness and truth of what I am saying. This is for me and I am friendly to myself and understanding, can say anything. Can say how upset I've felt today without despising myself. Upset because it is Celia's forty-fourth birthday – awful, awful. No husband, lover, children, home, I mean real home. Awful. Can't bear it, can't and yet have to. Find myself thinking stupid thoughts, like at least she is healthy, not poor, likes her job. Can't keep out of my head memories of her birth – boring, sentimental nonsense, Rosemary would say, but letting them run, the memories, gives me intense pleasure. Can't always run my memories as I wish, can't always choose, so annoying. Silly memories, painful memories, frightening memories – they pop up unselected. But births, they are choosable, like records. Just take them out and put them on. They never change, they are made to order, I made them myself and put them carefully away. Forty-four years ago tonight, there I lay, cocooned in care, Oliver at my side, myself at the centre of a great tangle of warm flesh, baby, husband, small child, all of us together in one room, a family complete, such joy. Today, all I've felt is grief, suppressed grief, grieving because Celia's life is so bleak. Rosemary says I am stupid, Celia has the life she wants, why do I fuss. Has she the life she wants? Wherein lies her happiness? Show me, I tell myself. I rang her, wished her happy birthday, was glad she liked her present, glad, glad but miserable, too. Started to weep as soon as I put the telephone receiver down. Asked her what she was going to do on her birthday. She said just relax. Just relax. Stoical Celia, her life static. No development, no progress, no change. Rosemary says it is her life. It doesn't feel it, it feels like mine. Why? Why to lots of things. What a dreadful day. Done nothing, been nowhere. Hurry on tomorrow.

*

I'm like a burglar, even though I have my own key. I move like a burglar, on tip-toe, yet this flat is empty. I feel like a burglar, my hands clammy, in spite of my right to be here. Mother knows. She's out, but she knows. I told her I would pop in and look through some more photographs. She offered to look herself, but I said she wouldn't like what I like. Slide open the bottom drawer, feel at the back and of course it's still there, this file of papers, these notes of my own. Undisturbed. What did I expect? Though Mother would be cunning. If she realized I had found the file and was reading its contents, she wouldn't necessarily say so. What I should've done was to paste a hair over the opening of the file, or some equally ludicrous trick from a crappy detective story, but being me I'd have forgotten I'd done it anyway. I'm sure nothing's been touched. But where did I stop? Never thought to mark the place. At a different colour and type of paper, I think. Now that's helpful. About half an inch in, at the first pale pink sheet. And what in hell's name was it? Some totally boring diary entry for last year. It makes my head ache even to consider its significance. She was up to adopting Jess and then the war. Yup, the jolly old war.

*

— a betrayal, direct and deliberate. A betrayal of the family so dear to us both. Oliver did not need to go to war. He was a doctor, he was already doing valiant war work. By 1941 the casualties were streaming into London's hospitals. There were hardly enough doctors available. The danger for Oliver, on duty night and day in a central London hospital, was as high as, if not higher than, it was for a doctor serving in the Medical Corps anywhere in Europe. He worked so hard patching people together (obstetrics mostly forgotten) that whenever I did see him he was utterly exhausted. All he did, at home, was sleep. All I wanted to do was sleep, but it seemed the very thing denied to me. Rosemary and Celia were no trouble at night but Jess regularly woke, screaming, and took hours to comfort. Then there were the air raids, and the endless rush to the shelter, usually on my own with all three children. Talk was one of the many luxuries denied to us. If we'd

23

talked, Oliver might never have joined up. All we discussed, if our snatched conversations at that time can be called discussion, was the necessity for me to move to Brighton.

I refused to leave Oliver. I read somewhere that the Queen had been urged to go to Canada with the Princesses but that she had said, 'The children cannot go without me and I cannot possibly leave the King and he will never leave his people.' That was more or less how I felt: my place was with Oliver and, if Oliver believed his to be with the war casualties in London, then in London I would stay. But Grandmother Butler was ill, and on her own, and when, in the Spring of 1941, her companion of several years died this created a crisis for us. What were we to do with Grandmother Butler? She was seventy-five and in poor health. We could not possibly have brought her to London. However hard we tried, we could find nobody to replace her companion (a post we had had to fill and re-fill many times, since Grandmother Butler did not inspire either devotion or loyalty in any of her staff). Oliver thought the solution was simple: his mother must go into a Home. But that was a monstrous suggestion which it shamed him to make. I would not sanction it. So we were obliged to take the alternative and move ourselves down to Brighton, at least for the duration of the war. It would get us out of the raids, which were increasing in intensity, and, though the south coast was hardly a healthy place to which to move – a little like going from the frying pan into the fire – we believed it to be not quite as dangerous as London. It was at this point that Oliver betrayed me. He joined up. He applied for and was given a commission as an MO in his father's old regiment. He told me the night before we moved to Brighton, *told* me, as a fait accompli. It was the last night we were ever to spend all together in our London house, and, as Rosemary tried inexpertly to toast crumpets, at the fire, where the wood we had collected that afternoon was burning and while Celia banged on the tray of her high chair with a spoon and Jess was for once asleep in her small pram, Oliver quietly stated that, when he had escorted us to Brighton, he was leaving London to join his regiment in France.

It is no use. I cannot write about it. My pen congeals even now with bitterness. He did not have to go, but he went. We could have stayed together, as the Royal Family did. We might all have died in the Blitz but we would have been together. He told me I had to realize there were some things more important than one's own family. The war was being fought to make the world safe for families like ours. Surely I could appreciate that if —

*

No, she couldn't. What an awful send-off my poor papa must have had. There were other women, bursting with pride at their husband's courage at joining up when they didn't have to and there was my mother talking about betrayal. I really don't need to read all the pros and cons, all the arguments she's about to relate. I know exactly what stance she would adopt, all of it based on this family-is-sacrosanct stuff. She would go haughty and stiff, the way she does when one dares to go against her. Unyielding, contemptuous. No wonder my father waited until the last minute – so have I, often. What a hellish time my father must have had moving us down to Brighton, with my mother speechless with rage. And what madness, what insanity to go there. There can be no justification for it. Of *course* Grandmother Butler should have been slung in any Home that would have her – she deserved no better. They should have tied a weight round her neck and dropped her into the sea. But my mother was full of these Sydney Carton ideas of it being a far, far better thing she did, and so she sacrificed us all on the altar of the family responsibility.

I was only six when we moved and I don't remember it very clearly. But since we stayed there three years, a little over, my first real memories are of that house in Brighton. They are hideously dominated by Grandmother Butler's dreadful presence looming over us every-where. My very first clear memory that belongs to me, and owes nothing to things I have been told, is of Grandmother Butler blocking the entrance to her house with her corpulent body and shouting, 'Stones! Stones! I will not have them in my house!' and shaking her stick. I remember sitting on the step while my mother emptied our shoes of tiny gravel-like stones and then got a bucket of water and washed all our feet. Then Grandmother let us in. It became a ritual, in fact Mother left the bucket by the door for our return from the beach, where we went most days (illegally, never in the least put off by the snaking coils of barbed wire). Not a single microdot of a stone was allowed into the house. Of course I couldn't understand Grand-mother's hatred of stones. But such things were never explained, not even by Mother who was a great explainer. She made us accept our

Grandmother's most absurd obsessions and prejudices as law. She was Head of the Family and must be accorded unchallenged respect. This applied even to her attitude to poor Jess.

She constantly bitched about Jess. I grew up with it. She took against Jess from the moment of her adoption, probably before. She was outraged that the family blood should be polluted and the family name sullied. I see now that this was, of course, also an attack on my mother, but I didn't see it then – all I saw was Grandmother Butler being consistently mean to a small child. 'Rosemary sit here and Celia there. Oh, Jessica, do *you* want to listen too? Are you sure, my dear? Are you sure you will understand it?' she would say when she was going to read us a story (she was a bloody awful reader). Then she would pick on Jess for making a mess at meals when Celia and I had made much the same sort of so-called mess. Any noise and Jess would get shouted at – 'Jessica, you must learn that in *this* family we do not cry for nothing.' It was awful and very hard for my mother to combat. Mother was scrupulous about fairness – God, it was boring. She didn't let Grandmother Butler get away with anything, but standing up to her was hard. If Mother said something sharp in defence of Jess, Grandmother Butler would come the frail old lady lark. Either that or she would go all aggrieved and remind my mother it *was* her house and she had 'taken her in'.

When we arrived, I think my mother had had ideas about splitting the house in two so we would have some privacy, but something must have gone wrong with that little arrangement. In my memory, Grandmother Butler was ever with us – eating, sleeping, listening to the radio, everything seemed overshadowed by her. I always woke up to the sound of her banging her stick, and then I would hear my mother getting up and going in to her. Of course, Grandmother Butler's version of our move to Brighton was different: she had magnanimously taken in her son's family and waiting upon her like a slave was the least my mother could do. What a bargain she got. My mother looked after the old sod beautifully. She even coped with her incontinence. And she did all of this because Grandmother Butler was family and you couldn't neglect family, however horrible and loathsome and awful they were. Their claims were sacred, their crimes against humanity forgivable. Over and over again my mother would remind us that Grandmother was old and ill, she couldn't see very well and she couldn't walk very well and we must be kind. It would have been easier if Grandmother Butler herself had shown any evidence of kindness, but she did not. I say that with authority because I was her favourite. It was me she chose to show her Indian treasures to – ghastly tatty shawls and stuff. Grandmother must've been the Memsahib to end all Memsahibs – arrogant, uncaring, imperious, demanding. She'd drone on about her life in Hyderabad, all the usual stuff about the heat and the parties and how sodding wonderful the scenery was, and I was kept at her side supposedly entranced. I did quite like the stories about my dead grandfather and his daring deeds. He had been a general. She had some brilliant photographs of him in his dress uniform, one of them on an elephant, and, whenever what she was twitting on about got too deadly, I'd just ask her if I could look at the photographs. 'Rosemary is fascinated by the family history,' Grandmother Butler would say to my mother. 'So nice for her to be able to go right back. The Butlers have *such* an interesting history, don't you think?' Mother would flush a dark red and smile and say yes she did, how lucky Rosemary was.

I went to school in Brighton. It was a small primary school not far from Grandmother's Bedford Square house. My going there caused some trouble. I remember Grandmother Butler being scandalized when my mother told her which school I was going to. She need never have known, but the fact that I wore no uniform would've given it away. She thought I'd be resplendent in the green gymslip and blazer of the private kindergarten to which she had given the Butler seal of approval. 'Only riff-raff go there,' she said of my council school, 'and Rosemary is a Butler. I am sure Oliver would not approve.' Mother said he had fully approved. He believed in State education. I think Grandmother thought she was mad. She'd never in her life been in a state school of any description but she thought of them all as versions of Bedlam. My ability to read and write never failed to amaze her, but even that was turned against Mother. 'Think how well Rosemary could do if she went to a *good* school,' she would say. Mother would reply that I would do well wherever I went.

I used to long for Grandmother Butler to die. There seemed to me, as to most children, no sense in being alive if you couldn't do anything or go anywhere and if you complained about pains all the time. When I discovered she was seventy-five, nearly seventy-six, I was furious. She had been alive much too long, it wasn't fair. Nobody wanted her alive, what was the point. My mother told me not to talk about wishing people were dead when so many people were being killed in the war and in the bombing. But I couldn't help it. I used to fix Grandmother with an intense stare and repeat die, die, die in my head. She spoiled our life. She made Mother and Jess unhappy, she stopped us all from enjoying ourselves. We couldn't ever go off all together because we couldn't leave Grandmother alone. We couldn't jump up and down the stairs or play tag, because it would disturb her. Grandmother Butler, it seemed to me, was always put first. She interrupted all our normal family activities and yet Mother never stopped her. It was a case of endless reverential care. Grandmother Butler was not worth it. She had never done anything for anyone in her life. She'd always been waited on hand and foot, never done any work, ever, not even as a mother. She was old when she had my father, forty-eight – he was a menopausal miracle you could say – and she never looked after him at all. Out in India she had servants for all that. She simply didn't understand, as my mother repeatedly told me, what real life was like. But that was my point – that she did not and ought to. Every time I said I was going to tell her how thoughtless she was, Mother would beg me not to. She said she couldn't bear any rows and anyway it was a waste of time, Grandmother wouldn't understand.

She was right about that. Once I actually spoke up. Grandmother Butler had been especially vicious to Jess and then said to my mother, who had probably been too slow about bringing her wretched tea, something which implied that Mother'd been lolling around enjoying herself. I suppose I was about seven at the time and very rebellious. What I shouted at Grandmother Butler I can't claim to recall, but it was some defence of my mother. At any rate, I was reprimanded by my irate grandmother for being rude. Then I remember clearly what I did. I rushed up to her, very close, a brave thing in itself because I loathed her smell, and I thrust my face into her podgy, squashy one and yelled, 'Rude, rude, rude!' about a hundred times, covering her powdery old nose with spit as I did so. She hit me, one almighty whack with her heavy, truncheon-like arm, catching me on the nape of the neck so that I fell against her coughing and spluttering and then screaming to escape the nightmare feeling of being trapped by some scaly, oozing, heaving octopus. Mother pulled me away and carried me forcibly out of the room, out of the house, out across the road and onto the beach and

28

there she held me tight and kissed me and soothed me. She cried. *She* cried. I suppose with tiredness and humiliation and perhaps the awful certainty that she had made a terrible mistake: she knew Grandmother Butler hated and despised her and that I was learning to hate and despise my grandmother in turn. A cycle of hate, when all she had wanted was the family to close in and be sustained by mutual love and toleration. It was very hard for her.

My father, on one of his leaves, must have been aware of how hard — he would have had to be a total fool not to notice — and he did his best to ease the situation. A lady called Miss Clarke came to live with us. Where she came from I don't know but we were all glad, Celia, Jess and I, even though we didn't like her. Mother didn't much like her, either, though she was always very nice to her, and Grandmother Butler loathed her. Miss Clarke's sole function was to look after Grand-mother. Mother explained to me that she was not a servant and that her privacy must be respected always. We were never to go and knock on her door, even if Grandmother Butler told us to. We were to come to Mother instead. Miss Clarke had to have proper hours, Mother said. The mere thought of *her* companion having time to herself was enough to put Grandmother Butler into a permanent rage, but I suppose she had to accept it.

Miss Clarke was not the pathetic, weak creature that one might have expected to take on such a terrible job. There was nothing cringing or deferential about her. She was unmistakably in it, I now see, for the very substantial financial reward, a fact which Mother of course realized. Pay enough and there are always people who will do anything. Miss Clarke was one of them, a severe, strong, determined lady of about sixty who refused to be browbeaten by her difficult employer — not that it was Grandmother who employed her. If she had, she would have sacked her the first time her commands were not obeyed. I suppose one of the good things about having Miss Clarke, apart from the obvious advantage of freeing Mother and giving us all some life of our own, was that it put Grandmother Butler in a different and much more sympathetic light. Miss Clarke, as she was fond of saying, stood no nonsense. To hear her tell Grandmother Butler that she would certainly not pick up the handkerchief quite deliberately thrown on the floor, was at first thrilling — imagine refusing to do what Grandmother said! — but then it became somehow cruel, even to my eye. Mother would pick up handkerchiefs or anything else, because she pitied Grandmother. Miss Clarke didn't pity her and suddenly it made me see why Mother did. Watching Miss Clarke 'discipline' this cantankerous old woman so mercilessly made me see how sad Grandmother's plight was. I didn't feel any love for her, I didn't feel any real 'family' connection, but I did in the end, thanks to Miss Clarke, begin to feel that Grandmother's life was awful. The thing she had always enjoyed most in life was dominating other people. Now she couldn't even do that. She was at the mercy of Miss Clarke. Because of my mother, this couldn't get out of hand, but the threat was there: if the last vestige of family vigilance went, then she'd lost everything.

*

— worried about the prospect of invasion more than I did. If there was an invasion, Oliver thought we were even more at risk living on the south coast than he was. But I liked our life in Brighton in spite of Grandmother Butler. It was healthy. We prospered. All the children looked better and were happier.

The Brighton they knew was a Brighton of sandbags and sirens, of tin hats and water tanks, not of seaside jollity, and it is true that they were as familiar with the sounds of loudspeakers and guns as they were with the crash of the waves on the shore and the cries of the seagulls. All the same Brighton was still a pleasant place to live, it still had its charms. We had air raids, of course, fifty-six altogether and a great many houses were destroyed but, compared to what was happening in London, it was nothing. There was only one occasion when I was seriously frightened and that was in May 1943, when a bomb fell on a school and twenty-four people were killed, including some children. I did think then how ironic it would be if we were killed in Brighton after escaping from the London Blitz. But on the whole I felt confident of our safety and my confidence was subconsciously absorbed by the children. Grandmother Butler, of course, never for one moment imagined a bomb would have the audacity to fall upon her. She would point out the barrage balloons to the children as though they were absolutely foolproof protection and, when they told her of the big naval guns they had seen on the cliffs, she glowed with pride at how invincible we were. So the children were brought up feeling secure in very insecure circumstances. Their father not being with them was the only true indication for them that all was not quite as it should be.

Oliver had leaves, of course, six of them in all, each both agonizing and precious. The strain was unbearable both before and after, especially after. We would get little warning that Oliver was coming home, but that was perhaps fortunate – my own anticipation of his arrival I found hard to endure and would not have liked prolonged. I used not to tell the children until the very last minute and even then they would become almost hysterically excited, especially Rosemary. The emotion of those reunions was always traumatic, leaving me battered for days afterwards. I never got out of them what I most wanted, a normal, peaceful stretch of family life. Nothing was normal, how could it be? None of us felt normal, it was all a case of constant re-adjustment. Oliver was an interloper in our tight little unit: we had forgotten what it was to have a father in our family. His very maleness was perturbing. His physical presence made us shy and ill at ease for the first day. It made me see that a family is always more than the sum of its parts. Oliver changed the way in which we behaved towards each other. The children seemed to feel subconsciously that an alliance had been formed against them and were determined to break it up. Oliver could never be alone with me until they were asleep, and they even resented and fought sleep so long as he was with us. It was all very tiring and debilitating. The euphoria of greeting him would quickly give way to despair at the impossibility of *really* being with him.

This was particularly so on his last leave, before he was posted missing on D-Day 1944. He had come home, without warning, for a forty-eight hour leave at the beginning of January, just turning up, dreadfully haggard, on the doorstep in the early hours of the morning. All the household was asleep, to my immense relief. For the first time, he did not have to embrace four people all at once amid laughter and shouting and usually, also, crying. There was just me, bleary-eyed and shivering in my nightdress. We crept into the kitchen, whispering, like fugitives. I savoured every second of it, of this wonderful intimate privacy. There was time just to be silent together, to become accustomed once more to each other's features and expressions. Oliver talked more than he had ever done on any of his other leaves. He told me he was less convinced that what was being done in the name of a righteous war was worth it. He had been with a division sent into action on the Belgian-German border and had attended large numbers of wounded German women and children caught in the crossfire. His voice shook as he described their sufferings. The means were said to justify the ends, but did they? He spoke of his disgust at the hatred deliberately provoked against the whole German race, of the indoctrination of the troops. The only good German was a dead one. His mind had turned to all the 'good' Germans not only in history but those alive now. His fervour was lessening all the time. He wished he had stayed in London. He wished he had become a pacifist. Perhaps I had been right all along and there was nothing worth leaving one's family for: no cause was great enough. His misery was so acute that it hurt me physically. We clung together as the cold winter dawn lightened the kitchen and overhead we heard the first sounds of our children wakening. I told him he was worn out, that what he needed was sleep and more sleep.

Most of those forty-eight hours he did indeed sleep. When he was awake he sat with the children and played dominoes. Rosemary hung about him all the time, she even sat outside our bedroom while he slept during the day. She would not let him alone, forever stroking his hair and clinging to his arm and pressing herself to his side. She was terribly proud of him being an officer *and* a doctor and boasted endlessly to Miss Clarke (who was more than ready to hero-worship). Although it was all so understandable it irritated me. I had to try hard to stop myself telling her to leave him alone. And I was very glad when at the end of an exhausting day she went to bed leaving my husband to me. That night, Oliver began to confess once more his new terror that nothing could have justified the deaths and sufferings he had witnessed, that perhaps life, any sort of life under any sort of regime, was better. I found myself arguing strongly that it was not, that he *had* been right all along. He also began to talk about dying himself but I stopped him. I could not bear it. When he did die I regretted my cowardice bitterly – oh, how I would have welcomed some instructions. 'If I die,' Oliver might have said, 'this is what I want you to do, this is what I want my children to do . . . you must always . . . when they grow up I would like . . . tell them that . . . ' Who knows what things he might have said? I stopped him saying anything. I clung to him, as Rosemary had clung to him, and loved him. We both wept ourselves to sleep —

*

I don't think I can stand this. It *must* be rubbish, romantic twaddle. Nobody could be as slushy in real life. She's just doing what she likes with the past. Imagine a man, exhausted, on this short leave in this hellish house with his terrible old mother moaning on and three little kids driving him mad with all their fussing – does he really have these philosophical discussions with this Perfect Wife? I don't believe it. Every account of soldiers on leave I've ever read or heard always says how you were just too fucking tired to say a bloody word and, as for philosophizing, all you were interested in was food and sleep and, if you could get the energy, sex. No mention of sex from Mother. Love, yes, spiritual unions, yes, but straightforward sex, no. But sex there was because as we all know, little Emily appeared prematurely less than eight months later, two and a half months after my father's death. So there was undoubtedly sex to give him a good send-off.

I know it was painful. It was painful for me too. It was tragic and terrible for her but not, surely, as she describes it here. I don't know about her and Dad, whether they were the perfect match she makes out. I only know I've watched her turn every event into something it wasn't. I don't think she even sees things as they really are – I know she doesn't.

*

— and then next day, on the same sort of grey morning he had arrived, Oliver had to leave. Naturally, he had no idea when his next leave would be. He said he thought there was going to be a big push soon.

Grandmother Butler made reading *The Times* aloud to her one of the ordeals of the day. I did it, although it was meant to be one of Miss Clarke's duties, because I found it less demanding than some of the other chores she would rather I had taken on. I did it at the same time every day, eleven in the morning when Rosemary was at school and the other two were having a nap. I tried to make it a pleasant ritual. I made tea and toast, which I took into Grandmother Butler's sitting room, and we always had five minutes' exchange of pleasantries before I began. She so adored having *The Times* read to her – her own eyesight was by then very poor and, even with spectacles, she could not cope with that excruciatingly tiny print – that she was capable of some

33

degree of pleasantness. It felt quite cosy and I had a real affection for the poor old thing at that moment. She was so eager and attentive, straining her awkward bulk forward to catch every word, as though everything in the newspaper was meant personally for her. The news of the latest invasion of Europe in *The Times* of June 7th 1944 excited her tremendously. I had to read everything twice and she loved it all. General Eisenhower's message to his men, something about the tide having turned and the free men of the world marching together to victory, had her flushed and breathing heavily with emotion, even if he was one of the Americans she scorned. It sounded like the most dreadful kind of glib cliché to me but to Grandmother Butler they were truly stirring words.

I had no idea, and neither had my mother-in-law, that Oliver had already, while we were reading that account of D-Day, been posted missing. We thought it very likely he had been involved, but no regiments were mentioned. And since all the emphasis was on victory we did not experience that tightening around the heart which gripped us when I read news of devastating defeats. We were unusually buoyant and optimistic. I read out aloud of this 'mighty armada', which had sailed so nobly to regain France, and I could not help but feel triumphant. There was a message printed, I remember, from General Montgomery, in which he claimed to have complete confidence in success. Grandmother Butler was annoyed with me for laughing at how he ended his missive – 'Good hunting', I think it was, or some other banality, entirely inappropriate. There was even a piece on the role of the medical corps which I read with pride. Every column of that paper seemed filled with good news for a change. Churchill's speech in the House of Commons was cautious but more than convincing: the end of the war *must* be in sight. 'I think,' Grandmother Butler said, 'this calls for a celebration.' So we got the sherry out and solemnly drank a toast of Grandmother Butler's devising: 'To England and Oliver!'

How absurd. As if Oliver was in the least patriotic or jingoistic. But Grandmother Butler was. The days stretched into weeks, and then months. It became obvious Oliver must be dead (though I did not admit it until all the prisoners of war had finally returned and put to rest my mad theory that somehow he had been spirited from Normandy to the heart of Germany and put into a concentration camp). Grandmother Butler started saying things like, 'He died for his country and there is no finer death. All the Butlers die for their country.' I found it unbearable and that is why I left. There had been shock after shock ever since that heady D-Day. First the letter from Oliver's commanding officer saying he regretted he was 'unaccounted for', then the second letter saying he had been put on the official missing list, then another transferring him to the missing believed killed – oh, the categories were endless. Slowly, the dread grew, and yet I had faith. I never felt Oliver *was* dead in my heart of hearts. I was not pretending. And I believed that this feeling I had, that Oliver was safe, was to be trusted. So I said nothing to the children. They were used to their father being away, they thought nothing of it. I left them undisturbed and told them only happy news. The happiest news of all was that I was expecting another baby, to my great joy. At least Oliver knew that. There was pleasure and anticipation in every line of his last letter. It would be a boy, he was convinced (and so was I). A 'peace' baby, he was equally convinced. How clever we were, he wrote, to arrange our very own victory celebration. He even suggested a name, Alexander, after Alexander the Great.

I had to leave Grandmother Butler's house. It was sheer folly, but for the sake of preserving my own sanity I had to leave, after that final letter saying Oliver must now be definitely presumed dead. I was not going to presume anything of the kind, but Grandmother was. She wept, she wailed, she talked and talked about the death of her only son, and I hated her. So I came to an agreement with Miss Clarke. I agreed to double the lavish wage she was already receiving, if she would take sole charge of my mother-in-law for at least the following six months. I knew I was consigning Grandmother Butler to unfeeling, if not downright hostile, hands but I could not help it. She was appalled when I broke the news. She ranted and raved at my cruelty, my desertion, my unworthiness to bear the name Butler. Then she collapsed, and had to be put to bed, and clung to my hand and begged me to stay with her, for Oliver's sake, for the sake of the family because I was all she had. But I left. In July 1944, seven months pregnant, I somehow managed to transport myself and three small children back to London. My conscience tortured me but I was driven by such inner compulsion that I endured it. I wanted peace, and there was no peace, while I remained in Grandmother Butler's house, from the nightmare of Oliver perhaps being dead. I was forced, too, to run away from that house because, there, Oliver had been only a soldier. I never wanted to think of him as a soldier ever again. Once back in London, I had different visions of him and those who —

*

I thought this wasn't meant to be a memoir, an autobiography? I thought it was meant to be about choices, and how my sisters and I didn't realize what we had done to our own lives and my mother did? So far it has been *all* memoir, all self-justification for what happened in her own life. I can't see it has anything to do with us. Is she building up to something? Is this really all 'essential background'? I doubt it.

*

— time in my life when I most lacked family support. I had no relatives whatever who could help me. There was no one to whom I could turn, upon whom I could rely. Any friends I had made —

*

Ah. But this *is* relevant to all of us. Mother had no friends, I don't know what she means by saying 'any friends I had made', because there simply weren't any, unless she kept them secret. She has gone through her whole life without a single close friend. And why? Because friends in her eyes are signs of weakness. They get in the way. In the way of family – they come between you and your family who are the only friends worth having and should be *quite enough*. My mother has always been the cat who walked by herself and oh so proud of it. She never wanted any of us to have close friends – we had each other, did we not? No good pointing out to her that no four children had less in common than Jess, Celia, Emily and me. We couldn't be each other's friends because we had no common ground except our relationship. Our personalities clashed from the beginning, our temperaments were totally different, our interests poles apart. Mother wouldn't acknowledge this nor would she acknowledge the importance to us of outside friends – outside the family. She pretended she wanted us to make friends, but her resentment when we brought them into our joint life was perfectly clear. She could never accept them, nor be easy with them. She was hospitable, but never welcoming. Her most frequent comment, after any friend of mine had stayed the night, was 'isn't it

36

nice to be on our own again'. And she had strange notions of what having a friend entailed. If someone was your friend that had to mean one hundred per cent loyalty. You didn't dare say, in a flash of temporary irritation, such as all friendships are subject to, 'I hate Anne,' or whoever. Mother would pounce. If you hated Anne even for a day, she could not be your friend. And, if Anne asked you to do something and you said you couldn't be bothered or whatever, Mother was scandalized: friends couldn't be let down.

*

— had moved out of my neighbourhood. I returned to that London house, to wartime London, with nobody to help. The house, which we had left empty, was in an even worse state than when we had deserted it, and that had been bad enough. What gave me the necessary courage to carry on was the baby I was carrying inside me. People tended to pity me twice over because my husband was missing presumed killed *and* I was unmistakably pregnant, but none of them understood. Without that baby alive and kicking inside me I could not, at that point, have continued. The baby was my own life-saver. For the baby I ate as well as I could, rested as much as I was able, kept as calm and cheerful as possible. The baby made me go out and seek help instead of struggling on: it was for the baby's sake that I made the sensible decision to employ Linda, the sixteen year old daughter of my neighbour. She had just returned from her evacuated school and was pleased to have the job of mother's help. The coming baby was my hope, it alone kept my mind off death and destruction. As the time for its birth drew nearer I grew excited, feverishly so. I knew everyone looked at my pink cheeks and shining eyes and broad smile and wondered how I could, in the circumstances, seem so happy and well. But I felt happy and well, and the reason for it was the child they all pitied me for carrying.

Of course, I thought it was a son. I was absolutely sure. I succumbed to every kind of old wives' tale imaginable, even believing things as silly as the shape of the bump showing it was a boy. It seems elementary now to point out that I also had done what many bereaved women do who give birth posthumously: I had come to believe, tricked myself into believing, that I was carrying Oliver inside me. So long as my son thrived in my womb my husband was not dead. I was pleased, rather than alarmed, when I went into labour prematurely. On August 30th I

37

was rushed by ambulance into University College Hospital. I could hardly wait to see my darling son (and my darling husband in him). I treated childbirth like a party, laughing and triumphant all the way through. It shocked those around me. Their anxious, disapproving faces only amused me more. I knew they thought I was succumbing to hysteria, that they could not recognize euphoria when they saw it. Even to the end of that difficult labour I was smiling through the pain which only afterwards I acknowledged as agony. I thought the fact that it was all taking such a long time, and was so much harder than my other two easy, straightforward labours, was because this time it was a boy and before I had only borne girls. (Another ludicrous superstition.) When finally, at midnight, Emily arrived, a fine healthy girl, I could not take in the fact of her sex. Everything seemed to stop within me. I found myself holding my breath, struggling to understand. There was no son, no Oliver. And then the tears came, harsh, frantic sobs which racked my feeble body in which every nerve seemed to sing. They put Emily into my arms and pressed her to me, to give me comfort, but her tiny face was drenched with my tears, her scrap of a body shook with the force of my sobs, and they had to take her away.

Everyone was very kind. Now that I was miserable, everyone understood. I was allowed to lie there and cry for days on end. Nobody tried to jolly me along. When my baby was once more put into my arms, she was so vulnerable it shocked me. There was no question of rejection or blame, no shred anywhere in my heart of not wanting her, or of hating her, because she was not a boy. I came to terms with that at once. Thinking of a name for this new daughter was the first sign that I was healing myself. I thought of Alexandra, because of Oliver's wish that a son should be Alexander. But I knew every time I used that name I would be trying to make her into a boy. I chose Emily because I had been reading Emily Brontë's poem 'Remembrance'. It was not that I wanted Emily to be a remembrance of her father's death (which I had still not accepted), or even of Oliver himself, but that, like Rosemary, she was the embodiment of such happiness. The line in that poem which goes, 'Then did I check the tears of useless passion – weaned my young soul from yearning after thine', seemed to me what I must start to do. I would not wallow in what was past. I would indeed wean my young soul. If Oliver ever returned he would be proud of me.

By October I was better. I had stopped crying every day. All my energies were channelled into planning ahead. I went to the family solicitors to ask about my financial position and learned that the house was mine and there was no mortgage. Oliver's inheritance at twenty-one from his father had enabled him to buy the house outright. All that saving in our first few years had been unnecessary, but I suppose Oliver did not want to spend all his capital at once. I tried to be hard-headed and realistic. I had no immediate worries. But I saw, after I had done a few sums, that within five years, whilst I would never be penniless, I could quite easily be hard up, with four children to support. So I decided to divide the house and make a flat on the top which I would let, thereby giving myself an income. This proved a wonderful diversion. It gave me something unemotional to think about and I relished that particular kind of challenge. Linda's father was a carpenter, wounded at the start of the war and invalided out. He put me in touch with a good builder and decorator, and throughout the rest of the year work went ahead on the house. It meant workmen everywhere, which normally I would have hated, but in the circum-stances all the comings and goings, the banging and shouting, the general chaos, was good for me. The workmen were all rather elderly and clearly felt fatherly towards me. They helped me in all kinds of ways and I was touched. And the children loved having so many men around. Without all the activity that first winter back in London, with none of the wartime restrictions lifted, life would have been even darker and more dreary than it was.

I no longer cried at night, nor even felt like it. My grief had changed. When I came upon Elizabeth Barrett Browning's line, 'I tell you, hopeless grief is passionless', I knew that was the state I had reached, a state that lay beyond mere noisy sorrowing. And it was at this point that I was afflicted by a mysterious illness – not exactly an illness – more a disease. One day, when Emily was only five months old, I was brushing my hair in my bedroom, looking at myself in the mirror Simon Birch had given us as a wedding present, when I felt the bristles of my hairbrush seem to seize up. I thought I must have a knot even thicker than usual – my hair was extremely thick and rather coarse. I pulled the hairbrush impatiently and to my astonishment it came away bearing a great hunk of hair. I put up my hand to my head and found a patch of smooth scalp just below the crown of my head. I can not say I was frightened or worried: I simply assumed the sheer force of my

39

brushing had pulled these hairs free. I could easily spare them. The patch, the tiny bald patch, did not hurt. There was no rash or sore or lump. So I thought nothing of it, suffered no twinges of anxiety. But after that I could not help noticing that, although my hairbrush did not stick again, every time I brought it away it seemed very full of hairs. I grew tired of removing them from the bristles of my hairbrush. But I was still not particularly worried until about three weeks later when, after washing my hair, I found great clumps of hair in the basin and on my towel. My hair was black, the towel and washbasin white. The hair looked menacing and obscene stretched in broad swathes across the clean porcelain and the fibres of the towel. I was disgusted rather than frightened, even then. I knew women's hair often did fall out a little after pregnancies. I vaguely remembered that it was something to do with hormones and, heaven knows, my hormones had been in one sort of turmoil or another for nearly a year. I had never been vain, never given to studying myself in a mirror and, after Emily's birth, my woebegone countenance was a sight I tried consciously to avoid. But now I began surreptitiously both to feel my head and constantly to peer at it from all angles. Was my hair really thinner? Was something seriously wrong with me? My anxious fingers prodded my scalp, relieved when they had to push against thick, firmly attached hairs and trembling when, as I withdrew them, they took with them the long black strands. I would stare at my hands, transfixed by the ugly sight of hair apparently growing from between my fingers. Then came a day when I felt another patch of smooth, oh so smooth skin on the back of my scalp, this time above the nape of my neck. It made me feel sick. The word 'bald' sprang into my mind for the first time. For a week I pretended it must be the soap I was using. Shampoo was, like everything else, difficult to get and for some time I had washed my hair and the children's with ordinary soap. I stopped. From somewhere I obtained some mild baby shampoo and cautiously washed my hair with that, rinsing it very carefully and patting it dry gently. It made no difference. At the end of another week or so I was frantic with worry.

The doctor I went to, the kindly old gentleman I had been under for Emily's birth, was immensely reassuring. He said that he could see I had Alopecia Areata, a form of hair loss brought about by nervous disturbances. There was no need to upset myself – the hair would grow again. There was no treatment necessary. I must try to relax and rest and nature would do the rest. I left his surgery, scolding myself for the panic I had got into and embarrassed by my own fear. My heart had lurched at the thought of baldness: it was so utterly ludicrous. Bald, bald, bald I had repeated to myself until I wanted to scream at the ridiculousness of it. A bald woman. I thought of pictures I had seen of senile old ladies, their heads grotesquely knobbly without hair, their faces underneath made twice as hideous because of the lack of it. I thought of plaster models in shop windows and how even the most beautiful looked absurd until their wig was put on. I would be a freak, mutilated, pointed at in the street, tittered about, completely unable to hide, but, thank God, there was no need any longer to torment myself. I believed my doctor implicitly and went on believing in him until I had only the thinnest covering of hair left, which had to be carefully arranged to protect my bare, stark white scalp. Then I went back to him. I asked to be sent to a specialist. Yet again, I went to University College Hospital. The specialist confirmed my GP's diagnosis but was slightly less confident. He told me that in ninety-nine per cent of cases the hair grew back normally, given time and the removal of stress. I asked him about the other one per cent? He shrugged, said it did happen but really even then Alopecia Areata was no tragedy. It was painless, did not kill, did not impair any faculties. It was nothing to fret about, even if the worst came to the worst. Wigs were very good these days, getting better all the time. I had to stop him by rushing out.

It was the humiliation I dreaded most. I insist again I was not vain but I was proud. How could a bald young woman hold onto her pride? I tried repeating to myself what the doctor had said, about Alopecia Areata not being fatal. I tried to be thankful I had not got a heart condition or cancer. I tried contempt for my own fears. What did it matter how I looked? All around me were men with legs cut off, eyes gouged out, half of their faces missing, and there was I whimpering over the loss of my hair. But it was no good. I wept and wept and became more and more distraught. Nobody appeared to notice, or, if they did, they said nothing, they were tactful. I don't know to whom I refer by using this 'they'. I was intimate with no one. There were only the children, the workmen and Linda who saw me every day. Rosemary, of course, asked why I wore a horrid scarf all the time but Linda never commented. As I sat feeding Emily, weeping over the contrast between her own almost bald pretty head and my own ghastly

41

one, I felt I could not go on much longer and, if I collapsed, what would happen to my family? It was even conceivable that they might end up in an institution, because there was no one to take them in. So I steadied myself by making contingency plans. I asked Linda to ask her mother if she could go to Brighton to stay with my children, if I needed to go into hospital. She agreed. I wrote to Miss Clarke and explained only that I needed a rest and what I proposed to do. She wrote back at once, a stilted letter, but perfectly agreeable. Then I decided to send them all off at once, while I tried lying in the garden, ignoring everything for a week, to see if this would work what I had by then come to think of as a miracle.

I lay in the garden. It was the beginning of March, a wonderfully warm early Spring. The garden was completely wild and overgrown and I had to hack away thick weeds and branches to make a small space for myself. I lay in the sun, between Emily's feeds, and tried to empty my mind of all thought. I lifted each limb in turn and let it flop back. I relaxed. I had promised myself that I would not touch my hair nor look at it for a week. Each morning I shut my eyes when I made my bed so that I would not see the amount of hair clinging to the pillow. Then, on the last day, I steeled myself to face what I already knew: I had hardly any hair left. I was going to be one of the one per cent. Strangely enough, I took this verdict calmly. I decided that, before the children came back, I must find a wig as much like my own hair as possible and start to wear it immediately. It would give me confidence, it might even achieve a sufficient measure of relaxation to enable hair to grow. Naturally, I had no idea where to begin in my search for a wig. There must be wig-makers, wigs had surely always existed, but where? I looked in the telephone book and found several firms announcing they were makers of wigs – names I had vaguely associated with the theatre. In fact, the first shop I went to was a theatre costumier's in St Martin's Lane. I walked in, baby in my arms, eyes red with crying, I expect, and asked in a very haughty manner if I could see some wigs. 'For what period, Madam?' the man enquired. I wanted to say for the here and now but could not get out the words. 'For myself,' I said. 'I need a wig temporarily.' For the first time he really looked at me but I was wearing a hat, pulled well down. He apologized, even blushed, and said he was afraid they did not make wigs in contemporary styles. He gave me an address in St James's and another in Bond Street. I walked from St Martin's Lane to Bond Street.

The name he had given me was on a brass plate together with seven others. The doorway was narrow, squashed between two shop fronts, and the stairs inside were steep. I trudged all the way to the top, heart thumping with the effort of carrying Emily so far, as well as with nervousness, and at last I came to the name I wanted. I knocked and tried the door which opened into what looked like a cosy little village draper's shop. There were two ladies sitting in wicker chairs in front of a gas fire, both holding mugs of tea. All round the room were plaster heads, white and grey, some with wigs on, some without. A small desk was pushed into one corner. On it there were some papers and a bottle of milk. One of the ladies, wearing a blue nylon overall, got up, coughed and asked if I had got the right address. I said I hoped so, I needed a wig. And I started to laugh, with mortification. The other lady came over and said would I like a cup of tea – it was all so homely, so unlike anything I had expected. The relief was wonderful. Emily was put down on a cushion from one of the old wicker chairs, and I had my tea and blurted out my sad story, well, some of it. The ladies tut-tutted and smiled and frowned and there-there'd. Then the fatter one – they were both small and fat and bespectacled – took a tape measure out of her pocket and measured my poor head. A lot of cupboard opening went on and pulling about of boxes, before a wig was produced. They made wigs to order, they said, and nothing they could give me would really fit. Then they managed to find a wig, which they put on my head. I hated it. It seemed tight and uncomfortable and scratchy. Fearfully I looked in a mirror and, though I looked slightly odd, there was no doubt I also looked better. It was wonderful to see my face framed, as it always had been, by thick, wavy, bushy hair. I hated taking it off and once more exposing myself, even more than I had hated having it put on. I saw a wig might not be the joke I had assumed, that perhaps, as the ladies promised, a properly made well-fitting wig might help me a great deal. But once I wore it, if I was one of the one per cent, I would always have to wear it. It would be my secret. I could not shame my daughters by involving them. Night and day I would be doomed to wear it, forever and ever, and what would I do about small hands tugging and winds and swimming – the problems were endless.

Yet I left Bond Street happier than I had been for weeks. My head was measured, the hair chosen, the style agreed. I was ready, as I had always tried to be, to face the worst, if and when it came. Ready, too, to embark on permanent deception. The most important thing in the world was to protect my family from —

*

From what? *Oh, my God.* She expresses herself so badly it makes me want to squirm. I couldn't break in and interrupt all that stuff about her hair. I suppose even using the word 'stuff' makes it sound as if I'm being sarcastic or derogatory. I don't intend to be. What I find so upsetting is the pathos of it all. There she was, shut into herself, being brave again, and it makes me cringe.

We're getting near that point where my real memories begin, properly formed things with beginnings and ends, quite substantial and as trustworthy as memory ever is. But this Alopecia episode is a fraction too early for me. I have strained and strained to remember but I was only nine and I can't be sure of anything. I remember the scarf and how it annoyed me because it looked silly. I remember, as I said, going to Brighton with Linda. I don't remember anything about coming back. My next landmark is going to Primrose Hill School and being given some milk that was sour. I came home and cried and Mother said it must have got too warm in the classroom and it wouldn't be sour tomorrow. So there I was, demanding sympathy for something so trivial, and there she was with her hair falling out worrying about wigs. It's extraordinary that we never knew about the wig, or rather the significance of it, because of course I do remember the wig. It went into the dressing-up box on the top landing. Friends who came to play used to marvel at it – it was so beautiful, so real, a proper wig and modern, not one of those Woolworth's efforts made with horsehair. How can she have borne seeing us tripping about shrieking and laughing, wearing something that had caused her so much pain?

It was bloody ridiculous, it was laying down a whole pattern for our upbringing from which she *never* deviated. Nothing nasty in the woodshed for us, ever. What did she think we were, fragile bits of glass which would be shattered if the merest puff of wind blew in our direction? It was insulting. And it made us feel that to expose our own agonies to her was too humiliating, that we, too, had to be cheerful all

44

the time, take things on the chin, never say die and other ludicrous rubbish.

But she *was* brave, I do see that. It must have been hell. I bet, though, that any minute it's going to be 'but we were very happy' again.

*

— but we were very happy in spite of all this trouble. It took time, of course, to establish our new life. I will not say we were happy all the time. It was a whole year after Emily was born until I could find myself smiling at anything at all. I remember her first birthday, watching her stagger across the garden and thinking that the worst must be over, that the thought 'this time last year' made me shudder, but that it was almost a relief because it made me appreciate how much had changed for the better. My hair did grow again, but not until it had completely fallen out except for a long, pathetic wisp coming from the crown of my head. I wore my wig, which was uncannily like my own hair had been to look at, but not of course to feel. It fitted very tightly indeed. There was a sort of inner cap, like a swimming hat, which I had to stretch over my head, it gave me a headache long before each day was over. I was not supposed to sleep in it, and in any case it was too hot and uncomfortable to do so, but I had another, much looser, to wear in bed. I was always afraid it would fall off in the night and one of the children would come in and see this hideous, hairless monster in their mother's bed and scream and scream. I started to wear a ribbon, securely tied on top of it, to keep it anchored – oh, the distress it caused me when Rosemary laughed at my early morning appearance. But gradually I grew more confident. I never forgot I was wearing a wig – nobody could do that – but, because I looked normal wearing it, I began to feel more normal and not so terrified of public derision. And I suppose this achieved some sort of automatic inner relaxation, which did the trick. My hair started to grow. One night, removing my hateful wig, I ran my hand over my aching head and felt tiny pinpricks of stubble. I thought my excitement would produce an adverse reaction and tried desperately to stop myself feeling my head again and again, but I could not sleep for hoping. I made myself promise not to feel my scalp again until the week was up, and I kept the promise. A week later there was the softest down all over my head. I waited another week, and then another, and then at last I confronted a mirror without a wig, something I had not done for six whole months. I still looked bald, as though my scalp had been painted with a light brown brush. It was nothing yet, the new hair, but it was everything. Those lumps and knobs on my head which had loomed as large as Everest, when first I saw them, were now merely the gentlest of undulations. I could face myself. For another month I wore a wig, and then I told my children I was tired of long hair, I was going to have it all cut off, very short, so that it would be easier to look after. I was too busy to have long hair which needed so much attention and which I hated to see untidy. Don't cut it, said Rosemary, Daddy won't like it and I won't like it and you'll look ugly. VE Day was just over. I knew the likelihood of Oliver returning was now absolutely remote and that it was wrong to let the children think they would see him again. They could not grow up sustained on a diet of false hope (as I was). There were some things from which I could not protect them, and that was one. So I did two things I dreaded on the same day. I took off my wig, for good, and I told the children their father was never coming back. The telling was dreadful for me but not for the children. They accepted it quite calmly. Rosemary said, 'He was a soldier and he was killed in a battle wasn't he?' I said yes. She asked if he got a medal. I said no. Celia, aged five, asked if we would get another daddy. I said no. She said Ellen didn't have a daddy and neither did Phillip and James (all children in the same reception class at Primrose Hill Infants School). My shorn head was accepted in the same matter-of-fact way. Rosemary said I looked funny. I could not have looked as funny as I felt – lighthearted suddenly and glad and dizzy and slightly unbalanced. Instead of hoarding my wig secretly or destroying it I put it immediately in the dressing-up box. It made me feel triumphant to watch the children treat it as a plaything.

And now, at last, I am done. The background is sketched in, even if it has taken longer than I thought. I am ready to begin —

*

Thank Christ. But on what? That was all too depressing to make me want to continue. So I shan't. I'll leave, and ring her up later and say I had to go before she came in. She'll be disappointed but I can't help it.

Mother is having her hair done. I don't think I want to think about her hair, not after thinking all week about that Alopecia episode. It's the way she wrote about it that really fucks me up – so succinct and *tidy*. I know it was centuries ago, but I can't imagine myself sitting down in the future and making such a neat, sweet little story out of any of the unbearable troubles I've had myself. But, for Mother, it's no problem. It's as though she was glad to be giving this painless account. It's bizarre, and false. I'm sure it's false. This is where her diary for that time might be more helpful. I realize that I get angry, worked up to a ridiculous degree, whenever I think Mother is not telling the truth, and that's what makes me anxious to get to the point where I *know* I can remember better than she can. I can't possibly stop ferreting around in these papers until I've come to the important parts of my own life, read everything that comes in between. I can't be bothered with our early childhood any more – I want to get on.

February 15th

First straight, green shoots thrusting out of the damp black earth, first rounding of buds on the pear tree, such excitement, such happiness at the thought of spring. Every year I forget the exact sequence nature follows, every year I am amazed. Makes me cheerful and optimistic, regardless. Thoughts turn to meals outside and children shrieking in paddling pools and slow sunsets. Warmth and beauty. Wish Emily felt the same. But no, says spring means nothing to her, how corny. She says I cannot know what real grief means if spring makes me happy. She hates spring, hates new life. Life is an evil monster feeding on the dead and she wants only the dead. Being with her is an ordeal, I suffer, suffer humbly, feeling I must be her whipping boy. But slyly, my head lowered in the face of her continuing ugly resentment, I see the blue sky and feel the sun's warmth and hear the birds and I am comforted. Rosemary found me still in the garden. She'd been sketching, in Epping Forest, showed me some drawings of trees. I asked if I could have one. Chose one. She sighed, said it was the worst, she would be tearing it up. She thinks my taste deplorable. I fear her censure, almost forget what I do like in my effort to avoid it. And I no longer know what *she* likes. Her oils of nudes I suppose, large and blue. She kissed me, asked me how I was. Such a shock to realize she has almost no interest in me. I am her mother and I am not interesting. But what is there for Rosemary to be interested in? My thoughts on spring? My two hours sitting in the garden? We chat with such apparent ease, polite give and take. She wants reassurance that I am not a poor forlorn widow. I give her what she wants. That way, I keep her. I will make any terms to do that. Just keep them, keep them coming. Offer a refuge, uncritical, supportive, though they have all found a line beyond which I cannot go. Some mothers can. Mothers of murderers, of rapists. I stand by him, mothers say, and he will always be the same to me. Cannot go that far. None of them are the same to me, now. Don't get dragged down by this, no point. Firmly concentrate on the loveliness of the day, of this first real spring evening. Keep such reflections for my, for whatever it is I am struggling with. Keep this for happy notes, please, or not at all.

*

— 'The children of lovers are orphans,' wrote Robert Louis Stevenson. His own parents loved each other so passionately that he felt their love excluded him. That is my first point: my daughters made the death of their father the tragedy of their childhoods. But they chose to make it so later, when they were adults. In fact, not only was Oliver's death remarkably untragic for them, it actually brought them advantages they cannot seem to recognize.

Oliver and I were lovers. We were as close as two people ever can be. Already, before he left for the war, I had been given an inkling of how our much loved children might suffer from our intense preoccupation with each other. We fought to be alone, we —

*

Oh, God, not again. Next she'll be on to quoting from her treasured *Collected Poems of Elizabeth Barrett Browning*, his engagement present to her, if you please. Which will it be? 'When we met first and loved I did not build upon thee even with marble', or 'How do I love thee?' Either one is a real turn-off. I can, and will, do without it.

*

— created the ritual of Rosemary and me having a little meal together, sitting formally at the kitchen table with all the baby clutter cleared away. Rosemary would tell me her day and I would tell her mine and we would discuss the things that had happened. I took Rosemary's advice on all sorts of matters from what colour to paint the kitchen to what we should have for supper. She was a strong child, always, strong in her views and opinions, and quick and sharp. She never hesitated. Out would come her answers, very definite and immediate. She was bold and clear-sighted, cutting through many a tangle I had got myself into. Then, when we had eaten our private little supper, we would both read for an hour before she went to bed. She was an avid reader and so was I. It gave me such pleasure watching her read all my own childhood favourites and hearing what she had to say. Often, she would surprise me by her reaction. *Uncle Tom's Cabin* she dismissed as sentimental

49

and dull, and it annoyed her to be told how I had cried and cried over it, but she liked *Jane Eyre*. It was a bond I never had with my other children. Whatever happened later to us, it is an undeniable fact that there existed between Rosemary and me a wonderful closeness —

*

A myth. Typical of my mother, endless romanticizing to shape the past as she wishes to. I am on surer ground now. This is where I wanted to get to. Those evenings I clearly recall, and what I recall is that I always wanted to go out. Other children went out and played in the street or the park. I don't suppose it was more than hanging about, but I wanted to hang about with the rest. But no. Mother said I was tired and needed 'a quiet time'. She would sit at the kitchen table saying, 'Isn't it nice, just the two of us,' and I would squirm. I didn't want to be just the two of us, I have *never* wanted it, it was what I dreaded most. I much preferred the others to be about. When it was just the two of us I felt unbearably restless – I'd literally fidget about on the chair, desperate to escape. And the endless deferring to my opinion didn't flatter me, it drove me crazy. What did *I* care what colour the kitchen was, and, anyway, it always ended up the colour she wanted and had decided on before she ever opened her mouth. What she tried to do was persuade me that I actually wanted what she wanted. And as for the reading, I hated the books she gave me, even *Jane Eyre*. She liked melodramatic, sad stories. I like funny books, or comics. It was the same with the wireless, upon which we were heavily dependent. She liked me to like plays and stories but I liked all the light comedy shows and the serials like *Dick Barton*.

She is right about the closeness but not about it being wonderful. We could not help being close, thrown so much together, but I always resisted it, I didn't want it. It wasn't that I didn't love her or like her – I did. I was proud of her, I always liked identifying her as *my* mother at the school gate, but I didn't want to acknowledge any closeness. It was too intimate, I couldn't bear her need. It never struck me that she was using me as a substitute for my dead father, just that she needed from me what I didn't want to give. I wanted distance. The gain she talks about was no gain, except for her. I didn't 'choose' to make my father's death a tragedy – that was how it genuinely seemed to me and still does.

— that I allowed them to think we were hard up. They talk of growing up worrying about money, which they never did. They forget that in that post-war period, with rationing still in operation, everyone lived frugally. They say they would have chosen to spend their inheritances, saving themselves from the 'endless penny-pinching', as they describe the slight and entirely commonplace economizing from which they argue they 'suffered'. It was unnecessary, they claim. What they mean is that, after Grandmother Butler died, they were technically rich and yet I kept their wealth from them and denied them new tennis racquets and dresses and a pony and all manner of other luxuries. I deliberately made their life 'hard'.

That is nonsense. They have no conception of what 'hard' means. It is tempting to sketch in my own truly hard childhood but I shall resist it — it is what they bait me to do. And it is a weak argument, not one I care to use. It is better to stick to the facts and the facts are that we lived very comfortably and that I could not have used their money even if I had thought it right to do so. I never resented or contested Grandmother Butler's will. She died in the severe winter of 1947. She left her house and money in trust for her grandchildren, specifically excluding 'those who are not true blood relatives', which meant Jess, of course. I was appointed a trustee together with her solicitor and Simon Birch, Rosemary's godfather. To me she left her jewellery and clothes. The solicitor was embarrassed about it, but I was not upset. It seemed to me right and proper that my children should benefit and not I. I did think, briefly, of selling our London house and moving permanently to Brighton, but I decided not to. The children were settled at school and I could not face the upheaval. So the Bedford Square house, lovely though it was, was sold and the money invested. This left me in the strange position of being rather hard-up while being the trustee for children who would be rather well off when they became twenty-one. The solicitor was eager to start considering ways in which some of the trust could be released for expenses, but I took a pride in refusing to countenance this. In any case, to someone like myself, brought up as I had been, I never thought of myself as poor. Oliver had left me five thousand pounds and a house: a fortune, or so I thought. And by taking in lodgers I gave myself an income.

What I had wanted was a male lodger. We were a house of women and we needed that. I did not want my girls to grow up as I had grown up, so devoid of the presence of men that they seemed weird and fearful creatures. There were no uncles, brothers, or boy cousins to console them for the loss of their father. What I wanted was a man, or two men, going in and out of the house, joining us occasionally for meals, generally around to become part of the pattern I was intent on creating. They did not need to be friends, just familiars. The two large rooms at the top of the house made excellent bed-sitting rooms and a box room on the half landing was converted into a bathroom for the young gentlemen's exclusive use. No kitchen, however. I thought a gas ring and a kettle in each room enough. I would undertake to provide meals by arrangement but I thought most of their eating would be done at the hospital. At the hospital, because of course I imagined medical students would fit the bill. Quite why I don't know. It seemed obvious. Something to do with Oliver being a doctor I suppose.

I asked Simon Birch if he would be so kind as to select for me two of his quieter students who needed accommodation. He sent round an extremely earnest pair, both bespectacled and anxious looking, both from Somerset. I truly forget their names but they were very nice, caused no trouble. They had lunch with us on Sundays and usually two other meals at some time in the week. They were obliging about carrying heavy things upstairs and stoking the boiler for me and, in the summer, they tackled the garden enthusiastically. Both worked hard and were untypical of medical students in that they were not boisterous. I don't think they ever had any friends round and certainly never gave a party. They paid their rent promptly. When they left, they bequeathed the rooms to two of their acquaintances who were equally pleasant, and so it went on, until in 1950, when Rosemary was fifteen, two students of a different kind took up residence. I don't know how the system broke down. The two who preceded them were like all the others had been and I trusted their recommendation implicitly. I don't remember their names but I could never forget the names of the two they gave their rooms to. They were called Trevor Maxwell and Michael Pearson. And it was when they entered our life that Rosemary began to rebel, although she —

*

Before we get on to Trev and Mike, which I'm looking forward to, even if I have a very good idea of what she's going to make of that little episode without needing to read a word of it, let me interrupt and quickly point out that in fact she's strayed from her own point. The lodgers had nothing to do with us thinking she deprived us of the standard of living we would like to have had. Those lodgers were the good part of our Reduced Circumstances. We wouldn't have wanted not to have them, however rich we were. And Mother knows this perfectly well. What we objected to was her attitude to money, to all expenditure, however trivial. Everything got written down. There was an account book for the household expenses and another for personal expenses. Every penny spent had to be entered in one or the other. When we were each thirteen, Mother gave us our own account books, and made a big thing of showing us how to do a credit column and a debit one, and how to balance the two. I hated it. All those stupid figures – icecream 6d, fare to school 3d – it drove me insane. At the end of each week, we had to present our accounts and what a carry-on there was if we hadn't entered everything or if we were in the red. I really couldn't stand it. Mother called it instilling financial sense into us, but it did no such thing. It made me cheat. I just wrote down the first things that came into my head to explain where my miserable five shillings a week had gone. Usually I just wrote down exactly the same each week. It made me detest money, that awful solemn emphasis on accounting and budgeting. If you had it, you had it, and if it had gone, it had gone.

Mother used the words 'I'm afraid we can't afford' a lot. What we couldn't afford was just about everything that made life worth living. I was fiercely jealous of what other girls at school had (by this time I was at Camden High School, which is a state school, but there were lots of very well-off pupils left over from its recent private days and it went on attracting that type all the time I was there). Possessions were important then. I wanted a decent pen, a Conway Stewart, and not an awful Woolworth's fountain pen. I wanted new hockey boots that fitted me properly and not hardly worn second-hand ones. And I wanted to do all the things they did that cost money: I wanted to go ice-skating and to the cinema and up the Thames on boats. I wanted a gramophone of my own and a transistor radio, *the* thing, and a flash wristwatch. I'm ashamed to remember how much I wanted all this. But I never got them. Mother, quite rightly you will say and I myself now say, despised material things. She couldn't take seriously my wanting to have them, so she said she couldn't afford them. I didn't swallow bravely and come out with a touching spiel about never-mind-Mummy-I-don't-care. I raged at the injustice of it. And all the time Mother was saying money couldn't buy the things that really mattered – love, family, health – and we were rich in those. Dear God. What would one little wristwatch have mattered? I *know* she could have got money from our trust for all those things and more. But she didn't think it would be good for us. Self-denial was the order of the day for her and it was damn well going to be for us. Everything we had was threadbare – carpets, curtains, the lot. Our rather grand house, in an increasingly grand area, was furnished in the most spartan manner imaginable. I used to love going into Linda's next door, all jammed full of settees and leather chairs (her mother's pride and joy) and china cabinets with flowered cups shining in rows. I loved Linda's room, with its new, fluffy, white rug (nylon, Mother pointed out) and her posh kidney-shaped dressing table with the flounced surround. In Linda's house they bought things all the time, a constant stream of merchandise, and yet her father was only a jobbing builder. It was all on the never-never but that meant nothing to me then. I didn't care where the hell it all came from, I just wanted *things* then. More than clothes, which is strange, I suppose. Clothes never bothered me. They bothered Mother. She was obsessed with appearances. We were the sort of little girls who wore dresses with very white Peter Pan collars and always had matching knickers, *matching* knickers, and those hideous patent leather black shoes with ankle straps. When I think of the energy that went into all that.

How stupid she was. A thousand or so wouldn't have made much of a hole in the trust fund and it would have made all the difference to greedy little me. It would have brought some innocent frivolity into our serious lives, and that was what we needed. She didn't have to be so bloody boringly *worthy*.

*

— had nothing to rebel against. I was never a domineering, over-strict mother. I deny it absolutely. Ours was a free-thinking household, in which everyone was always encouraged to say what they thought. Yet Rosemary, at fifteen, acted as though she had been constrained all her life and must at all costs burst out of the bonds so unfairly restricting her. The effect on her sisters was disastrous. Celia and Jess were ten, Emily only six, when Rosemary entered this phase. Everything she did was admired and applauded by them. I tried so hard to keep a sense of proportion and humour about how Rosemary was behaving, but the sheer triviality of her attacks – because they were attacks, sustained ones – wore me down. Everything was why should I, I don't have to, will if I feel like it, don't care. She sulked and scowled and snapped so much I forgot what a smile had looked like on her face. She could hardly warm a chair for two minutes and only stayed in the house if she had a friend with her. For them, she was witty, amusing, good fun. We heard endless shrieks of laughter from her room all weekend. She seemed to hate us. Yet, at the same time as she made me angry and miserable, she also made me desperately sorry for her. She caused me endless distress, but time after time I held back from remonstrating because I pitied her. On the surface, there was little to pity. She was pretty, clever, talented, popular. But she was also unbearably restless, frustrated and tormented by discontent with her lot. The future, any future, was where she wanted to be. I longed to soothe and console her, but she was unapproachable. It was so difficult finding —

*

This is too much. I want you to see my mother when I was fifteen and so 'unapproachable'. Even though Emily was far too old for such babying she never seemed to have her out of her arms or off her knee for one minute. They were quite inseparable and invincible. Every time I came into a room that kid was being cuddled, literally from the minute she woke up to the minute she went to bed. Coming home from school I'd find Emily, whom I loathed for her winsome ways, clutched to her bosom and Celia and Jess demanding her attention. 'What sort of day did you have?' she'd say and instantly, *instantly*, Emily would start asking some inane question, and my mother would become utterly absorbed in answering her. Sometimes I'd start telling her about my day and she'd make some comment above the noise and Emily would actually put her hand over Mother's mouth and stop her speaking. It was a bloody farce. I wasn't the one who was 'unapproachable', she was. She could surely have organized things better with her wonderful talents in that direction. If she'd cared about me she could have made sure Linda or someone was there at four o'clock to take over the other three for half an hour. It was too late by the time we got to our useless suppers. I'd forgotten everything about the sodding day. But then she was always obsessed with Emily, physically I mean, always caressing and stroking and holding her. It drove me crazy. She was always saying I'd never liked being cuddled, as a sort of reprimand. She said that, even as a baby, I'd fight off embraces. Well, she's the only one who knows, but I doubt it and anyway babies change. I know damn well that, every time I saw Emily being gooed over, I wished I was her (I don't now, of course). 'You *are* lovely, Em,' my mother would say and give Emily an enormous hug. 'No, *you* are, Mummy,' Emily would lisp and they'd hug again. Christ, 'unapproachable'. If she thought I was so pathetic, if she pitied me with all her tender heart, why didn't she find some way of expressing it? Was it really so hard? Not that I concede I was pathetic – bloody patronizing thing to say, a well-known ploy when you can't handle someone, the ultimate insult. I've done it myself when I want to get at somebody, just looked disdainful and said they were pathetic. She never just got on with her own life and let me get on with mine. Never laughed either, saw no humour in the situation. It was all tension and anxiety because she was so law-abiding and virtuous herself, she couldn't bear the thought of her own reputation being sullied by my breaking potty rules at school or something. She was always saying my behaviour would be seen as a reflection on her, on the *family*. I used to ask her what family – this goaded her the most. I'd jeer and say we weren't a family, just a house of women, silly things like that. I'd go further and say I had no family feeling whatsoever, that I didn't understand it, that it must be a sense, like smell or taste, that I had been born without. Then her stupid eyes would fill with tears and I would know that, although it might be the truth, I had gone too far.

*

— ways of pleasing her. I would buy her some small thing I knew she wanted and leave it on the desk in her room. She never mentioned these little surprises. It wasn't that I expected her to come running down (as Emily later would) shouting her thanks and beaming at my thoughtfulness, it wasn't that I demanded such extravagant appreciation. But it is true that the total lack of response hurt. I would try not to mention it, but sometimes, to my own disgust, I would find myself blurting out, 'Was that the pen you wanted?' and then she would look abstracted

56

and say that yes, it was, thanks. I tried to have the sort of food she liked too. I tried all sorts of ways to get near her and failed. The only people near her were her friends (whom she kept very much to herself, getting them from the front door to her room as quickly as possible, before any of us could even see them and say hello), and the two students who came in 1950 when she was fifteen. Trevor Maxwell and Michael Pearson.

They were both only eighteen. Up to then, I had had third year students who were older than the normal third year students because the war had interrupted their studies. But Trevor and Michael were fresh out of school and of a different breed. They were not exactly impolite but they were not courteous as the others had always been. They took things for granted. Their thanks, if expressed at all, were offhand. I was not used to such brusqueness, except from Rosemary. Nor was I used to the hours they kept. Trevor and Michael came in at all hours of the early morning and made a great deal of noise. I objected strongly and I must say they were suitably contrite, so much so that I let it pass. But that was when I ought to have turned them out straight away, when it would still have been easy and could not have been seen by Rosemary as an attack on her.

Both of them had a sort of charm, I suppose, even if it was not of a variety with which I was familiar. They were very natural, very at home anywhere. The other students had always seemed awkward and gauche in my kitchen – setting them at ease was one of my pleasures. Without exception, they were shy at first. Trevor and Michael did not know what shyness was. They were also openly inquisitive. Nobody had ever asked me if I was a widow – either this had been assumed or Simon Birch had told the first two students, who had always passed it on – but Trevor asked me straight away if my husband had been killed in the war. Then he asked me if I got lonely, still being young. It was ridiculous of me but I was deeply embarrassed. I felt as if my house had been invaded by some strange force I didn't understand, and I saw straight away that Rosemary felt the same. The only difference was that, whereas it made me alarmed and uneasy, it made her excited. From the very beginning, she adored Trevor and Michael. In no time at all, worries about uniform and homework and manners were the merest nothings. I had something much more threatening to cope with.

57

At fifteen, Rosemary was at her prettiest. She was never unattractive when she was young but later, until she was about twenty or so, she went through a stage when she seemed to devote herself to defiling her body and face in every way, and she almost succeeded. But at fifteen she was a pleasure to look at, far more beautiful than her sisters at that age. Her hair was long, straight and thick, with a thick fringe, and her colouring, as I've said before, definitely mine. (I don't know where that complexion has gone.) Her skin was always brown, her cheeks pink, her teeth very white. She looked like an exotic gypsy child, except she was not a child but a rapidly developing woman. I seemed to watch Emily's body change week by week but with Rosemary there were no stages – she suddenly seemed to have gone from being flat as a board to having breasts. I had to pluck up my courage to ask her if she would like me to buy her a brassière. She told me fiercely to mind my own business, she didn't want to be put into a *harness*. In 1950, that was quite daring but, though she must have aroused some comment at school, she never gave in. It was perhaps fortunate that she never wore tight things.

As soon as Trevor and Michael set eyes on Rosemary they were captivated. At first, perhaps they did not realize she was only fifteen, since she was tall and always looked older than her age. Unfortunately, their first glimpse of her was not in her school uniform but in white shorts and a loose tee shirt. I remember making very pointed remarks to show them how young she was, but these fell on deaf ears. Instead of being either moody or argumentative at mealtimes Rosemary became vivacious, putting herself out to amuse and entertain the two new students. She had never shown the slightest interest in any of our lodgers before —

*

Of course I hadn't shown the slightest interest. You should have seen Mother's lodgers, awful, boring, middle-class snobs the lot of them, all with hair that looked as if their mothers had combed it. They made me sick. And what my mother has carefully not pointed out about Trev and Mike, but what she really wants to say, is that they were of a different social class from the others. Trev was from Halifax and Mike from Workington in Cumberland. Nor were they the sort of working-class product my mother was used to. They weren't overwhelmed by our gentility or humble or embarrassed. They were just themselves, quite comfortable in their own skins. She says, in effect, that they had no manners – my mother was always very keen on manners – but she is wrong. The difference was that they did not have the *same* manners, but that doesn't mean they were uncouth or yobs.

The other thing Mother doesn't mention, except obliquely, is sex. Trev and Mike were sexy. My mother hates that word and so, as a matter of fact, do I, but it is the only one that will do. All our other students had appeared quite sexless, believe me. If the reason for having them there, apart from the money, had been to give us an idea of masculinity, it had failed. This quality never manifested itself, except for the odd moustache or beard or the ability to lug a heavy load up the stairs. But Trev and Mike (how my mother hated those abbreviations) were sensually male. No wonder my poor prim mama felt her kitchen had been invaded. It was, by sex, for the first time. They both had this way of standing, this basic cockiness, that was very masculine. Cocks were the first thing I noticed about them, no other way of putting it. Naturally, my mother had hardly been able to arrange for us to be familiar with naked cocks but at fifteen I spent a lot of time thinking about them. I could never work out where they went to, trousers being the flat-fronted things they are. Did the cocks hang down one leg or did they get folded away? Did they get bent up or down or sideways? And, when men sat down, how did these protuberances re-arrange themselves? Sometimes I thought they must be a myth, since no man I had ever looked at seemed to have anything there except zipped grey flannel. But Trev and Mike did. They had definite bulges there and suddenly I could believe in what this male equipment was supposed to do. I make it sound as if they both went round indecently exposing themselves, but all they did was wear rather tight trousers and do a lot of strutting about with their hands in their pockets. They also leered. Apart from men in novels I had never come across a man leering – leers were as mysterious as cocks. When Trev and Mike caught my eye and made a joke and stared, I became acquainted with the Leer. I loved it. My little girlish heart raced beneath my bra-less breast. I blushed, tossed my hair, flirted. What a pretty picture I must have made.

But they were harmless, Trev and Mike. And nice. They sussed out the situation in our house in no time at all and were really much kinder than all those dutiful young slobs who mended plugs or whatever.

They livened things up no end. They played wild games with Emily and carried her on their shoulders and, if I was besotted by our young heroes, she was their abject slave. They introduced pop music to our sedate household. Wherever they went, Radio Luxembourg blared out, and they taught us their favourite terrible songs. The other thing about them was that they were so affectionate and demonstrative – they were always slapping and pushing and hugging the younger ones, always chasing and grabbing them and making up silly games. Like most medical students they adored practical jokes and dressing up. Oh, we were lost in admiration at their childish wheezes. When they were on a hospital carnival float dressed as Good Queen Bess and Queen Victoria, we nearly died of pride. We were all their groupies, all except Mother.

It never entered my head then, but it enters it now: did Mike make a pass at my mother? She was only thirty-five, 'only' now that I am myself forty-nine. But was she an attractive older lady to them or someone like their own mothers? I've studied the few photographs she has of that period and it's so hard to tell. The clothes weren't flattering to that age of woman with those pinched, clinched waists and ghastly long 'new look' skirts. Hair was terrible too, all stiff and bunchy. But who can tell, except those who were there? She had good features and her famous beautiful complexion. She wasn't either too fat or too thin. And I suppose there would have been something attractive about her position: the tragic young war widow, I mean, with all these children and no man at all in her life. Probably it fascinated them, speculating whether she missed 'it'. Her stiffness and general air of convent girl purity would be another come-on. I always thought she wanted to get rid of them to protect me but it might have been to protect herself. Yet, surely, they would never have had the nerve even to try to flirt with my mother?

*

— in bed with Linda. It was the early afternoon, and I suppose they thought the house was empty. Usually I took Emily out for a walk then and stayed out until it was time to collect Celia and Jess from school. But there was a sudden thunderstorm, minutes after we left the house, and we dashed back out of the rain. I had no idea anyone was in the house. When I heard faint noises, I thought it might be burglars and so I shouted, 'Who's there? Michael? Trevor?' and, when there was no reply, concluded I had been hearing things. I went up to my bedroom to change my wet clothes, taking Emily with me, and there were Linda and Michael Pearson. In my bed.

I was rather proud of my self-control. I made some comment aloud to Emily about this being like the story of the three bears, and then I closed the door and went up to the children's room. My heart was thudding and I was absurdly upset. Like Lady Macbeth I kept thinking what, in my house, as though that mattered. They were both grown people. Linda was twenty-two by then, a mature woman, there was nothing shocking about it, but I was shocked. Michael did not care for Linda, that was what upset me. He teased her, as he did all of us, but it was perfectly plain that he thought she was a joke. From being plump at sixteen, when I first employed her, Linda had become very overblown indeed, and her fetching, easy ways had degenerated into laziness. She trudged about my house, supposedly helping me, but doing very little except having constant snacks and singing. At least her singing was pleasant. Michael told her she had a wonderful voice and had she ever thought about having it trained. That was the level of his flattery and Linda loved it. And there they were, in my bed.

I hated the idea of having to talk to either of them about it. I dreaded explanations. All I wanted was to act as though nothing had happened and hope it would not happen again. But Michael came to find me within minutes and could not be evaded. He said he was sorry, it was unforgivable of them to have used my bedroom, that what had happened was – but I cut him short. I said the matter was closed, let's not talk about it. I was sorry I had interrupted. He annoyed me by not leaving me alone at once and, indeed, by talking in front of Emily at all. I was afraid of what he might say next, so I deliberately left Emily getting dressed and went downstairs to the kitchen. He followed me and hung about. There was no sign of Linda I remember. 'All it was,' he said, 'it was a bit of a romp.' I suppose I winced. 'It isn't a crime you know,' he persisted. 'I mean, we shouldn't have been in your bed, that was wrong, but apart from that I don't see why you're so furious and disgusted.' I denied that I was either, of course. Then he began to get angry himself. He said my attitude to sex was puritanical. I said I *had* no attitude and, in any case, I had no wish to discuss such things with him. Then he got hold of me, grabbed me, said he wondered why not. I

61

pushed him off with such force that he crashed back into the kitchen table and the plate of fruit sitting there went flying onto the floor. I told him not to dare to touch me again. I said he was impertinent and stupid, and that he could keep his half-baked theories to himself. Emily came in at this point, furious because she couldn't find matching socks. I was so relieved to have an excuse to escape upstairs with her. I was shaking with rage and with fear, not fear because I thought that for one moment Michael had wanted to do more than engage my attention, but because his nearness had sent a wave of excitement through me. Not sexual excitement exactly, just general adrenalin. I had grown so used to feeling nothing that it scared me and I —

*

Well! No wonder dear Trev and Mike left in such a hurry, no wonder Linda found herself another job at long last. I can't blame Mike for this. Linda presented herself to him on a plate. It's pathetic to think puny little me ever had a chance. Why should Mike or Trev even notice me when the luscious Linda was there for the asking and I was jail-bait? And to think I imagined they were attracted by me, that they might any minute ask me out properly to the cinema or a party and would *certainly* kiss me goodnight. I wonder if they were booted out that very day? The atmosphere must have been awful but I don't remember noticing any change in Mother's attitude. She was always her usual grave, cool self with them. What a pity. What a pity it wasn't Mother in bed with Mike. She wrote at the beginning of all this that we did not realize how we have shaped our own lives, and yet she doesn't see what she did to her own. She denied herself sex. How wonderfully virtuous. How wonderfully silly. She makes me so *tired*. Self-denial for *our* sakes, of course. Couldn't have a mother enjoying herself like that, could we? Wouldn't have been proper.

Trev and Mike lived with us for not quite a year. I look back on it as a halcyon period. I used to fantasize that, if they could not be lovers, they could be brothers and then 'family' might not be the dreary thing it was. I loved both of them in a way I did not love Celia or Jess or Emily. Even apart from fancying them, I had all kinds of contact with them – we talked the same language, or, if that's putting it too strongly, they talked the language I wished to learn. Nobody in my family did. They didn't admire orderliness and obedience, they weren't conventional, they didn't plan and save industriously. I suppose I can't also add that they didn't admire the work ethic, as my mother tried to make us do: they must have worked to get themselves into that Medical School, and I don't remember any talk of them failing examinations. When *they* left I was devastated. The house was like a grave. I suppose, not knowing why they had actually left, I hoped they would still come back to see us, but they never did. They just disappeared from our lives, not even a letter or card as far as I know. My mother didn't seem surprised. She shrugged when I complained bitterly about not hearing from them and said they were very young and it was to be expected and we were just an incident in their lives. It wasn't, she said, as if they were family upon whom we had claims, or even friends. They had come as an economic arrangement and, however devoted we had become, it wasn't the same. What I hated was that she seemed quite pleased about it, as though she was using it as a demonstration of what *family* really meant so that at last I would see why she revered the institution. Well, I didn't. I hated it all the more.

March 5th

Just the sort of Monday morning I've been waiting for, cold, bitterly
cold, cheerless, dreary, perfect for going to the Royal Academy to catch
the Genius of Venice exhibition before it closes. Pleased me just to
think of going, didn't put me off a bit that Rosemary said it was a
boring exhibition, pleased me to be there while others trudged to work,
pleases me now to think back upon. Thinking about Arrigo Licinio and
his seven children. The mother in the picture flanked on both sides by
dark-clothed children. She was separate but part of them, gold silk to
their black velvets. Substantial in size and presence. Calm. Paint us, her
husband Arrigo had said in 1535, paint us as we are, a family. Put on
your best dress, he had said to her. None of them smiled, even the baby
was grim-faced. It was the importance which made them severe, the
presentation of their joint, enclosed family world to the painter. Not a
fidget anywhere, not a joker. What effort went into organizing the
sittings? What threats and cajoling? Never did I manage it, the posed
family group, though I tried. Plenty of individual photographs of us all
but no group photo, except one taken at Emily's wedding, and even
there we're not just on our own. But that was another era, another life,
family sacrosanct, free will within it unheard of. Nothing to prize
really, those brooding Italian groups. Bought a plate, olive covered. I
shall eat very white fish from it or arrange goat cheese and figs upon it
and admire the colours before I eat. How nice to be in London, within
reach of exhibitions and distractions. Move to the country, my
children said when I was sixty, move to somewhere beautiful and calm
and peaceful, move to a place where you can walk as you love to walk,
in real countryside or along seashores, you love the country, love the
sea. No. How far sighted I was. I need London more now I am getting
old, not less. Oliver and I could have lived happily in the depths of the
country, arrogant in our love, smugly self-sufficient, then. Swiss Family
Butler. But not now. London's bad parts I can take. The traffic, dirt,
crowds. Small price to pay for its compensations. No need, in London,

to fear bleak days, to shudder at grey, leaden mornings. Out. I can always go out, somewhere, there is always a *treat* available.

*

I didn't get as far on as I wanted last time because Celia arrived long before Mother got back. She was bringing Mother some smoked mackerel pâté she'd been making and dropping some shopping in. There was I, all hot-cheeked with guilt I expect, tripping out of this room clutching a photograph of Emily's wedding as an alibi. Celia wasn't even interested, she couldn't have cared less what I was doing. She has so little curiosity, it's extraordinary to think we're sisters. I stood watching her as she unloaded all the goodies she'd brought. Her pride was amusing. She set the pâté down with such care and *affection*, sort of stroking the cloth that covered the dish it was in. 'Mother *will* enjoy it,' she said. I didn't dare speak. Then she turned to me. 'Would you like some, Rosemary? It would be no trouble.' I said no thanks, I wasn't really into eating much. She was offended. Oh Christ – she was offended. I wonder what Mother has to say about Celia? I don't think I can stand the boredom of reading it. Celia's illness as a child, bound to be yards on that. The mere thought . . . but perhaps it might be fun, a useful test, for me to get in first here for a change. Now what do I remember about dear Celia?

Well, for a start, Celia was a surrogate father to us all. If Mother went through a phase, before I became bolshie, of imagining I could replace her dead husband so far as companionship went, she certainly went through a much more prolonged one of thinking Celia could stand in for him as a father. It was not fair that my sister should have had to spend her adolescence bolstering up Mother's idea of a family but she didn't seem to mind. I rejected my role, but Celia loved hers. She was five years younger than I but seemed much older by the time she was twelve. Partly, it was her appearance. Whereas I was like Mother, Celia was like the Butler women: short, heavy and with something Slavonic about them. I'd only seen Grandmother Butler when she was old but I'd seen photographs of her when she was young, and of her mother too, and they were exactly like Celia. Weight and girth always makes young girls look older, but Celia's nature also aged her prematurely. She was (is) phlegmatic. Her expression is deadpan. Her great, moon-like face with its large pale eyes rarely has much

65

expression in it. She looked like a middle-aged frump, even when she was young, and it never seemed surprising to find her acting like one. The only surprising thing about Celia was how sporty she was – a demon at any game, especially tennis. She had a walk like a duck-billed platypus but she moved with amazing speed on a tennis court. She and Mother played together. I always laughed when I saw them going off side by side.

Mother, who had wonderfully long and shapely legs, always wore a decorous tennis dress very nearly covering her knees, whereas Celia, who had terrible legs, terrible, fat, red, wobbly thighs, wore shorts. They looked so funny, like Laurel and Hardy. They started playing when Celia was about ten, soon after Celia's convalescence. She had rheumatic fever, or was it glandular fever – oh, I can't remember, I've never been interested in illness – some long-drawn-out, debilitating thing, anyway, which took ages to diagnose, never mind cure. I recall Celia collapsing all over the place and being very white. None of us could believe it, big, strong Celia going down like a ninepin and then weak as a kitten. If it had been Jess or Emily, both frail and delicate-looking in their different ways, then it would've made more sense.

Mother moved Celia into her bedroom. It became their special sanctum. Celia's bed was placed by the window, where Mother lined up all sorts of plant pots for her to look at while she had to lie down so much. They grew all kinds of things in them and had endless boring conversations about the health of each sodding plant. I could hear them droning on when I went to bed next door. I can't say I was jealous of all the attention Celia got, but Jess and Emily were – they were furious. They hated hearing Mother and Celia talking, hated hearing them laugh on the other side of the closed door. Later, when Celia was up to going out, she and Mother gardened. Celia had her own little patch and spent hours planting things and hoeing away and generally grovelling about in the earth. Mother encouraged her. Every time a flower bloomed in Celia's patch you'd have thought it was a bloody miracle. Best time of Celia's life, I should think. The only time she ever felt close to Mother in the way she wanted. It's pathetic, really. Celia and Mother want to be more than absolutely devoted to each other, but they can't be. They are incompatible and it's not a bit of good them pretending that, because they are mother and daughter, that does not matter. It does. Mother has always been able to argue and shout with

Emily and me but she's never been able to do so with Celia. She's afraid to: it would be too dangerous because Celia might, indeed would, take her seriously.

*

— when they were small people often mistook Celia and Jess for twins even though Celia was very much bigger and older looking. They were both fair, both had large blue eyes, and Jess was simply thought the 'weak' twin from whom Celia had greedily taken a double share of strength. And of course I exaggerated their closeness because they were so much of an age, I treated them the same. They always shared a room (and a pram before that) and no distinction was made over bedtimes and so forth. But by the time they were five I knew how very different they were and that it was no good treating them the same. Celia was clever and Jess slow, Celia solid and dependable and Jess scatty. But I still thought that they were close and that such difference of temperament and personality, far from separating them, might actually draw them even closer. I did see that Celia took the lead and that Jess depended on her, but there seemed nothing abnormal in that. I saw that, without Celia, Jess was unhappy, that she needed her, but that seemed to me natural. I thought it quite touching —

*

If only Mother would cut this out. None of us dared tell her the truth about Jess because she was so besotted with her. Jess was some kind of atonement for Mother, her way of placating the gods. I don't pretend to understand Mother's complicated rationale but I am absolutely certain that she invested Jess with some kind of mystical significance. It may even be that she thought of Jess as herself.

Mother thought that Jess's adoption should be formally broken to Jess and to Celia when they were seven. She didn't see how Jess could be brought up successfully as her own, if, right from the beginning, the word adopted was used. But at seven they would be old enough to understand and yet Jess would have had time to become a secure part of our life. Mother had some muddled ideas derived from the famous Jesuit saying about the first seven years being the most formative. She thought the habits and beliefs of those years were fixed forever. I had it formally explained to me first – God knows what kind of garbled version I'd been fobbed off with at five. Mother used all the predictable patter. Jess was special, she had been chosen, she was every bit as much my sister as Celia and Emily. I was dumbfounded. The sole bit of information I took in was that Jess was not really my sister. Again and again I said to Mother, 'You mean, you aren't Jess's mummy? She didn't come out of your tummy', stuff like that. I wonder if, when Celia and Jess reached the magical age of seven, she told them together?

*

— told them together. It seemed the natural thing to do, but perhaps I was also hiding behind Celia, who, when I had finished telling them, pleased me by taking Jess's hand and holding it tightly. The subject was never mentioned again, not for years. I suppose I congratulated myself on how well I had managed the whole business.

I have looked at Celia and listened to her and thought about her and wondered how she could be the daughter of Oliver and me. In temperament and personality she is not like us. Because Rosemary and Emily are in different ways like me, I used to let Celia think she was like Oliver. I think she liked me to do so. But I knew she was not. She was more like Grandmother Butler, after whom she was named. And so I knew, always, that even children who are indisputably the offspring of two particular people can often appear not to be. Celia was just as much a cuckoo in my nest as Jess and, yet, the difference was crucial. Where Jess was concerned there was a different kind of blame attached, a different kind of agonizing worry to trouble me. However different Celia was from me, from us, from the rest of the family, there was nothing that could have been done about it. But where Jess was concerned, there was. I could not bear to think that Jess might have been happier in another family if I had not so greedily claimed her for my own.

When I told Jess that she was adopted, and why, I had stressed again and again how precious she was to me, how desperate I had been to have her. Not for a second can she have thought her adoption was done reluctantly, or grudgingly, or even as a kindness. She had no curiosity about her mother, she positively detested any mention of her. I thought I had painted such a wonderful portrait of her – young, beautiful, sweet-natured and brave. Jess would have none of it. 'Don't tell me,' she would say and that mulish, closed look came into her face. 'I don't

68

want to know, I don't want to know anything.' It was not because she wanted to think I was her real mother, I am sure of that. The whole subject of adoption was simply taboo. There was nothing I could do but leave it untouched, hoping all the time that as she grew older Jess would be reconciled. At least, I comforted myself, she had Celia to support her —

*

She had Celia. Unfortunately. Celia was like Mr Plod the policeman (how appropriate in view of Andrew Bayliss later). She never appeared in need of help or support herself, except when she was ill as a child, that was the maddening thing. She irritated me totally, I always longed for her to crack up. And I loathed her self-righteous attitude towards Jess. I didn't give a damn for Jess, but on the other hand I vaguely sympathized with her position.

I find it hard to describe Jess. As a child I have said how whey-faced and colourless she was and what a pest, always moaning. She didn't figure much in my life. But later I became more aware of her as she herself became more troublesome. She was Mother's cross. This joyous babe mother had taken to her bosom, and upon whom she had spent so much care and lavished so much love, became her cross. She didn't know how to make Jess happy and, even if she didn't realize, as she says, the full extent of her misery, she knew she was a misfit. The simple truth was that, as Mother now has the courage to acknowledge, Jess *would* have been better off absolutely anywhere but in our family. In one way which Mother never appreciated, Jess being an outsider, even though brought up from birth by Mother, proved that there was indeed a family identity which was rejecting a non-family member. It proved heredity was quite clearly stronger than environment in our case. That was Mother's bad luck, and Jess's too. But of course nobody could acknowledge that, nobody could possibly admit that the whole adoption was a ghastly failure and, quick, let's get this wretched child into another more congenial family or else into a Home. I'm not saying that would have been the solution, or advocating that it should have been. I'm just stating the facts as Mother seems unable to do. After she was ten years old Jess was in torment in our house, most of it internalized but manifesting itself in scores of well-known ways – well known, that is, to those who do know them.

She started truanting early, certainly before the end of her first year at secondary school. In that, as in so many other ways, she was stupid, entirely lacking the cunning needed to get away with it. She never thought of getting her registration mark first, she just didn't go in at all and so it was extremely easy for the school to discover she was bunking off. Celia told mother, even before the school did, and Mother went into a complete spin worrying over where Jess had gone, just as much as why she'd gone in the first place. It seems Jess just went to the nearest playground and sat there until four o'clock. Later, once she had met up with two other truants, whose names I forget, the pattern changed. No more innocent sitting in the playground, which was about Jess's real level. She moved onto shop-lifting. She got caught, inevitably, whereas the others didn't, and I'm not just echoing my mother when I say Jess was definitely set up by them. Then it was a policewoman and a social worker and Mother making herself ill with worry. I hated seeing my mother so upset. It was disgusting – yes, I do mean disgusting not heartbreaking. Her immense distress disgusted me. Her face seemed to cave in and wobble, and there was panic in every frenzied gesture. I didn't help by saying in my best world-weary sixth-form way what the hell did it matter, for God's sake, it was only a bloody pencil, don't make such a fuss. It certainly wouldn't help Jess, I pointed out, to carry on as if she was a mass murderer. Get some sense of proportion, I told my mother. I heard Mother go in to Jess that evening – she'd been sent to bed after all the officials had gone and Celia had, for once, been told to stay out – and I knew Mother would be attempting one of her famous heart-to-hearts, and I felt for Jess. I knew how infuriating it was to have Mother telling you how much she loved you and how ready she was to understand, and all that shit. I could deal with it. Jess certainly couldn't. What she needed was psychiatric treatment but that was the last thing she was going to get, with Mother acting already as the ultimate amateur shrink. It was a test of the family, Mother told the rest of us. *We must all close in and help Jess.* That is what families were for and what they meant: the world might reject and condemn you but not your family, not ever. *They* understood, they supported you through thick and thin. This didn't mean condoning whatever form your misbehaviour had taken, oh no, but it did mean going on loving you *in spite* of it, quite uncritically and unconditionally. That was the nub – family love was unconditional. Nobody bargained in a family, nobody said they would love you if you stopped truanting or shop-lifting or whatever, they just loved you.

Well, Mother may have believed that load of crap. None of the rest of us did, not even Emily, who was at that time only about seven or so. But we all kept quiet and didn't voice our heresy, because Mother's state was pitiful. We didn't really care about Jess but we did care about Mother.

*

— perhaps unwise. Jess was so very weak. When all the trouble began it drove me, once more, to wonder about Jess's mother. Had that been her trouble? Had she, too, been a drifter, someone always pushed along and shaped by others? Jess ought to have been luckier. She had us, a close and loving family. In particular, she had Celia. But, once the outside world started to intrude, she was terribly unfortunate. She was picked up by girls much smarter than herself at school and went along with them, hardly knowing what she was doing. The policewoman, who brought her home the first time she shop-lifted, smiled wearily when I said that, but it was true. Jess had already started sleep-walking through life.

I tried so hard to get through to her. There she was, lying on her bed, hands behind her head, just staring at the ceiling. No tears, absolute stillness. I did not ask her why she had taken the pencil, but how – how it had happened. She shrugged, not defiantly, just helplessly. I made a conscious effort to take her in my arms and hug her, but she kept her hands behind her head and her body was unyielding. I said to her that all she needed to know was that I loved her and always would. She did not say anything or move a muscle. As I left the room, defeated, she said, 'Can I have the radio on?' Going downstairs I could hear Radio Luxembourg blaring away. It struck me that pop music was Jess's sole interest. She did not read or play any games or musical instrument or draw. She did not belong to any clubs or societies. When I had tried to talk to her not very helpful teacher about this, she seemed to think this inactivity quite normal. Lots of young girls were like that, she said, there was nothing unusual about it. But in our house it was unusual. Nobody else just sat. I began to suspect there must be something wrong physically with Jess to account for her ennui, and took her to the doctor, half dreading he would diagnose pernicious anaemia or worse.

He said Jess was a little on the thin side and small for her age, but perfectly healthy. Fatten her up, he said, but that was impossible. She hardly ate anything.

She was about twelve when all this trouble began, still a child, and I was so thankful she was a late developer. I knew that, once she became mature, another element would enter life that she would be unable to cope with and which was likely to wreck her more thoroughly than any other influence up to then. Boys would be able to do what they liked with Jess. It would not be a question of morals, she was just used to going along with whatever stronger people suggested. I suppose today I could have put her on the pill – though I would not have done so – but in the 1950s that was not an option for teenage girls, or anyone else for that matter. I did not know what to do when, at the late age of fifteen, Jess at last started to menstruate and generally develop. The odd thing was that Jess and I became closer during that time than at any other. She was very, very frightened by menstruation, even though she had had it all explained to her and had been surrounded by menstruating women. It was hardly a mystery to her with Celia sharing a room, and Rosemary at one stage making a point of talking about it loudly, because she thought it was ridiculous that it should be whispered about. But, when she began to bleed, Jess literally collapsed. She and I were alone in the house. I was in the kitchen and I heard a thump from above which I ignored, thinking it was just Jess knocking something over. But then I heard this sort of keening sound, a high pitched repetitive wail and I ran upstairs to find Jess on the bathroom floor, ghastly white, and the lavatory bowl full of blood. It wasn't in the least comical and I never even thought of laughing. The girl was genuinely terrified and made ill by the sight of her own blood. As luck would have it, Jess was the only one of my four who, right from the beginning, had exceptionally heavy periods. They lasted ten days and for four of those she practically lived in the bathroom changing sanitary towels. I felt desperately sorry for her and quite unable to take the brisk attitude I had with her sisters, who were brisk about it themselves. She clung to me, her little thin narrow face even more pinched and miserable than usual, and she liked me to cosset and indulge her and in general treat her as though she were facing a terrible ordeal. She would not go to school at first and I did not make her. She wanted to hole up in her room like an animal in its lair or, more aptly, like one of those women who belong to tribes that banish women when they bleed. I don't know why it was so traumatic. I sensed Celia despised Jess and, of course, Rosemary strongly disapproved of my allowing her to be what she called 'so melodramatic'. But, for once I think, even now, I did the right thing.

Jess as an adolescent was never very attractive. She always looked bedraggled and cowed. I so yearned for some kind, earnest young lad to take Jess under his wing and give her that confidence she had needed all her life. I thought it was probably her only chance. But how can parents engineer such things? They cannot, not for any of their children. Jess was no different in that respect from Rosemary or Celia or Emily. For all of them I wanted most a partner who suited them exactly —

*

Here we go again, the old tune. Don't you think it is strange that a woman who goes on so much about partners should have spent the majority of her life without one? I mean, if partnership is so great, why not make more of an effort to start another?

By the time I was twenty, I was asking my mother this a lot. I remember her fortieth birthday rather well. We were all amazed that she could be so old, we all thought forty sounded so terrible. Emily in particular hated Mother for owning up to being such a dreadful age – it quite worried her, at eleven, to have a mother with one foot in the grave, as it were. It really did seem too near old age and death for comfort. Mother laughed and said she couldn't help it, she *was* forty and that was that and she didn't mind. I suppose that was what made me angry, that she professed not to mind. I wanted her to mind, a lot, I wanted her to rage, rage against what I comically saw as the dying of the light. But she accepted ageing so philosophically, it was indecent. When her hair began to show some grey she didn't even remark upon it, and the lines on her face never bothered her. She never seemed to think it mattered whether she looked good to other people. I knew, by then, that she did. I knew men *did* find her attractive, forty or not. And I knew that she deliberately rejected all advances, however harmless.

There was the teacher who lived in a flat across the road, who ought to have been just my mother's type and, God knows, the poor man tried hard enough. He was absolutely respectable, had lived there five years and more than served his apprenticeship in getting to know us, in the way Mother thought 'natural'. He said hello, as he got in and out of his car, offered lifts when appropriate, picked up Emily when she fell off her bike, brought our newspaper over, when he got it by mistake (his name was Buckley, Gerry Buckley, and ours was Butler and his number was 8 and ours 18, so a certain amount of mixing up did go on). He did everything right, I would have thought. He wasn't a wet either – he was quite good-looking in a conventional English old-fashioned way, and rugged with it. He played tennis and ran in the park. He had a nice smile, and he was the right age. But Mother wouldn't let him become a friend. Worse, she positively put him off.

I happened to be there when Gerry came round once, to ask her if she would fancy the occasional game of tennis with him. Mother smiled and said she was afraid she wasn't up to his standard. He said that didn't matter, he wasn't actually much good himself, just liked the game and the exercise and it seemed such a waste having a possible partner so near – no, said Mother, I really don't think I could, thank you. Then she must have had just a slight prick of conscience, when he flushed and looked hurt, because she added something like, 'I haven't really the time, you see, it's all I can do to find time for a game with Celia.' I waited until he'd gone and I said, 'What a lie.' I suppose I must have said this – as I did most things at the time – with unnecessary vehemence, because she started defending herself, saying it was perfectly true, there was this to do and that to do and every day was hectic. I cut into her spiel. I told her it was obvious she just didn't like Gerry Buckley because she was always distant and off-putting. More denials, and then I can't remember how we got onto the next bit, but she was suddenly saying she had no desire to get involved with anyone, she had her family and that was enough. I argued heatedly with her, along the lines firstly that it was *not* enough and secondly, which I thought cunning, that it wasn't enough for her family either. Oh, nothing crass like we wanna new Daddy, but that we wanted her to have someone apart from us, that it would make us feel better. If bloody Emily hadn't pranced in at that point, we might have got somewhere, but she did and that was that, subject never returned to in quite the same way.

My mother was funny about sex. Now that's a laughable statement. All mothers are funny about sex, especially mothers on their own, who in the nature of their situation haven't had any themselves for ten years.

74

But she was odd in that she rated it, without participating. On the whole, Mother was a puritan. No excesses, endless control. You might have thought she would bring us up to shudder at the thought of sexual intercourse, but not a bit of it, she went out of her way to acknowledge its existence and the power of this human act. We'd be discussing some newspaper case about lovers murdering rivals, or something, and I would say how unbelievable, and my mother would chip in and say no, people who loved someone passionately would do anything to keep them and sometimes were almost unhinged just by the act of love itself. She would say we would be surprised when we experienced the force of attraction. So what happened to this force in her? That's what I want to know.

*

— exactly as Oliver had suited me. Naturally, when everything began to go wrong with Jess, I longed for someone with whom I could share my distress, someone who would be as concerned as myself. I used Rosemary and Celia. I knew I used them, and I knew I should not, but there was no alternative. Jess needed a father, I needed a husband. There was no one who could be both.

It would have been easy enough, I suppose, to provide the girls with another father. I know Rosemary thinks I chose not to do so and that she resents my 'choice'. But she forgets, or perhaps has never known, that marriage is not just an economic arrangement. If I had held that view, I could have married one of several men, men like Simon Birch or Gerry Buckley. Simon came back from the war uninjured. He went back to University College Hospital where he became an eminent anaesthetist. He came to see me often at first, anxious to stand by his dead best friend's wife and, though his embarrassment at my grief inhibited him, he did manage to comfort me in a curiously clumsy way. He brought me flowers and took the children out for the occasional treat. I knew he liked me, because Oliver had teased me about it, and I knew he had no girlfriends. He was shy and rather nervous and found all human relationships difficult, and so I was well aware of how important our friendship was to him. Simon would have married me any time I chose but I went to great lengths to avoid humiliating him by letting him ask me. In the end, inevitably, he grew tired. He wanted a wife and family. I was not going to give them to him. So he married someone else (and was very happy). I never felt guilty about this. Why should I? I hadn't loved Simon, I hadn't even been attracted to him. There was no basis for anything but a marriage of convenience.

Gerry Buckley was another matter (and so, much later, was John). He was a neighbour of ours, a handsome, lively man, very kind and considerate. I was *slightly* attracted to him, or at least felt I could become so. He was very attracted to me. I knew he was my age, unmarried, that he shared some of my interests, that he was a decent, good man, highly thought of at the nearby boys' school, where he taught English. It might have been pleasant to get to know Gerry better. The children would have been glad. I was afraid, I suppose. It was simple fear that made me keep Gerry Buckley at arm's length. I was afraid to put myself to the test. It hurt me to think I might, after all, find a substitute for Oliver – I did not want to be able to substitute him. I really did believe that in my case 'love strikes one hour – LOVE! Those *never* loved/Who dream that they loved ONCE.' I just could not believe my love had stopped even after all those years. It was there, somewhere. If Gerry, to whom on one level I was indeed attracted, if he had been stronger, more determined, and if Jess, if Jess – that is, when Jess – everything that summer was bound up with Jess. Afterwards, everything was tainted by it. I did not even notice when Gerry Buckley moved away. What happened was —

*

I know what happened. I neither need nor want Mother's version. I'd rather set down my own and not even read hers. It'll get it over a bloody sight quicker.

Jess went from bad to worse. Nothing dramatic. More truanting, though no more shop-lifting (discovered, that is). As the time for her to leave school grew closer and closer, Mother grew more and more desperate. I'd taken 'A' Levels and gone to art school, so that was all right, *just* (she really wanted all of us to go to Oxford). Celia was obviously going to go into the sixth form, but Jess was just as obviously going to be out on her ear, without a qualification to her name. She was incapable of taking charge of herself, had no ideas about what she would like to, or at least could, do. Mother had awful visions of her in a factory, doing some mechanical job like packing cartons. Jess did once venture to say that she liked shops, that she would like to have a go at

Marks & Spencer. This was followed up eagerly, but Jess hadn't a chance. Her arithmetic was terrible, she would never have been able to cope with a till. This might have been a surmountable difficulty, if she had impressed in other ways by being keen, but she didn't. Nobody, giving Jess an interview, would take her on. Then, there was her professed love of babies – she 'wouldn't mind' being a nursery nurse or a nanny. Poor Jess. She had no idea how very well qualified a girl had to be if she wanted to be either. Loving babies was not enough. What Mother most wanted for her was some kind of proper training, even if it wasn't for anything very grand. She needed, Mother said, to be given some sense of pride, or her confidence would never be established. She would drift, as she had drifted through school, attracted to all the wrong elements.

It was Celia who suggested cookery. Celia herself was a brilliant cook, up to her elbows in flour, making cakes by the age of five. Jess 'helped'. Celia pointed out that Jess was actually good at doing all the little jobs in the kitchen that no one else would do. She liked chopping vegetables or grating cheese or any of the other bloody boring, menial jobs Celia graciously allowed her to do. In fact, she was probably at her happiest helping Mother, or Celia, prepare meals. Once Celia had suggested it, Mother couldn't imagine why she had not thought of it, too. I suppose there was something horribly patronizing about the way we all leapt on this solution, something insulting in our enthusiasm, but Jess didn't seem to notice it. She seemed quite taken with the notion of becoming a cook. At least, I remember she said she 'didn't mind'. It was easier said than done of course – not even a poly was going to snap Jess up, even then. But Mother at last had a bit of sense. She realized she'd have to pay to get Jess trained and she was prepared to. She enrolled her for a six-month course at quite a reputable cookery school. There isn't much to the rest of this story, however long Mother has managed to make it. Jess started in the September of 1956.

She did well. One of the few things in Jess's favour was her efficiency when she *did* concentrate on a job. That was part of Mother's training that *had* stuck. Jess was never self-motivated but, if confronted with a task, and especially if supervised, she was extremely neat and methodical. Then, she could've passed for a True Blue Butler. She thrived on the cookery course. And it was at that point, precisely when everything should've taken a turn for the better in Jess's life, that it took a turn for the worse. Celia had a lot to answer for. Oh yes, she bloody had.

Celia always pleased Mother by being so protective of Jess. Suddenly, Jess didn't want protection because she had a boyfriend. Jeremy, he was called, as pretty as his name and not the ogre of Mother's imagination. He was on the cookery course, too. Celia detested him from the moment Jess brought him home. She was forever trying to make jokes about him – spiteful, unfunny remarks about his general weediness and his rather squeaky voice – and, whenever she came out with them, Mother would be furious and aghast: how could any daughter of hers, etc. etc. We had some classic family rows over Jeremy. I wasn't living at home then, but whenever I came for a meal we'd have one of those ding-dong sessions in which family love is so rich. It would go roughly like this: Celia would make some heavy-handed observation about the length of Jeremy's eyelashes, say; I would tell her she was just jealous because Jess had a boyfriend and she didn't; Celia would then say jealous was the last thing she was, that nobody could be *jealous* of Jeremy; I'd say he seemed rather attractive to me; Celia would say anything in trousers was attractive to me, I'd say no, I prefer *no* trousers, they do get in the way so. Oh, what larks! It would end with me calling Celia a cow and Celia at her most self-righteous, saying all she wanted was Jess's happiness and she *very much doubted* if Jeremy could make her happy.

He didn't, of course. He lost interest, or found other ones. Celia ostentatiously comforted Jess who was devastated and stopped going to the cookery class, even though she was more than half way through and certain to get a diploma. Instead, she lay listlessly in bed all day, eating biscuits and listening to records. Nothing would move her. Celia would manage to force her to get dressed and washed and to comb her hair, but the minute Celia left for school Jess either got back onto her bed or lay in a hot bath for hours and hours, claiming she was cold and that was the only way she could get warm. Mother said she was simply depressed because her first boyfriend had let her down. All she needed was kindness and help to get over it. I said she was sick and something drastic had to be done. Mother's mind leapt ahead to mental institutions. I think she had a picture of a kind of Bedlam with Jess in a canvas strait-jacket locked up in a padded cell. I couldn't bring myself to start a train of events which might lead to such horror, so I left it.

Mother went on making tasty morsels for Jess, soothing and comforting her, wilfully ignoring all the signs. She had no excuse. She wasn't ignorant. She'd trained as a nurse, knew something of medicine, yet she behaved like a peasant. Her faith was in rest and care and camomile tea. Jess died. Aged not quite seventeen.

She didn't have the slightest intention of killing herself. It was quite absurd to think that she had. What happened was that we had a sudden cold spell in February. Thick snow, ice, howling east wind from Siberia, the lot. Mother's house was like an igloo. We'd never had central heating and the 1940s' electric wiring wouldn't stand up to more than a two-bar electric fire in about three rooms. In spite of Mother's precious log fire in the sitting room, two lethal oil stoves in the kitchen and another in the hall, there was no real warmth anywhere. Nothing in the bedrooms, naturally. It was heaven going back to my bedsitter, where I could easily get a good fug up. Jess was wretched. Even her hot baths weren't very hot and in the ancient bathroom there was ice on the *inside* of the window. So one day, when Mother was out, she took a one-bar electric fire into the bathroom and balanced it on the washbasin, facing into the bath, and plugged it in. I didn't even know there was a plug there – it had certainly never been used. Then, with the blessed heat beating onto her, she got into the bath and the fucking fire toppled over into the water. She was electrocuted. Mother came home an hour later and found her. Burned, drowned.

I need hardly say that my mother suffered terribly. She never spoke of finding Jess. I suppose I ought to read what she has to say about that but I can't bear to. I can't bear to experience her horror, even at second hand, even at this distance of time. I imagined it all at the time – the body floating, the burn marks, the hell of trying to get it out, the ringing for ambulances, the presence of the police, the statements that had to be made and nobody there to cling to. Celia was on some course, part of her Biology 'A' Level syllabus. I was in London but it took four hours for me to be located and told. Not even Emily was there – thank God, Mother always said. I forget where she was but, anyway, Mother was quite alone until I got there. I hadn't been told Jess was dead, just that my sister had had an accident and would I come home as quickly as possible. I didn't even know which sister. The house seemed full of people when I got there, all curiously silent. My mother was sitting in a chair, bolt upright, transfixed by some sight only she could see.

Somebody told me Jess was dead and I went into the usual routine that people do, bumbling on about how did it happen and so on. Mother didn't speak. I went to her and knelt down and laid my head on her lap. I couldn't look such suffering in the face. Eventually Celia got home and between us we cleared out all the people. Our doctor had left sleeping pills, but Mother refused to take them. Emily stayed at her little friend's for the night so she didn't come into it at all, then. We all sat up until the early hours of the next morning, with first me then Celia taking it in turns to say to Mother she mustn't blame herself, it wasn't her fault. At least neither of us was crass enough to suggest it might be for the best. That was what I was thinking, of course. Appalled by my own callousness but thinking it all the same. Where Jess was concerned I was stone. She meant nothing to me. But my mother loved her, and was deeply wounded and scarred. I saw, with fascination, how close the bond had been. She looked as if her own heart had been torn out, as though beneath her ever-neat blouse was a great, gaping, bleeding hole. We put her to bed, Celia and me. Celia was very shaken, quite unlike her usual solid self. Her hands trembled when she tried to pour some water for my mother and she spilt it over the eiderdown. I think now it was guilt but then I thought it was shock. There is nothing more to say.

April 2nd

Can't quite decide whether Rosemary invented her errand or not but won't quibble, will just be grateful (have I always been grateful enough?). I know I am being 'taken out', no need to feel patronized. Even supposing she said to herself, it's been ages since I took Mother out, better take her, why should that matter? It does, but there is no rational basis for it mattering. I was thought about, was taken, enjoyed it. Enough. Good just to sit beside her and be driven, talked to. So competent, Rosemary, in spite of appearances to the contrary. All thought out, knew exactly how to get to Cambridge, how to find Ely, where to find the engraver. Walked round while she looked at his work, arranged terms. Quite happy on my own, no need for her to feel anxious. Made great efforts to understand the whole deal she was negotiating, what was being engraved and then what would be done with it and how the plates would be designed and marketed. Not the sort of thing I'd buy myself. None of Rosemary's products ever are. Astonishing that they make money. Would have liked to treat her to a nice lunch in some quiet country restaurant but she doesn't like that, doesn't care for the kind of pretty dining rooms I like. So we had a picnic, and ate it sitting on the car rug near the river. Rosemary hardly ate anything. She makes me feel guilty for loving food, for thinking it ought to be artistic and a pleasure to look at as well as to eat. She smoked. Once, she used not to in my company, in my house, but I urged her to do so. I hate her smoking, hate it. The need she has for it offends me. I hate to see her snatch at the cigarettes, at the matches, hate the urgency with which she lights up. If she has to smoke I wish she did so with elegance and ease, gently not frantically. She's never even tried to give up. Still surprises me that any daughter of mine can want to smoke. We never discuss it now, like so many other things. No point. Must struggle to co-exist, as I would with a guest, a stranger. Must remind myself I have no rights, none whatsoever. Must stop feeling I have to sing for my supper or a day out, must stop that, too. But I feel beholden, always, sensitive to any imbalance in my relationships with my daughters.

*

This isn't good for me. It must've been good for Mother or surely she wouldn't have carried on. It isn't good for me because it not only depresses me, it *upsets* me and that's worse. What upset me is the uselessness of all this. Mother writes with the apparently supreme faith that everything important is in the past. There she is, anxiously raking over supposedly crucial scenes, looking for evidence and clues and Christ knows what, to help her untangle the mess she thinks we're all in. Quite apart from her getting things wrong she is evading the issue. And that issue is *now*. Mother, Celia, Emily and me *now*. To hell with the past.

*

— all went away in the summer of 1957, the summer after Jess died. It was Rosemary's idea.

Holidays are trying times for widows. They are the times when one feels most alone and unlike other families, and, in me, they induced feelings of panic. I had little experience of holidays, they were mysterious to me, there was no residue of experience for me to draw on. But, as in everything else, I was determined to give to my children what I had never had, and so I worked myself up to tackling holidays quite early on. For several years we went to Devon and then in 1950 we embarked on our Great Adventure. We went abroad to —

*

I was fourteen when we went to Brittany. It was purgatory. God knows, all the trailing to dreary little English 'family' hotels was bad enough but at least Mother was fairly relaxed, she could cope. The hotels were always slightly genteel, whispers in the dining room and that kind of thing, even though the family tag was attached to them. All 'family' hotel meant was that they would give children house room and throw a few fish fingers at them around five o'clock, as a 'special' supper. These hotels were always on beaches miles from any village or town. Where the hell did she get them from? Perhaps they looked enticing in brochures but, when we got there – oh, what a drag that

82

always was, standing waiting for buses outside some small branchline station – the paint was peeling and the curtains drab, not at all the gleaming white-washed façade pictured in the brochures. Mother's disappointment was tangible, though never voiced. If only she'd said what a bloody dump, let's go home but, no, it was 'Isn't it near the sea – even nearer than it looked in the brochure – aren't we lucky.' We might have been, if the sea had been blue and sparkling and the sodding beach hot, but of course it was England in August and mostly cold and windy. We crouched in polo-necked sweaters behind windbreaks and moaned because it was too cold to swim. Mother tried to make us run races – gosh, what fun. If it rained, as it frequently did, it was ludo and snakes and ladders in our bedroom, because the hotel sitting room was always being cleaned and Mother didn't think we ought to get in the way.

There was never anyone to make friends with, nobody else had a loony mother who chose geriatric establishments for holidays. My friends mostly went on joint holidays, sharing villas with other families. But not us. We were self-sufficient, had each other, wanted peace and quiet – dear Christ, what ten year old and under wants peace and quiet? Why did *Mother* in her position want it? I don't know what she can possibly have got out of it. Certainly not a rest, because it was bloody hard work for her entertaining us. The only thing I think she can have got out of it was the walking. She always genuinely loved the walks, any old weather. I hated them, even when she tried to make them interesting by collecting shells and wild flowers and so on. They just seemed so *pointless*, walk to A to walk back to B. It was the monotony which made me want to scream. I didn't commune with nature at all. None of us did, except Celia of course, who collected whatever revolting thing was the taste thrill of the day, and, with her sickly love of Nature, could at least pass for enthusiastic with the light behind her. But Jess whined she was cold and tired all the time and Emily would only go if she was bribed with Smarties or chocolate drops or the promise of an icecream. Mother had to rise above all that, which she did. She shut her mind off and always loved our walks and, for once, to hell with us.

But Brittany was an entirely different fiasco. When Mother asked us if we would like to go abroad that year I was amazed. It just didn't seem to be us. I couldn't hide my excitement. I imagined France as a kind of paradise, full of sunshine and attractive suntanned boys with neckerchiefs knotted jauntily round their necks and meals under vines and singing everywhere. I was passionate about change then, any kind of change, the more violent the better and the more complete. What I hated most was routine, sameness, and now we were going to fling our hats in the air and be different. I saw how anxious Mother was and, for once, I tried to help, I'm sure I did.

In the end, it was almost exactly the same as every other rotten holiday we had ever had. Only the Channel crossing from Southampton to St Malo was different and measured up to our fevered imagination. We crossed during the day and we all stayed up on deck all the time. It was brilliantly sunny and the sea ahead was blue and endless. I remember suddenly hugging Mother and shouting, 'Isn't this great?' and she was all pink-cheeked and smiling. But it didn't last, neither the weather nor the euphoria. By the time we had docked the sun was clouded over and, as we caught the Vedette boat to cross to Dinard, it began to rain. We got a bus at Dinard which took us to St Jacut-de-la-Mer, or rather a mile or so beyond it to a small hamlet with a good beach: yes, Mother had done it again. Isolated hotel, no other habitation near. It was dark when we got there. All the way there I had watched the countryside out of the bus window and worried: it looked no different from millions of places in England. Every now and again Mother would point and say, look at that lovely clover, isn't it pretty, and I would think *clover*? What's French about clover? The trees, the roads, the animals, even the buildings looked to my panic-stricken eye utterly unremarkable. Our reception at the place we stayed did not help. No jolly striped-tee-shirted-beret-wearing patron, but a sour-faced old woman who told us we had missed supper and showed us to a spartan pair of rooms, opposite each other, in a dingy corridor. Never mind, said Mother. I cried myself to sleep.

Next day was no better. It wasn't raining but there was half a gale blowing. We could hardly see the sea for misty spray. We set off, as ever, for a walk. The coast there has lots of little inlets with pine woods coming down to the sea. It was difficult to walk along. We picked aniseed, and Mother said we would press it and start a scrapbook of French flowers. We trudged on looking for bloody French flowers, and finding only buttercups, until we got to St Jacut. Big deal. A pretty enough place, I'm sure, but not the Cannes of my imagination. Mother said to look at the interesting architecture, look at the old stone and the wide archways and the narrow bridges . . . We looked and yawned.

*

— and said what I needed was a holiday, a chance to get right away from the house (which she said I should sell). I sat and listened with only half my mind, not caring what anybody said to me, alert only to the tone of Rosemary's voice and nothing else. Usually, she called in on us every other week or so and stayed at the most half an hour. It was always obvious that, as soon as she came through the door, she was wondering how quickly she could go back through it. She would perch uneasily on the edge of a table or simply prowl about, all the while giving me what amounted to a report on her doings. Never once did she ask what I or Celia or Emily were doing. If I tried to tell her what I thought were interesting bits of news about the family, she would interrupt and say that reminded her and she would be off on another story about herself. It was a varied and entertaining record (she was in her last year at the Central School of Art). But when she left I would feel flat and hollow, we all did. It was pathetic to see Emily's eagerness to please her glamorous big sister and her disappointment when Rosemary failed to show any real interest in her. All the time I told myself I was lucky that Rosemary came at all, that I should not complain (not that I did except to myself), that she could quite easily have cut us off. And I knew that, if I betrayed how aggrieved I felt at the way she treated her family, I would alienate her altogether. She was offering what she was able to offer, and that had to be accepted. But it was hard to control the bewilderment I felt at the failure to maintain a close bond with the child who was most like myself.

Rosemary astonished us by returning the next day with an armful of holiday brochures. It was a Sunday and she had lunch with us for the first time in months. Afterwards, we spread all the leaflets out on the kitchen table and Emily grew very excited at the idea of doing what Rosemary suggested and going somewhere really different, to the Algarve in Portugal. It was all terribly attractive, but I hesitated. I still had no energy, didn't want to go anywhere or do anything, didn't really want sunshine and strong light. It was offensive to me to talk about good times. It was too soon after Jess's death. But Emily begged

85

and pleaded, and Rosemary said sharply that I was always going on about families pulling together and, now that she was trying to do it, I was rejecting her. She said couldn't I just for once let go and let others take charge. So I agreed.

In fact, there turned out to be quite a lot of arranging for me still to do, not that I resented this. Rosemary was not quite as efficient as she made herself out to be. When it became a matter of actually booking a villa she was vague and offhand – one would turn up, not to worry, that kind of thing. And she hadn't thought out details like how we would all get there. She spoiled the idea of a family holiday, for a start, by saying she planned to drive down to the Algarve with two friends, was that all right. I could hardly say no. In fact, once she had initiated the holiday, Rosemary did nothing to advance it. I found and booked the villa, I made aeroplane reservations and studied train timetables as usual. All Rosemary did was turn up – late.

The villa was beautiful. It was near the village of Porches, three miles up a sandy track which I thought we would never reach. The people whose advert in *The Times* I had answered had indeed said their *casa* was isolated, but they had not impressed upon me just how isolated. It was perched on a cliff top with no other building visible for what seemed miles around. It was whitewashed, one storey, with a long verandah going round three sides of the house, smothered in bougainvillea. The rooms were all small. There was no running water, of course, and no electricity. It was extremely primitive. The furniture in the small living room smacked of Cheltenham and would have been ludicrous in that setting, if it had not also been so pretty. There was a tiny button-backed sofa and a walnut writing-desk and even a fringed standard lamp, which was never likely to have light shining from it. On the walls were Constable prints and a framed Oxford rowing blue and, in one corner, an enormous grandfather clock highly polished and working.

The ground around the villa was flat, studded only with fig trees, but we discovered, going to and from the beaches, that it was not as flat as it appeared. The ground around us undulated. As we walked half a mile or so to the path which dropped steeply to a sandy cove, we realized how deceptive the landscape was. The beaches were so unexpected. Looking from the verandah of the house to where the sea must be, it seemed that the dry, rough grass simply went on as far as the horizon and it was such a surprise to find, down below, a series of small, but beautiful, sandy beaches. When the tide was out, we could walk from one to another but, when it was in, each was separate and reduced to a yard or so of sand.

We waited all that first day for Rosemary who, like us, had been due the evening before. When we went to the beach, we carefully left a welcoming note. What concerned me most was how would we manage if she never turned up, stuck as we were without food or drink (there was no drinkable water). We would have to walk to Porches and carry everything back and, though I loved the isolation, I did not want to become a beast of burden in that heat. But it was more than that. For once, I would not have chosen a quiet spot, if it was not to be shared with others, and I would never have agreed to a villa without prospect of company such as even the most inhospitable hotel can give. As I waited for Rosemary I was anxious.

Late the next afternoon we heard the car from a long way away and rushed out onto the track, and there it was, a Dormobile, not the saloon car we had been looking for, and there was Rosemary waving from the window. I was so relieved I hardly took in the fact that there were three people with her, not two, and that they were all men. It had never occurred to me that Rosemary's friends might be men. I had automatically assumed they would be girls, was sure Tanya, a friend of hers since early Camden days, had been mentioned. She had never indicated her companions would be men, and men whom I had never met. But she was perfectly at ease. She jumped out, hugely pleased with herself, actually hugged all of us and then casually introduced her friends, Tony, Seb and Matthew, as an afterthought. They all seemed large, thin and unkempt. Only Matthew shook hands. Suddenly, the *casa* seemed noisy and full. Everything about it had changed and for once I was glad of the lack of privacy. When it grew late, and we had eaten and drunk everything the new arrivals had fortunately brought with them, there was some discussion about sleeping arrangements. There were four bedrooms, each with two narrow, rather short, Portuguese beds. I slept with Emily and had thought Rosemary would sleep with Celia but no, she said she and Tony would share and Matthew could kip with Seb. And that was how it was.

Rosemary was then twenty-two. She was not a child, not even a dependent. At twenty-one, she had inherited her share of Grandmother

Butler's money, which had come as a tremendous surprise to her. All through their childhood I had concealed their expectations from them, especially from Rosemary, believing no good could be derived from knowing about their inheritance too soon. But, when she was twenty-one, I was powerless to stop Rosemary inheriting £10,000. I watched her reaction nervously. She was astounded, and awed by the possibilities before her. At first she said she would travel when she finished at Central, then that she would buy a cottage in Ireland and go and paint all day, then that she would buy a car. What she did do, to my relief, was leave it untouched. She decided to finish at Central, then decide what she would do next. So far as I know, she spent nothing at all. She still dressed in the worn rags she had always liked and decorated herself with cheap baubles from street markets. There were no signs that the money would go to her head. I advised her to tell nobody, not even close friends, and asked her also not to tell Celia and Emily, whom I wished to be equally unprepared when the time came for their own inheritance.

But, of course, having that money did alter our relationship. I had never discussed money with my children. I hope I never moaned about it. After Trevor and Michael left, Rosemary complained bitterly about having to have lodgers and said she hated them, why did we have to have them. I replied, truthfully, that the money was useful. It paid for luxuries, like holidays. We were not poor, I said, but nor were we even moderately rich. We had enough, if we were careful. Rosemary protested she hated being careful, what was money anyway, she hated it, it was horrible. But I was pleased to notice some small consideration, as she grew older, in the way in which she asked for money when she needed it. She took a Saturday job when she reached the sixth form, as a waitress in an Italian icecream parlour, and seemed proud of earning her own spending money. When she started at Central and wanted to have her own room somewhere she was diffident about the finances of it, about whether I could afford to pay her rent. Luckily, she qualified for a full grant which covered most of her expenses. This pleased her, but she still saw herself as beholden to me. In the Algarve, on that holiday, I realized this was at an end. She felt truly independent and that independence was based on having money in the bank. Now, she did not feel beholden. She was a free woman and expected to live like one.

It would have been quite foolish of me to protest about Rosemary sleeping with Tony without being engaged or married, equally silly to say I did not like the effect on Emily who was not quite thirteen. In theory, I did not disapprove of pre-marital sex, so long as there were no children. It was not, in the late fifties, by any means common for young people openly to sleep together, but I had never supposed it did not go on. Again, in theory, the freeing of taboos pleased me. But it was not easy for me to accept. I had been brought up in an old-fashioned institution and married afterwards to a highly conventional man. I found it difficult to watch my daughter rebel against a tradition I myself had followed and the hardest part of all was watching her do it and knowing she had no idea of the damage she was doing to herself. At sixteen, she was made for sex. It was as crude and simple as that. All the vulgar hateful phrases about 'being ripe for it' were so shockingly appropriate. Unlike Jess, Rosemary did not long for love and companionship – what she craved was sex. Then a young man called Alan gave it to her and her disillusionment was total. She did not conceal what was happening from me. She told me, defiantly, that she was tired of trying not to sleep with Alan when she wanted to. (At the time she had known him about three weeks, I think.) She was going ahead. I was appalled at my own distress. I tried to reason with her, to ask her what kind of love affair it could possibly be, when they were both still at school, when neither of them had any place to go. I said I would not have Alan staying in our house. And I told her that she must go to our doctor and consult him about contraception, with my permission, because if there was one thing I would never, never forgive, it was an illegitimate baby.

What a terrible start it was, how different from my imagination. It was not that I tortured myself with erotic images of Rosemary and Alan but that I was haunted by the lovelessness of it all. Their affair was not worthy of the name. It was merely a coupling between two people who found each other physically irresistible, nothing of Romeo and Juliet about it, not in the least. Perhaps I myself was the result of such barbarity. Perhaps Jess had been. I cried the first night she went to stay with him, when his parents were away, but I did not try to stop her. She looked so vulnerable as she left the house, smiling, excited, a little embarrassed, a little thrilled with her own daring. When she came back she was offhand. Nobody, least of all me, asked if she had had a nice weekend. Every time Alan appeared at our door I wanted to hit him. I cannot even remember now what he looked like, but then I saw his face leering everywhere. In the end, Rosemary dropped him. Six weeks I think he lasted. He used to ring up and she would tell us to say she was not in, in the classic fashion, and I began to feel sorry for him. He had not suspected quite how ruthless she could be. And I swear she was ashamed to have made so much of so little. All she had scored was a technicality and she knew it. Her virginity could not have been worth losing —

*

Of course it had been worth losing. I should have lost it long before, the way girls do today. What a *bore* it was being a virgin. The very word makes me squirm, so prissy. Mother's perfectly right: all I did think about was sex. It dominated every waking moment and entirely took over my dreams. And, as for Alan, he was useless, totally. He'd be finished so quickly it was hardly worth taking my clothes off. It wasn't until I found Mick that I got any real relief. And that was what it was, such a relief to have sex properly and feel satiated. It calmed me. I could think about other things again, get some sense of proportion, of perspective. I found, looking back to those feverish pre-Mick days, that I despised Mother for her attitude. Lovelessness indeed: what had that to do with anything? I didn't want love, last thing I wanted. I wanted sex. What on earth is wrong with that? She tried to make me feel cheap and disgusting and I hated her for it. And all the time, behind this 'do you love this boy' stuff, she was really flaunting her own perfect love affair with my father. Sex without love, she told me, was nothing. What a fool. Sex without love can be marvellous. Sex with love can sometimes be hell.

*

— and then there was a gap. Perhaps there were others but I never knew about them. In her final year at school she met Mick, much older than her, with his own place. He was a house decorator, a cocky, cheerful, energetic fellow, whose attraction was difficult to fathom. He played the saxophone and most of their time seemed to be spent sitting in pubs – I think Rosemary fell in love with those rather than Mick, with the ambience rather than the man. But I knew she was still confusing passion with love. I watched and observed and had almost become convinced that Rosemary was a different species from myself, that she was not interested in love, when in 1957 she brought Tony Morgan to the Algarve.

Rosemary loved Tony. She was in love with him. This was perfectly plain within ten minutes of seeing them together. What was not so clear was whether Tony loved Rosemary. He was certainly not nearly so wrapped up in her as she was in him, something all of us saw. Whatever he wanted to do, she fell in with. No, she would say, she did not want to go to the market in Portimão and then Tony would say he'd like to and she would instantly change her mind. Whatever stupid scheme Tony came up with, she would applaud, and he was an expert at thinking up stupid schemes. It was his speciality, the sillier the better. Emily adored him and I admit he was very good with her, too good for Rosemary's liking. It annoyed her to see Tony fooling about with Emily, throwing water over her and generally being boisterous. It annoyed her even more to find Celia and Tony had things in common. Tony played all sorts of instruments including the guitar and Celia, who had brought her oboe with her, used to improvise with him. We sat out on the verandah till late at night with Tony strumming away and Celia joining in. It was nice for her.

In fact, the whole holiday was nice for Celia and Emily. I remember very little about Seb and Matthew except that their presence was important. They were quieter than Tony, they lacked his charisma, but they each had things to offer. Seb was sporty, played all the games I had struggled with for years and introduced Emily to surfing, though the waves were not really big enough. Matthew was a botanist. He was the most unlikely friend for Rosemary. Whereas Tony and Seb joined in, he was always on the outside, observing, like me I suppose. I could never quite make out why he had come, but I was not supposed to ask such boring questions. I was glad he had. The atmosphere was at times so raucous that without Matthew I would have found it quite unbearable. Tony had a radio in his van which was tuned to some incomprehensible station giving out loud pop music and, when we went on trips together, it drove me mad but the others loved it. They all sang to it and banged on the sides and roof of the van and screamed and laughed. I hated to be thought a kill-joy. I tried so hard to join in but I felt incongruous in such company. My age was a burden when we were all together. I felt sad. Nothing had ever brought home to me so violently the pathos of my own situation. I was forty-one, my children almost all grown up and about to leave home. I was left with the feeling that my life's purpose had been achieved: I had brought my family up. They would not cease to be my family, but I could not expect to occupy the same position in their lives. What would happen next? What did women like me do? The louder Rosemary and her gang roared with laughter along the beach, down the hill, the louder and more insistent became my own questioning. I could not expect them to notice or —

*

Dear Christ, it hit us all in the face all the time like a stinging wet towel – Mother's depression, Mother's silence, Mother's bloody maddening wistfulness. She was such a curse, so reproving and distant and aloof, and there was I, giving her what she had always wanted, a bloody great big family party with everyone happy. When else had she ever seen old Celia *laugh* all day? When had Celia's great big solemn pudding of a face cracked with smiles and her cheeks, her huge white flabby cheeks, turned pink with pleasure? My, what that holiday did for Celia. She even came out of her regulation black swimming costume and into a bikini and, wow, how suddenly luscious she looked. Her body tanned beautifully and all that blonde hair came to life. I bet it was the best two weeks Celia ever had and, if she hadn't been such a puritan, it would have been even better. Seb wanted to sleep with her straight away and she was definitely hot for him, but of course 'it wouldn't be right', silly cow. It couldn't have been righter. And, as for Emily, she was thrilled with her little self. Lolita had nothing on her. Twelve years old and just beginning to realize what it was all about, and three men amused by her and ready to flirt and encourage her, thinking all the time what a raver she could be in a few years' time. She loved the action, the noise, the lack of any timetable: who wouldn't after years of holidays with Mother?

But yes, I hated it, I was miserable. 'Whatever he wanted to do she fell in with.' Yes, I did. Yes, I did pander to Tony's every wish. Mother despised me and he despised me, but I couldn't help it. I loved him and I knew he loved me: if people love each other why can't they show it? What's wrong with that? Tony found it 'too much'. It made him feel crowded. That was why Seb and Matthew had had to come. He didn't want to be alone with me all that time. He liked groups, crowds. And he got bored so quickly, with everything. My desire for change was nothing compared with Tony's – he wanted to be up and off and round and about every five minutes. Almost any room gave him claustrophobia after an hour. He could never live in one place for long, preferring to kip down where he found himself. God knows why the idea of coming on a family holiday appealed to him. When I happened to moan about it, he jumped at it like one of the Lost Boys in Peter Pan, said he'd love to be part of a family. Like Mother, he'd never had one. I don't know why. Asking questions about the past was something he hated. He would say it wasn't relevant, he was him, now, take it or leave it. I worried he didn't understand about families, about Mother. I dreaded him offending or, even worse, hurting her. All the time I was on guard, sure he was going to shock her with some outrageous act. He might hit me and she would be appalled and not understand. Violence was violence to Mother, there were no extenuating circumstances, she wouldn't understand Tony as I did. Theft was theft, too. She only had to see him nick some wine, or leave a restaurant without paying and she would be disgusted. Tony's attitude to life was not Mother's: she had no sense of humour, didn't begin to appreciate why Tony ripped people off. If ever they got onto any discussion about how he lived, we would be in real trouble. Tony drew unemployment benefit as his right and saw nothing wrong with it, complained it was peanuts anyway. Next to illegitimate babies, Mother thought going on the dole, if you were young, fit and strong, the unforgivable sin. There is *always* a job, she would say primly, you can always wash dishes or scrub floors. Tony would have had hysterics.

We had a meal up at Monchique, outside, at a funny little restaurant on a bend in the road, with a stupendous view all the way down to the coast. The meal took an hour to come and we drank ourselves stupid. It was so warm, the air smelled so pungently of eucalyptus, we were all in such good spirits after a great day. When the meal came, it was great plates of chicken piri-piri, mounds and mounds of it, all piled up, a jumble of legs and wings and quartered breasts. We fell on it like Robin Hood and his merry men, flinging the bones over our shoulders, eating faster and faster, calling for more cold wine and rough, vinegary bread. Mother sat at the end of the table, picking at a salad, head down. She was worried that we were throwing the bones around, about the mess we were making. Then Tony got onto the table and started dancing and we all clapped and jeered, and Emily got up beside him and he lifted her up so that she could hold onto the trellis affair overhead and swing. Mother was frantic. She stood up, pleaded with Tony, but nobody could hear her above the row. I was so tired of her. That face, the fussing, the absolute refusal to relax. 'Oh, Mother for chrissake, stop it!' I shouted. Nobody else heard me. She turned and went across the road to where the van was parked and disappeared into it. I could have cried. It wasn't her age that held her back, it was everything else and most of all her sense of *position*. We offered her the chance to be herself and she didn't even know who that was.

The boys called her Penny. They were the only people who ever used any variation of her Christian name. Everyone else has always called her Mother or Mrs Butler. I couldn't even think of anyone who called her Penelope except my godfather and he hardly counted because we never saw him. Not even Trevor and Michael had called her by her name. But Tony certainly wasn't going to Mrs anyone. 'What's her name?' he said to me and when I told him he nodded. He called her Penny the first day, casually, absolutely normally. Seb and Matthew automatically followed suit. I thought it was nice, friendly, but every time Penny was used she flinched. Who was this sunburned Penny, wearing so few clothes, doing so little work? Did she sing? Did she forget about the time? Mother wasn't sure. She floundered about, nervous. I kept looking at her and thinking she looked interesting, worth knowing. I don't think she had ever shown so much of her body to us children, even if her mind was still locked up. She had such a fine, intelligent face, such a direct gaze. Tony was amused and intrigued by her. I was terrified he would go too far and become familiar. Mother hated familiarity. She was always stiff and jumpy, do-not-touch-me written all over her. 'Can't be much fun for her,' Tony said one night, 'lying next door to us all night.' I wished he wouldn't say things like that, calling to my attention something I was already too well aware of. I didn't enjoy sex that holiday. I couldn't stand the thought of her listening. It fascinated Tony, in a prurient way, I felt, that Mother hadn't had anyone since my father died. He couldn't credit it. I told him repeatedly that I didn't want to discuss it but he returned again and again to the subject. I raged at him, asked him why for fuck's sake people like my mother were *pitied* because they had no lovers, it was wrong and unfair, just shut up. Poor Mother, eternal victim of speculation. It was unbearable, that holiday, to realize the extent of her sacrifice for us. I dreaded above all else her coming to the conclusion, as I had done long before, that she had wasted her life. I did not want those protective scales to fall from her eyes, it was too cruel.

I wasn't happy again till that awful holiday was over and I was sitting in the van looking out on the green fields of France as we made our way north. All I wanted to do was drive with Tony forever through foreign lands, singing, stopping when we wanted to eat and sleep, no ties. I thought of Celia and Emily sitting on either side of Mother in the train. I thought of them arriving home and resuming their boring structured lives. Not me. Sometimes we drove all night and slept all day, sometimes we ate and drank hugely, other days we fasted. It was an erratic progress, exhausting. And when we got back to London it was to nothing permanent. We didn't even know where we would stay. All our stuff was in plastic bags in the back of the van. We would find somewhere, and then somewhere else, always makeshift. That cute little town house Mother saw me with would never materialize – she would have to wait for Celia to do the sensible thing. I would not trip out of it, terribly elegant in a smart suit, jangling the keys of my new Mini Minor, on my way to *such* an interesting job at the National Portrait Gallery or the Courtauld Institute. None of that was going to happen, nor the handsome husband like my father, nor the 2.5 children.

As we crossed the Channel I said to Tony, 'How about driving across America? I've got some money.'

May 7th

A cold, blustery Bank Holiday. I hate Bank Holidays. Nothing to be disrupted but feel disrupted. Knew I would so had made plans. Very clever of me, love my own forethought. Got the eight o'clock train to Brighton. Walking along the sea front by ten, wonderfully invigorating. Flashes of sun, quite big patches of blue sky, strong wind making the waves scud along. At the West Pier crossed over to Bedford Square. The old Butler home covered in scaffolding. Sat in the square's garden and looked up at the bow window where I spent so many happy hours. Did a few calculations, sitting there, entirely unsentimentally. Forty years ago today would have been sitting there, pregnant, staring at the sea, daydreaming about Oliver returning soon. Grandmother Butler would be shouting in the background, the children playing behind me. Felt so sad for my young self. Not for myself *now*, but my young self who had so much unhappiness ahead. But she, the young self, didn't, doesn't, feel connected with me. A peculiar sensation. How can I be so divorced from my young self? I think about her, study her in retrospect, and feel nothing, nothing except that kind of comfortable compassion one feels upon reading some touching story in a newspaper. Didn't yearn to be back there, aged thirty. Didn't want to be at that point again. Felt detached and also puzzled, not so much about what has happened to me since I was thirty, but about what has happened to my children. Cannot reconcile what they were then with what they are now. Doesn't fit. The record I am making, writing, isn't explaining it as I hoped. Good to have a day off from what I am finding exhausting work. Should I give it up? Sun came out quite strongly. Walked back to the Palace Pier. Odd that, as I sat on the end of the pier facing out to sea, I should find myself thinking my life *began* rather than ended when Oliver died. Left the pier. Zig-zagged my way back towards the station. Sat in a café and had tea and poached egg. Found myself staring out of the window into a second-hand furniture shop. The furniture spilled out onto the pavement. Wasn't that Grandmother Butler's mahogany wardrobe? How had I got rid of it in the end? Heaven knows. Of course, it wouldn't be hers. Hundreds like it. Caught the four-something train back. A good day.

*

A rest, I think, a break, before we get on to Things Really Going Wrong. A long gap. Mother must be wondering why I have turned suddenly into such a dutiful daughter. Never away, am I, now there's all this secret entertainment. In and out of this room like a cuckoo in a clock and about as silly. I don't even pretend any more that I'm looking for photographs. I say I'm scribbling some notes and *she* says, 'It's a nice little room to write in, isn't it?'

*

— Rosemary disappeared. There was no official leavetaking. She telephoned from Gatwick airport but that was all and, with the pips going every third sentence, it was not easy to take in what was happening. All she said was that she was off to America with Tony and that they were going to 'travel around'. She would write. I panicked and kept asking, stupidly, where she could be contacted if necessary. The pips went and she screamed over them that she did not know. I did not even say goodbye or wish her luck, and it was this that distressed me most afterwards. My last words were that I thought she was being rash. It was shameful. I so badly wanted to have been the sort of mother who could reply, 'How lovely, darling, what fun, bon voyage, good luck.' Instead, I was aggrieved and grudging. So when, after a month or so, Rosemary again rang up (in the middle of the night) to say she was in the Blue Ridge Mountains of Virginia and having a great time, I was so eager to play the right part that I did it too well. How marvellous, I said, what a wonderful journey she must be having. I was all hearty cheerfulness and encouragement. After I had put the telephone down I felt wretched. I had not asked anything I really wanted to know. I had not found out where she was going next. I had not said how I missed her and loved her and thought about her all the time.

That was the pattern of the next eighteen months. When Rosemary rang, I was filled with such a tumult of emotion that it took days for me to return to normal. Her voice seemed to excite me to inexplicable tears. Face to face, Rosemary was formidable in any confrontation but her disembodied voice was light and gentle and even tremulous. She sounded defenceless and helpless, and instantly my imagination created pictures of her forlorn and dejected, in need of me. It was foolish. If she had written, and I could have replied, I think I would have behaved better. I know I would have loved to write to her, but she never gave me the chance. The last thing she wanted was a letter from me. No address was ever revealed, no destination suggested.

It was difficult to piece together, from Rosemary's rare and fragmented phone calls, exactly what she was doing and whether she was enjoying herself. I never asked about how her trip was being financed because obviously she was spending her inheritance. Sometimes in the middle of the night I found myself doing experimental calculations: if she and Tony were driving round America spending, say, £10 a day, then in a month they would get through about £300. On top of that were two air fares and, presumably, the purchase of a car, say, £5,000 minimum. What she had would not last more than a year at a frugal rate and six months at a more comfortable level. I told myself that I must see it as a Grand Tour of old, an excellent way to spend one's inheritance, seeing the world before settling down. But was she seeing the world? She spoke of long, exhausting drives, of being 'shattered'. There were no comments on any of the places from which she telephoned. San Francisco? Haven't really looked at it yet, it's great, though. Washington? Didn't really see it, it was pissing down. Mexico? The roads were bad. She spoke a lot about people, though, endless lists of meaningless names. Sometimes it sounded as if she and Tony were travelling in a circus and of course I found myself, inevitably, wondering how generous my feckless Rosemary was to them. My £10 a day for two people seemed ludicrously insufficient when she mentioned giving great parties for what sounded like hundreds. I asked her once if she had been drawing or painting and she was exasperated. Why? That was what she said, why, and when I replied so that she could keep her hand in for when she returned and was looking for a job, she burst out laughing.

She never asked how Celia or Emily were, though she always enquired politely about me. If I passed on some bit of family news she would say, oh really, or that's good/bad/a pity, and then pass on. I excused her on the grounds that there was no room in a transatlantic telephone call to go over everyone's lives but it upset me all the same. I would have liked some sign from her that she knew she had two sisters. She did once send Emily a card, a month late, for her birthday. I allowed myself to think that, as the card had been posted in New York, perhaps Rosemary was on her way home. But no. The next call came from Australia and plunged me into despair. Australia was just too far away, and the cost – I hated to think of it. From then onwards Rosemary seemed to recede in my mind. I had difficulty conjuring up her exact expressions. The snaps we had taken in Portugal seemed lifeless and flat. She was gone. Once, I had had a daughter and now she was gone: that was how I felt and it bewildered me.

One afternoon Emily came home from school and said she had met Tony. The hurt leapt up in me when I thought Rosemary had not at once come to see us. Emily said, looking at me oddly, that *Tony* was back. Not Rosemary. Rosemary was still in Australia. I made her go over exactly what had happened very carefully. She had been walking along Camden Road when she saw Tony. She asked where Rosemary was and he smiled and said still in Australia. He hadn't liked Australia, it was boring really, so he'd come home. He'd been back in London a week or so. Emily had had the wit to ask where he was living but, predictably, he'd just said 'around'. She'd also asked how Rosemary was. It seemed she was fine. The bold Emily's last query had been was he on her own? Yes, Tony had said, as far as he knew.

We went over it, the three of us, all night. For once even Celia was intrigued enough to speculate. What none of us could decide was whether it was a good or a bad sign that Tony had returned alone. I was filled with hope that Rosemary had tired of him and that she might have found someone kinder and more suited to her. I felt it was a sign of maturity that she had let Tony return on his own and not come running after him. But Celia thought Tony might have abandoned her, Rosemary might have been left high and dry and would not come home until she recovered from the blow. Instantly, my image of a triumphant, independent Rosemary, happily striding some Australian beach alone, vanished and was replaced by one of her lying on a bed in one of the big cities, weeping and distraught, too distressed to be able to get herself home. Emily told me not to be silly. She was sure Rosemary would come home soon.

In those last few weeks before Rosemary came back, it was strange how vividly she returned to my mind. The shadowy creature of the six months before grew flesh again. I would have liked to seek out Tony and talk to him, but I did not, and of course he never came to see us, and yet, in spite of no further news, I felt released from the worst of my anxiety. It was ironic, really, and unbearably naive. I was simple minded enough to think that with Tony's 'bad influence' removed, Rosemary's life must have become calm again. I told myself I would not be surprised if the next we heard was that she had got a job and fallen in love with a new man. I practised accepting that she might settle in Australia. I even looked up the names of her Grandfather Butler's relations, who I knew had descendants living there still. And I could see her as Australian, she fitted in with my concept of the country. She was forthright and daring and could not stand artifice of any sort. She would do well there. I was determined to face up to it bravely. Perhaps I could go out to see her every other year, and she could come to us; perhaps once she was permanently settled, she would like writing letters. I found myself going round the house, smiling, just thinking about it. Then, in the early hours of one April morning in 1959, Rosemary returned home and reality exploded like a bomb destroying all my absurd fantasies. I heard the doorbell ring, looked at my watch, saw it was four o'clock and could not imagine who it was (we had no lodgers by then, and Celia and Emily were both safely in their beds). I got up, wrapped a dressing gown round me and went downstairs. When I opened the door, there was Rosemary, paying off a taxi.

It was dark, of course, and she was some distance away when I first saw her, but even so I did not recognize her. The huddled shape bending down meant nothing to me. I peered out, shivering in the cold early morning spring air, apprehensive and vaguely alarmed. A strange memory came back to me of Oliver arriving in just such a way on his last leave. She picked up a bag in each hand and walked slowly towards me. Even then, I did not recognize her, did not go forward and fling my arms round her. Instead, I drew back, my hand on the catch of the door, ready, I suppose, to protect myself by shutting it if necessary. 'Hello, Mo-ther,' she said, in the old way, teasingly, stressing the last syllable. I said her name, faintly. We embraced. Almost at once she began to weep. My heart raced with distress and shock. I led her into the kitchen, murmuring all sorts of inanities and fussing about with kettles and coffee pots. Why did I not just hold her, hold her . . . I put the light on, turned anxiously to scrutinize her and was appalled. She had changed beyond belief. I felt almost hysterical, wanted to tell her to take that face off, put her own back on, be herself. What I was looking at was not my daughter but a middle-aged, drawn, exhausted, *ill* woman. I suppose it all showed in my expression. She sat down, put her head in her hands and said, through her tears, that she was just tired, it had been a hellish flight. That helped. It gave me something to cling on to, something to justify her appearance, and, even though I knew no flight in the world could account for this transformation, I took refuge behind it. I was soothing and then masterful. I filled a hot water bottle and gave her a hot drink and some aspirin. I urged her to go now, at once, to bed, not to say another word. She let me lead her upstairs, to her old room. In no time at all she was in bed, only her coat and the sweater underneath, a great bulky hairy thing, and her boots removed. I pulled the blankets over her and kissed her wet cheek and said – I'm afraid, I remember I did actually say – 'It will be all right in the morning.'

She slept until just before midnight the following evening. I did not even try to go back to sleep myself. I dressed and sat at my desk, writing my diary for an hour, and felt steadier for it. When Celia and Emily came down I told them what had happened but did not say anything about how their sister had looked. Emily accused me of not seeming very excited and I said I had not taken it in yet. All day I tiptoed about the quiet house waiting for some sign of life from the back bedroom on the top floor. Up and down the stairs I went, pausing, listening, flying to answer telephone or doorbell, so that Rosemary would not be disturbed. Her luggage still lay in the hall. I eyed it speculatively, trying to read significance into its very size and shape. I thought of opening it: there would be dirty clothes I could be washing. I did unzip the side pocket of the larger bag and took out the wallet inside it, feeling guilty. All it had inside were old airline tickets and some money, English, Australian and American. When the girls came home they were amazed I had not woken Rosemary. They both thought I ought to. But I insisted sleep was what she needed and must have, a natural, deep sleep for as long as her body needed it. They were cross that she had not appeared by the time they went to bed themselves.

Usually, I went to bed with them, sometimes before. I was never a late night bird – the morning was always my best time. But I felt quite alert as the evening went on, keyed up as I was. I settled down in the sitting room, consciously arranging myself for a long wait. I lit a fire, once the central heating had switched itself off, and put only one lamp on. My mind could not concentrate on a book. What I did in the end, to stop myself fidgeting, was arrange photographs. I had stacks of them in cardboard boxes, filling the drawers of my desk, all ready to put into albums. All the time I was sorting them, I was listening and, when I finally heard footsteps coming down the stairs, I admit I held my breath and my fingers trembled. What I most wanted was to be natural but what was, what is, natural? There was nothing natural about the situation. I had no idea how to behave and that in itself upset and inhibited me, not to know how to behave with one's own daughter.

She said hello as she came in, asked the time, kept well away. I got up and said I would get something to eat and she said irritably she did not want anything, just a drink, something cold, like orange juice, would do. I flew to get it. Once she had the glass in her hands, she seemed calmer. I did not know whether to start asking her things or wait for her to tell me, and there was an awkward silence before, inevitably, she started talking at the same time as I did. We both told each other to go on which produced more confusion. There was so much that needed telling, that was the trouble. I did not want to sound accusing. Finally, I said that it was lovely to have her home, to see her again, but that I was so surprised I really had not got used to it. That started her off. Out came a long, rambling account of her journey, of all the things that had gone wrong, of how good her intentions had been about phoning to say she was on the way. All the time she was describing her misadventure with airlines, I was studying her closely. There were certain dramatic structural changes that accounted for my failure to know her but these did not explain everything. Her hair had been cut off, cut badly. The long, thick tresses had been viciously cropped to within half an inch of her ears. She had put on weight. Always slim, she now looked hefty, almost Junoesque, and her bone structure had disappeared under a layer of fat. Her complexion, which she had inherited from me, had mysteriously vanished. Nobody would have believed she could possibly have had healthy red cheeks or that she had been in the great outdoors for so long. It seemed neither Californian nor Australian sun had ever touched her. But, worst of all, was seeing that the transition from child to woman had been irrevocably made and that it was to her disadvantage. I never saw Celia or Emily age. I look at them now and of course, I see that they look different, but I never saw the time at which it happened. With Rosemary, I did. She had gone away, aged twenty-two, young. She had come back, twenty-four that month, not really young. Something had gone, something not accounted for by the changes I noted. It is not too sentimental to say that I sat there silently saying goodbye to a child of mine.

When she seemed to have come to the end of her account of her travels, I made sympathetic comments. There was another hiatus. She suddenly said she knew she looked awful but she felt awful and then in a great rush out it came, I might as well know, there was no point in hiding it, she would need help, she hated asking, it was not fair, there was no one else she could depend on – she was pregnant. She was nearly four months pregnant and she felt like death and she would have to move fast and that was why she had come home, for an abortion. Then she started to cry, softly, not trying to hide it or deal with her own tears. I do not remember what I said, nothing much. I did not move. I felt frightened. Hiding my own fear was the hardest part. I was frightened not just *for* Rosemary but *of* her, of her whole predicament. Abortion was a terrible word to me. Today it is bandied about so easily and often that the fear has gone but then, more than twenty years ago, it was shocking to most people. I felt faint and sick. Dully, I was aware that something more than comfort was expected of me. Rosemary had come to me so that I could take over. While half of me rejoiced that she had such faith, that I was not, as I had sadly imagined, a person on the periphery of her life now, the other half rejected the role she was giving me. She was grown up, an adult, with an adult's problems. She could not return to being a dependent. It was unfair, she was asking too much. Yet all my concern was to suppress that reaction and advance eagerly towards doing what she wanted.

She kept saying she was sorry, she did not know how she had got into such a mess, she knew it was an awful thing to do, to come back like this but she had not known what else to do and she felt so ill. Over and over she said those last two things, and over and over I assured her she had done the right thing, that was what homes were for, that was what family meant. I said she must not look on it as some kind of disgrace or defeat that she had had to come back to us – we would always want her to. Then I tried to be practical. I said she must eat a little or she would feel even worse and never get her strength back. I made her have some soup and bread and then, when her eyes began to close with fatigue, I once more led her back to bed, but said I would waken her at nine in the morning, and that she must get up and we must start thinking. She was docile and unprotesting, falling back into bed with obvious relief. Before she fell asleep, I asked if it was all right if I unpacked her bags and found some clean clothes for tomorrow. She smiled faintly and nodded, smiled, I suppose, at my absurdity, worrying about cleanliness. Before I went to bed myself, I sorted out the contents of the bags and loaded the washing machine. As soon as I unzipped those bags, the smell of stale tobacco seemed to permeate the whole house, the stench was dreadful. And, oh, what a sorry heap of soiled and stained clothes came tumbling out! It was a kind of torture dealing with them, grieving over fine waistcoats matted with, with I do not know what. Why had she bothered to bring any of it back?

It was when I woke up, at seven, that a whole new perspective presented itself: an abortion? A baby, but an abortion? Why was that the solution? I lay and thought about it. Rosemary did not want a baby. There was no place in her life for one. Becoming pregnant had been an accident, for which I did not blame her. But I could care for her baby. I was only forty-three years old, perfectly fit and healthy. Abortion, if it could be obtained (and I had no idea how it could) was dangerous, especially if, as she said, Rosemary was nearly four months pregnant. She might die. Would it not be better to have the baby? The family, all of us together, could bring it up. Emily adored babies. She was the one who would be most affected by a baby in the house and how lucky that, alone of the three, she had always loved babies. Yet, as I dressed and started the normal morning routine, I could already imagine Rosemary's fury if I announced it would be better to have the baby, safer . . . It was not what she had come home for. Nothing had yet emerged about who was the father, but I imagined Tony was and certainly he would not want a baby, even if he knew of its coming existence. Perhaps it was what he had run away from. If I even tentatively suggested she should have the baby, Rosemary would hate me. I think she had to hate —

*

I hated reading that part. Who wouldn't. Surprisingly, it's more or less accurate. In matters of natural and great drama my mother always shows unexpected restraint – she's nearly always reliable then. If anything, she has underplayed the hell of my return and she hasn't mentioned at all just what she had to put up with, because I didn't just weep, I shouted and snarled at her and very nearly became violent. The kinder she was, the more impossible I became, and she never once turned on me.

I don't know why I did go home. I could have stayed in Australia and had an abortion, I'm sure. It would probably have been a lot less trouble in the end, because it certainly wasn't easy in London in 1959. Mother rang up Simon Birch, very embarrassing for both of them, I suppose, as abortion was still against the law. He came round to see me, first time in years, and I thought what a cold fish he was and how I disliked him and how I hated putting my proud mother under his obligation. He arranged for me to see a gynaecologist straight away. God, what a wretched fuss it was in those days, absolutely stupid and humiliating. I felt quite wild, mad, with resentment which was fortunate, because it meant I shouted and ranted at this man in his Harley Street consulting rooms and asked him who the fuck he thought he was to suggest I was healthy enough to bear a child. I told him I'd rather kill myself than have it. And I would have done, too. The mere thought of a baby filled me with loathing. What would I do with one? Managing my own life was hard enough without taking on somebody else's. And it hadn't been my fault: I had done everything to prevent having one. Every time somebody goes on about the dangers of the Pill now, I just wish they had had to use the diaphragm, and then they would know they were lucky. I don't care what the Pill does to you, it's worth it and that's after a lifetime's, well, half a lifetime's, use. Maybe the damn diaphragm got punctured, a hole so small I never saw it. Maybe I changed shape inside and it no longer fitted properly. I don't know. All I'm sure of is that I made no mistake, not ever. I was never tempted not to put it in. I always went for check-ups, wherever I was. So I accepted no responsibility for an accident I had done my level best to prevent.

Tony said ridiculous things. When I suspected I might be pregnant he said, 'That would be nice, a baby.' I was livid. Nobody could ever have meant anything less. Tony hadn't the remotest idea of what having a baby entailed – he couldn't even begin to envisage it. When I said so, furiously, he just said he liked babies, children, he wouldn't mind one of his own. He asked what would be so awful, they were lovely and I wasn't a kid myself or anything. I was speechless. We had a terrible row, worse than any of those we'd been having ever since we left America (that was another mistake, also not my fault) ending with him calling me 'unnatural' because I didn't want to be a mother. He sulked afterwards. He said I had depressed him. I started not to care about anything any more. I lay in bed all day, not speaking, feeling sick, not bothering to dress or eat or go out. We were in Sydney, in a house about two miles from the centre, a ramshackle, suburban-looking place with a large overgrown garden. It belonged to somebody we met in California, a man who had gone round with us for a while, to whom Tony took a great liking. He was just the usual bum going round the world but older than most. Tony thought it was so funny that back home in Sydney he had been a chemist. There is nothing remotely amusing about being a chemist, but to Tony there was. So when we went to Australia, to Sydney, Tony insisted on looking this guy up, descending on him. He wasn't there. The house was locked up, but we broke in. Some neighbours came to check us out and Tony flourished our friend's written invitation to stay (which Tony had written himself). We were left alone and stayed there the whole time we were in Australia except for rather unsuccessful trips to beaches and parks and stuff like that. We always planned to go off into the great outback but we never did. Like lots of things we never did.

This house was in a rundown district (rundown then, anyway) called Randwick, near Coogee Beach. It was actually at the top of Coogee Bay Road. I thought, as soon as we arrived there, how much Mother would have liked that house. It looked like a large English country vicarage (except for the palm tree at the front and the frangipani trees to the side and the lantana growing wild all round). It had two sorts of gables at the front, edged with white scalloped boarding, and a porch running between them. It was solid-looking, with long, narrow windows, a family-looking house, as Mother would surely have said. The roof wasn't the garish red of most roofs around there, but a kind of greyish colour that toned in well with the yellow sandstone from which the house was built. Geraniums flourished in the matted undergrowth all round the garden, mixing in with the red flowers of the lantana. It looked pretty in a decadent sort of way. What it really needed was a dull English sky behind it to complete the vicarage impression, but instead there was the relentless blue of the Australian summer. There were none of those misty, soft English colours – everything was brilliant and hard, even brighter than California had been.

Inside, the house was dusty rather than dirty, and full of creepy crawlies. Tony said he would get some stuff to kill them, but he never did. We stuck to two rooms, both with verandahs. When we flew in over Australia, we noticed what everyone notices: how much space there was, each house with so much land to itself. Nothing cramped or mean. It really appealed to us. But the odd thing was that, as soon as we were on the ground and in that house, we felt the opposite – shut in, claustrophobic – and yet we knew all around was land, land, no endless high buildings, everything brilliantly light and bright. But we lolled in our dark rooms, finding it hard to leave. Every time we tried camping on the beach, we got driven off and ended up back in the only place we knew, that house. It was one of the few times I ever had Tony to myself, and it was fatal. All the memories I describe of Tony seem to be bad ones, and that is so unfair. Mother and everyone else never knew what he could be like, and I couldn't tell them. Tony was original. He had spirit, a spirit I tuned in to. We would do quite terrible things together and they didn't feel bad. I could steal, cheat, lie, destroy and run away with Tony, and none of those things would feel bad. He made every other man seem feeble. And yet I didn't hero-worship him. I knew he was no hero. I knew his faults, his lack of centre. But Tony loved life, he had a joyousness and acceptance that permanently excited me. I had a great yearning to make things go right for him and, if that is not love, I don't know what is.

But I couldn't make things go right, not for either of us. Tony grew bored. We knew nobody before we took off for America, but never lacked for company of every sort once we got there. Every day we met new people, people just like us. We drove hectically all over America, without rhyme or reason, and always found friends. When we went to Australia, on Tony's whim, mysteriously we found none. I can't explain it, it just happened. It meant we were together alone, for weeks on end, and it was boring for Tony. I discovered I was more of a contemplative than I had guessed. I *can* take great slabs of peace and quiet if I have the right person with me. Tony had nothing of the contemplative in him. Peace and quiet were anathema to him. Once he'd tinkered with whatever car he had and played his guitar for several hours (badly), he had nothing to do. He didn't daydream. He didn't read or draw or even talk – he hated talk for talk's sake. Within a month he was saying Australia was a disaster, let's go back to America. That was when I said the money wouldn't run to it.

Now Tony did not leave me either because my money was coming to an end or because I was pregnant. He was *never* greedy, never exploited me. Mother thinks he did, but then she would. I don't wish to read what she has to say on that subject. It doesn't actually matter because I know he didn't and he knows he didn't and that's all that matters. Tony didn't value money. When we had it, he spent it, but, when we didn't, he turned his hand to something and got some. He didn't dislike that kind of hand-to-mouth living either: in fact, it suited him. In a curious way he hated waste as much as my mother. People who paid too much for things disgusted him. He despised flashness, wouldn't have had a new Jaguar if I'd bought him one. He most definitely was *not* at all materialistic. People saw him as a parasite on me, but nothing could be farther from the truth. But, when he was told I had perhaps a thousand pounds left out of ten, he was horrified. He kept on and on about where the hell had it gone, and I quite enjoyed reminding him that one of the points of our odyssey had been to do just that, to let it go and not even have to notice. I didn't know where it had gone. I had no accounts. I had bought and given for a year and a half, and that was that. I said, if he wanted he could perhaps tot up a few sums but I couldn't and wouldn't and I didn't care. Tony did. He went very serious and started lecturing me about being more careful. He seemed to feel that the money being nearly spent was a sign that we should go home, if not back to America. Maybe we had had enough. Maybe we should stop pissing about. I asked what would we do if we returned to London? And then he surprised me: he said I had a career to think about. That made me laugh. I'd never mentioned any career, what career, what was he talking about. He said it was obvious, I was clever and educated, I wasn't going to sit around all my life doing nothing. Some day, he had always known, I would turn my attention to what I could do. We had another row. I said I saw no reason why we shouldn't move on somewhere else, even go back to America, but our life style would change, that was all. We would have to work our way round the world instead of travel freely. Tony said if he was going to do that he'd rather be back in London. Might as well be, he said.

He said, I said. How trivial and squalid it all sounds, but it wasn't. It was grand and tragic, two people who loved each other tearing themselves apart wilfully. If I hadn't been pregnant, I might have managed my life better. But, instead, I turned myself to the wall and wept and slept and snivelled and Tony left. I gave him the money for his ticket home of course. He said he'd pay that back. I said I didn't fucking want it back. He tried to get me to go back with him but I refused. I wanted to see how completely he would abandon me, what circumstances he would leave me in. It was all a game. Tony knew I was strong really – he was fond of saying my mother had programmed me too well. He knew I wouldn't lie there and let myself starve, he knew that, however I appeared, I was always able to take care of myself. He knew that what stopped me from being practical during those last weeks was his presence. My apathy was a kind of threat. And he was right. As soon as he had gone, I got up, showered, dressed and went trudging out for food, even though I didn't feel like eating. But I didn't go and buy myself a ticket home for another month. Instead, I lay on my bed and looked out at the frangipani trees. They had been in flower when we arrived but now their leaves were gone and they looked distinctly phallic. I stared at them for hours and wondered if I had any feelings left any more. I thought about Mother after Father was killed. Perhaps all feeling left her then, except for us children, perhaps that other sort of feeling died, as it seemed to have done in me. Maybe I should have the baby and get some feeling back. To escape such thoughts I went out in the evenings. I walked on the beach, Coogee Beach, hating it. The main road ran right next to the sand. There was nothing lonely or lovely about it. I suddenly longed for the windswept, isolated beaches Mother used to drag us to. All the time I stared out at the silly rock they called Wedding Cake Island, I was thinking of Devon and Suffolk and mourning the lack of wildness. The colours everywhere began to offend me. I loathed the bright red flowers of the coral trees and even the hibiscus seemed ugly. Only the dark, shiny, menacing leaves of the Moreton Bay fig pleased me. It wasn't like European fig trees. It grew to a vast size, twisted and gnarled and in some ways like a really old English oak, and its fruit was inedible. Sometimes I would pass cars parked under such a tree and the sight of them covered with revolting bird droppings (from the birds who alone could eat the figs) pleased me.

I cried a lot in my room. All the time I knew I was being stupid not going at once to a doctor, but I hadn't the energy to do it. I couldn't stand the thought of explanations and examinations. There really wasn't any point to anything, nothing mattered, day slid by into night and I was paralyzed with fright. Yet inside my head there was a small, vivid image of my mother, shrunk a million times but distinct and dominating. I hated to see it, but it would not go away. She didn't talk to me or do anything, she was just there, like a very strongly lit still photograph. I didn't have visions, there were no voices. I just saw her.

Coming home to her was the greatest possible relief. I wouldn't want to deny that. All the same, I wish I hadn't done it. I never did it again, because afterwards I remembered the price I paid and she paid and it was much, much too high. The lure of Family was something I learned the hard way to deny.

*

— to hate me anyway. Perhaps I would have lost nothing by daring to suggest she went ahead and had the baby and I would care for it. But I did not. My head knew it would be foolish, even when my heart cried out to do it. My responsibility, as I judged it, was not just to Rosemary but to the unborn child. I was not brave enough to think I could take on a baby, to insist on it being born, and be sure I was right. And, of course, inevitably, those old, weary thoughts about my own origins and Jess's reasserted themselves. I was glad I had been born. But I looked at Rosemary, a comparatively fortunate young woman with every kind of support, and I saw her fear and anger and distress, and I thought of my own mother as I had not done since Jess's birth. It is so tempting to minimize the anguish of any woman bearing an unwanted child. In comparison with all the millions born, what does it matter if one woman fights against adding another? But it does matter. To me, life itself was, and is, *not* sacrosanct. I cannot go along with the Right to Life campaigners of our day. And yet I, of all people, revere the family. It seems a contradiction that I should appear to sanction the killing of unwanted babies. I would not hide behind disputes as to the point at which life begins. I want all babies to start off life in a family and that is why I helped Rosemary. She did not have her own family and mine would have been no substitute. It was no fault of mine that my own children were deprived of a father. Nothing makes me quite so angry as young women wilfully deciding to impregnate themselves artificially, or knowing they are never going to see the father of their child again. It is an attack on all I hold most precious, and I condemn their arrogance.

Well that is high-minded, I suppose. There were no discussions with Rosemary, no ifs and buts or worrying about rights and wrongs. It would have been a waste of breath. Emily was terribly upset – it was one of the hardest things to tell her – but Rosemary was adamant that she would not hide behind secret operations. Emily and Celia had to know the truth. She told them herself and, to their credit, neither of them criticized her —

*

What an outrageous lie, neither of them criticized her, indeed. Dear Celia was *all* criticism and, Christ, how I hated her for it. She said she felt it her duty to tell me I was making Mother terribly unhappy. She asked me if I realized that. I said I realized she was a shit, and told her to fuck off, but she wouldn't go away. I remember her standing in the doorway of the room where I lay, feeling like death, and lecturing me on my sins. She ticked them off on her fat fingers. She summed up with this appalling sentence about my having made nonsense of all Mother believed in, and then said I hadn't even the *decency* to be *grateful* and at least *behave nicely*. I stared at her and thought murder was certainly a possibility. What the hell did Celia know about gratitude? She thought it meant saying thank you every other minute. Like when she was young, she'd bleat 'Thank you for having me' all the time to anyone who'd let her cross their threshold for a second. It was 'thank you, Mummy', like one of those talking dolls. Where she got that kind of unctuousness from, I can't imagine. Not from Mother, that's for sure. Her parting shot was that I could at least get up and not lie in bed all day *worrying Mother*. She, Celia, would rather die than be a worry to Mother. Dear Jesus, to think she hadn't a clue that she was one of the biggest all-time worries Mother has ever had.

*

— to me, Emily said she did not know why Rosemary had let it happen, if she didn't want a baby, but she didn't go on to say she was against the abortion. She did not think Rosemary ought to have a baby and neither did Celia. Neither of them were comfortable with her in the house, until after the abortion was over, but then neither was I. I loved her and felt for her but the very sight of her trailing from one room to another, alternately yawning and sighing, and looking all the time so *derelict*, was unbearable. We all wanted her out of our sight and felt guilty about it. What we really wanted most of all was the abortion over and the chance to start again. That foetus haunted us all each time we looked at Rosemary.

In fact, the whole business was managed with amazing speed, thanks to Simon, Rosemary's godfather. I never contacted him again after that date and he never contacted me: the minimal contact we had disappeared. He was not censorious, but only concerned for his professional integrity. The affair had to be handled properly, all the correct channels gone through. His value lay in knowing which gynaecologist to send Rosemary to and then which nursing home to select. We paid, of course. It turned out that she was not as pregnant as she had estimated: she was thirteen weeks when the abortion was performed. For some reason, quite apart from the fact that it made it safer, that helped me. All those charts of babies in the womb swam before my eyes and I was relieved to realize how small a thirteen-week foetus is. Rosemary could not have felt it move. It was possible, with an effort of will, to regard it as mucus and blood. But there was no need to point this out to Rosemary. She had no sentimental notions about her unborn child. All she fretted about, as we drove in a taxi to the private nursing home in Surrey, was having to be in any kind of hospital at all. It was the thought of white walls, white beds, white uniforms, of disinfectant and steel instruments and polished floors which terrified her. And she was afraid, too, of the pain, though I had assured her there would be virtually none. She would go to sleep and wake up in half an hour or so, feeling slightly sore and bleeding. It would be no worse than a heavy period. She said that in that case she wanted to go home straight away, but I put her right. She had to stay in for two days, at least, so that the danger of septicaemia and of haemorrhaging was past. She turned green at the mention of these and was half fainting when we got out of the taxi.

I stayed during the operation. I didn't weep, nor did I feel unduly anxious. I had faith that Simon would have sent us to somebody competent. I sat there, watching the pale sun make patterns through the slatted green blind, and thought about how things went wrong in the most unexpected ways. How many times had I looked forward to grandchildren? How many weddings and happy sons-in-law had I seen in my imagination? How many phone calls had I taken in fantasy land announcing, it's a boy, it's a girl, both well? And now I was sitting waiting for a scrap of unborn flesh to be incinerated. I did not feel bitter, only regretful. It was Rosemary's life but it *felt* like mine. When they wheeled her in she looked so childlike, with all her hair covered and only her face showing above the sheet, that I could not believe what had been done to her. I sat beside her until she came round and held her hand. 'Is it over?' she murmured and I nodded. I told her to sleep, not to think about it. 'I want to think about it,' she whispered, 'it's such a lovely thought. Thank God. Never again.' I went away feeling bowed down and old. Most of all I felt —

*

I, on the other hand, got up the next day feeling wonderful. There was, as Mother had correctly divined, not the smallest shred of remorse about it all. (Later, I had an abortion Mother never knew about, when I did feel destroyed, but that first time I felt euphoric.) I was annoyed at having to stay in that place a minute longer than the abortion took, but I saw sense and managed to last the statutory two days. Then, unfortunately, I had to go home again because I'd nowhere else to take myself. I was horrible to everyone, selfish, nasty, cruel even. Most of all to Emily who was, at that stage, fifteen I think, particularly beautiful and still so close to Mother. Everything about her annoyed me: she was so *acceptable*, so bright and that loathsomely apt word 'trendy'. She had to wear the vile, bottle-green Camden High uniform but, whereas I had flaunted all the things I wore which were not part of regulation kit, Emily was much more subtle. She was one of those girls who could wear uniform but wear it differently, so that teachers would be exasperated because it appeared correct but somehow wasn't. She had cunning little tricks, ways of tying belts, of tucking up skirts or tucking in jumpers, which made her stand out. She was so pert with it, too. Bandbox fresh. She made Celia look dowdy, but then old Celia, tiller of the soil, was dowdy. Yet I noticed that some kind of rapport existed between them. They were fond of each other. I hoped Mother was gratified.

I honestly can't remember how long I stayed there. A couple of weeks maybe, every day hell. The house could not contain me, I had no place there. Every time my mother referred to 'my' room, I could have screamed. There was nothing mine about it. But it took a while to find myself a bed-sitter and also a job. Now that pleased Mother: I actually got a job. It wasn't a very good job, but it was something. Well, I had to. I only had a hundred pounds left after paying for my return from Australia and the abortion. I got a job in a design team, a small firm, started by two friends from Central, designing anything they could get their hands on, from taps to Christmas cards. I did the graphics for them and got paid according to what we made (not much). I took a room in Fulham to be near them, a tiny, top-floor room with a spectacular view over Chelsea. And so I moved out of the family's cosy little life again, apologizing for disturbing them. It was a shame they had to hide their pleasure at my departure. Mother told me to come and see them, often, I was always welcome.

Mother thinks that was the worst 'phase' in my life (she is fond of dividing time up into so-called phases). She might be right, I don't know how to measure these things. Lying in that house in Sydney, knowing Tony had gone and I was pregnant, was certainly rock bottom. But there have been other rock bottoms, some of them more prolonged. The difference is that next time I didn't involve Mother. I managed on my own and got going again. My family could not be a wonderful warm blanket wrapped round all my angles, fitting me snugly, protecting me effortlessly when the storm outside raged. They were simply people to whom I was related, who were kind to me, whom on the whole I liked and even loved and would always want to know about, but they were indisputably not a part of me or me of them. I didn't know whether acknowledging this made me happy or sad – a bit of both. From the age of twenty-four, I didn't choose to stand on my own feet. I just looked down at last and saw that was where I was.

*

— felt empty. I felt that in spite of being unable to fault what we had done we had rejected her. We three, Celia, Emily and I, were ashamed of how comfortable we were together, how easy and effortless in all our dealings. We could not give Rosemary what she needed and wanted. We had been like a friendly hotel to her, nothing more. We wanted to be more but she would never let us: we would not do. The idea of sitting all evening, chatting to us, horrified her. She was not remotely interested in us, then. I would have said with certainty that as she drove away in the summer of 1959 she was, this time, really leaving us, consciously getting out. 'I don't feel I've got another sister,' Emily said. 'She doesn't mean anything to me any more. She doesn't even like me and I don't think I like her' —

*

God, I'm popular. I hadn't realized Em decided so early she didn't like me. Lucky I didn't really appreciate this then. Oh, I wouldn't have cared, people not liking me doesn't bother me. What's 'liking' anyway, feeble emotion in my opinion, but I would probably have been influenced by my little sister's openly avowed *dislike*. I wouldn't have tried so hard later, and I emphatically did try. I didn't with Celia, not ever. Mother asked me to, but I wouldn't.

Now why does she interrupt herself here?

May 16th

Couldn't *not* go to the Pre-Raphaelite Exhibition, but went with misgivings. All those historical paintings, all that mythology, not to my taste. Stared helplessly at Hunt's *Rienzi Vowing to Obtain Justice for the Death of his Young Brother Slain in a Skirmish between the Colonna and the Orsini Factions* . . , dear me. Quite unable either to admire or to make anything of it. Sat and rested in front of *The Children's Holiday*, showing a Mrs Thomas Fairbairn and five children. Not a friendly family. Heavy gilt frames on most of the pictures irritated me. Pictures ponderous enough without them. Thought, when I reached the end (and saw *Chill October*, now that I could enjoy) that I'd walk round once more in case I'd missed anything. I had. No 21, a portrait by Ford Madox Brown of Lucy Madox Brown, painted in 1849. A head and shoulders study of a child about seven years old. A round, apple-cheeked face, a sturdy child, rather plain and solemn. A wilted rosebud tucked into the neck of a navy blue garment. Immediately I saw it, I thought of Celia: her exact image except for the colouring. Remorse and panic both at once. Wanted Celia back, as she was then. To treat differently. Lucy, Celia, looked at me accusingly. I am too serious, I am too grave, she said, what are you going to do to help me?

I did not enjoy the exhibition. I don't wish to write any more about it.

*

Last time I was here, a whole week ago, I stayed with Mother's every golden word. It has its advantages. At least at the end of her account of my infamous abortion I did feel she'd given me more insight into certain aspects of it than I'd had before. It didn't give me the courage to walk out of the room later and tell her what I thought, but it shifted my perspective slightly. I can feel it shifting all the time now. It makes me feel queasy, as though I was wearing someone else's spectacles for driving and looking at a road which I know to be straight but which suddenly appears to tilt.

But Mother is bound to be finished with me, for the moment. She's out there in the garden with Celia. Every time I look up she waves. Celia is helping Mother 'tidy' the garden. It looks painfully tidy already to me – they're both mad. It makes me smile, remembering. How devastated Mother was that Celia didn't become a doctor, like dear Daddykins, how she'll pour her heart out, but I don't know if it'll be interesting enough to arrest my attention, until we get to Andrew Bayliss, that is.

*

— was academic. She had a natural mathematical, scientific aptitude. I needed no one to tell me she was Oxbridge material. I suppose all the way through her schooldays I automatically assumed, the way parents of such effortlessly gifted children do, that Celia would go to University. In fact, I assumed more, I assumed she would become a doctor. She seemed to accept my assumptions, even encourage them. And then, the summer she did so spectacularly well in 'A' Levels, Celia made her announcement. She was not going to try for Oxbridge. She was not going to try for any University.

It was like that: an announcement. Celia stared at me steadily and said she was not going to go to University, in spite of these results. She was glad about them, but they were irrelevant. She was going to be a gardener. Not a horticultural expert, but a real gardener, starting at the bottom. She was sorry, she knew I would be disappointed. Perhaps I surprised her by being more violently angry than disappointed. I surprised myself by the force of my rage and bitterness. It was so *stupid*, so apparently affected, even though I knew Celia was the least affected and the most straightforward person in the world. But I did not move her. She became, absurdly, a gardener, on the staff of the Royal Parks. For three years she picked up paper, cleared out drains, swept paths. Eventually, she was promoted to tying up roses, raking, hoeing and other menial jobs. She said she was learning all the time. She could tell when plants needed attention, she had the knack. She was officially appointed a Grade II gardener, the lowest grade, on her twenty-first birthday. Her first real gardening job was propagating geraniums in the Hyde Park greenhouses. I could make no sense of her life. Her wage was tiny and her satisfaction difficult to see. The main excitement seemed to be watching the building of Duck Island in St James's Park, a subject she lectured us on again and again. To become an assistant to the Bird Man became her greatest ambition. She made no friends, belonged to no group. Yet she maintained she was 'quite happy'. Every day she came home at five, had a bath, helped me cook, watched television, helped Emily with homework. She no longer played her oboe, nor did she belong to any sports club. Occasionally, she played tennis or swam, but not regularly. Emily's friends treated her like an aunt, although she was only four years older, and I could not bear it. But what could I do? I could not be cruel and point out to her what she already knew: that it was unnatural for a girl of her age to live so sedately, that it was not good for her, that life was meant to be more fun. I could not organize her, force her to join clubs to replace those she had left at school. Once, when I was pushed into worrying aloud about her lack of pleasures – pushed by my own exasperation – she said, '*You* don't do anything either. I'm just like you.' That was what frightened me. She is not in the least like me. And, at her age, I had met Oliver. But Celia, living as she did, was never going to meet anyone. And then Andrew Bayliss came along, the answer, it seemed, to all my prayers. But he turned out to be an evil, selfish, arrogant man. He always knew what he was doing which was quite the worst part about him. There was no question of him falling helplessly in love with Celia. There were no excuses, I accept no extenuating circumstances. And, once he had wormed his way into her affections, he made no attempt to protect her from the realities of his position. He never mentioned that he was still married, nor that he still visited his wife nor, later on, that she had had his baby. He presented himself to Celia as a lonely, much wronged divorcee. He was the original schemer, cruel, calculating, corrupt —

*

All that is absolute rubbish, a clear case of paranoia. Andrew Bayliss was none of those things. I only met him a few times but that was enough to show me he was just a dull, boring, harmless jerk. But Mother had to build him up into this sadistic figure because she couldn't bear the thought of the shabbiness of it all. She wanted Celia to be involved in a great drama, instead of a squalid little affair, which is what it was. Everything had to be Andrew's fault. As if the fact tha he 'waited a year' before he asked Celia out was a sign of plotting and scheming – my God. All it was a sign of was his doggedness, his stubbornness. He looked a policeman in or out of uniform: big, solid, square, but not so much powerful as immovable.

He wasn't very nice, Andrew Bayliss. I'll grant Mother that. He wasn't thoughtful or kind, though she forgets he appeared so at first. Probably his greatest virtue was his patience and I expect it was this that appealed to Celia, who was herself pretty patient. She had a horror of people like me, always rushing, never finishing things, never able to queue or stand still. I imagine it was Andrew's ponderous quality that first attracted her. Mother may, as ever, have had the best intentions in the world when she put Celia up to buying a flat with her inheritance, but she made a big mistake. The night Mother suggested to Celia that she should buy a flat for herself, Celia came to see me. It was probably one of the two or three times in her life that she's ever done that and I was so surprised, when she rang up asking to come, that I kept saying what, *what*, in the most offensive way. I invited her round and she pedalled all the way to Fulham on her bike, there and then. She hadn't been to my bed-sitter before, though Emily and Mother had, and she was nervous about it, which made her even more inhibited than usual. I did think of doing a quick tidy up on her behalf but then I thought, Christ, how stupid, so I did nothing and she saw it in all its glory, mess and everything. She couldn't take her eyes off the mattress, piled with grubby covers, just as it was when I'd crawled off it. I knew she wanted to put a sheet on properly and smooth it straight, and plump up the pillows, and make it look like a sofa. The place was littered with open packets of this and that, which upset her too, and the general grime offended her. She tried so hard not to make any comment, to keep her eyes on my face and not to look anywhere else, that I felt sorry for her. It was quite a small room, so we couldn't help being close to each other as we talked, which was a weird sensation. Celia repelled me physically. Mother would be so upset if I confessed that to her and it upsets me to admit it even to myself, but it's true. My sister's marble-like flesh repels me. I want to jump up and run away, and yet I feel no animosity towards her: it really is a physical sensation. I don't dislike or disapprove of her any more. In lots of ways I admire her, especially for not going to University which Mother had programmed her for, for choosing to be something crazy like a jobbing gardener and not a doctor. But sit me beside Celia and I am almost beside myself.

She asked me if I liked living there, what it was like. It was such a dumb question, I couldn't think how to answer. Finally I said that if she meant did I prefer it to home, she didn't need to ask because she already knew the answer. Anything was preferable to home, as far as I was concerned. She stared at me a long time, unnerving me even more, and then she said, 'Do you think I'm abnormal?' I so badly wanted to burst out laughing that it hurt to control myself, and I'm sure I must have gone scarlet in the face. It's impossible to tease Celia out of that sort of question. It wouldn't have helped to mimic her and tell her not to be such a loony. I knew that, for once, I had to reply with equal seriousness. So I said, no, of course not. Loads of people lived at home and weren't in the least abnormal and it would be absurd of her to think there was anything wrong in liking to live with her own family. Then I added, very carefully, knowing each word would be deliberated upon, that all the same her situation *was* a little out of the ordinary. It wasn't entirely normal for a twenty-one year old to be so deeply devoted to her mother and sister. Maybe a break would be a good thing, maybe she would enjoy a little freedom. Then out it came in a long, rambling stream of only half coherent words – how she was afraid to leave home, afraid to be on her own, afraid she would never be able to make a life for herself. She hated change, loved routine, didn't ever want to do anything she wasn't already doing or be anywhere else, but Mother wanted to be rid of her, she liked Emily better, was easier with her . . .

I interrupted her there, said she was being silly. I told her Mother worshipped her family and would never want to be rid of any member, not even me. Celia calmed down and said she supposed so but it didn't really help. She still didn't want to do what Mother wanted her to do, but she supposed she would have to. I saw suddenly how little confidence Celia had. She seemed so capable and organized, and indeed she was, but in herself, in what she was, she was a mess. But what could be done? It was like pushing a baby out into the cold. I spent the rest of the time she was with me flattering her, telling her how proud Mother was of her using her inheritance sensibly, unlike me. I tried to get her to see how much fun it would be choosing and preparing her own nest and how thrilled Mother would be to help her – all that curtain-making and painting and carpet-laying. She smiled rather sadly and said she supposed so, and then she thanked me fo listening. I said what else were sisters for, trying not to sound sarcastic or like a parody of mother.

For weeks afterwards Celia was on my conscience, which made me furious. I worried about her in a vague sort of way but didn't do anything about it, except ring Mother up, which I did pretty frequently, and ask her how all the moving was going. They were all moving: Emily and Mother to one small flat and Celia to another. It was about six months before I visited Celia in her new abode. I'd had lunch at Mother's, as she had, and I went back with her, genuinely curious to see what she'd got together. The flat itself was brilliant – all that garden down to the canal and the big, spacious rooms – but what she'd done to it in the way of decoration and furnishings was awful. I saw Mother's influence everywhere – itty-bitty, sprigged wallpaper in the bedroom, carefully matching tiles in the bathroom, gleaming Formica units in the kitchen. Foul. And all immaculately, frighteningly tidy and arranged, so much so I felt there must be chalk marks on the floor in case anything got accidentally moved. Celia seemed small in this flat. Of course, I gooed and said how lovely and how lucky you are and God I wish I had this space, what I could do with it. I even went so far as to admit I wished I had bought something, it was bloody awful paying rent for what I had. I was going to have to leave my room that summer and start looking again and I hated that. Celia said I could stay with her, if I liked. I was so horrified at the thought I couldn't think what to say, so muttered something about not being tidy enough and having noisy visitors.

I didn't see Andrew that time but I heard about him quickly enough. Mother forgets how terribly pleased she was at first. 'Celia's got rather a nice boyfriend,' she told me triumphantly over the telephone and there was more satisfaction in her voice when she said he was a policeman, a police *sergeant*. I roared at that, it was so fitting. Mother prattled on about it being nothing *serious*, goodness me, but it was so nice for Celia and, oh, if I could see the difference in her already and what a lot of interests they had in common. It was Emily who told me, the next time I dropped in, that he was old and boring, and, frankly, she couldn't see what Celia saw in him. I took Emily up on this verdict at once and got her to describe Celia's policeman. Mother was listening all the time and was furious at how Emily put him down. Mother said he made Celia very happy and that was all that mattered, that was all she had ever wanted for any of us, just somebody to make us happy. 'He doesn't make Celia happy,' Emily said. Mother told her not to be so arrogant. How could *she* tell? Emily shrugged and said, quite calmly, that it wasn't worth arguing about, she just could tell and she didn't care what Mother said. By that time I was so intrigued I made immediate arrangements to come for lunch and meet this Andrew Bayliss.

He was dreadful. The lunch was purgatory. He was pompous and prim and, worst of all, a fascist, if not made then in the making. We had several arguments verging on the political – it was the time of the Profumo scandal – and his views and opinions ran so counter to our own that it seemed unbelievable that he could be connected with any of us. He sat there, coming out with this hang 'em and flog 'em and castrate 'em drivel. It was extraordinary. And Celia at his side didn't bat an eyelid. Discipline, order, authoritarian rule, that was what the country needed. Celia looked at him adoringly, once or twice, and I saw him squeeze her hand under the table. I thought that was rather sweet. When the meal was over, he sprang up and insisted on cleaning up, said he was highly domesticated, wouldn't be put off by Mother's protests. I liked him for that. He did a good job, too, left the kitchen gleaming. Then he and Celia went off for a walk and I didn't see him again for quite a long time, not until he was very involved indeed with Celia and Mother had stopped being pleased and was beginning to be frantic and frightened.

*

— and devious. Once I grew to recognize this, and I admit it took me a very long time, I did not know what to do. I, a mother, was not supposed to interfere. I have noticed this attitude in general, noticed people talking on buses or trains about family matters almost boasting that they 'kept well away', as though this is a matter for congratulation. Of course I should have liked, these last twenty years, not to have been implicated in the tragedies which have befallen my children. I should have liked to excuse myself of all responsibility, to have successfully assured myself that not only was I not called upon to do anything, but that there was nothing I *could* do. I do not know where people get the idea that family catastrophes are a kind of spectator sport from which any member can avert their eyes if the going gets to rough. They are not. They are quite impossible to sit through without leaping up to staunch the blood. So I am not going to apologize for 'interfering'. I had no alternative, witnessing what I witnessed.

And what I witnessed was Celia's incarceration. Andrew Bayliss began to dominate and crush her from the very beginning of their association and she seemed incapable of extricating herself from his clutches. I would never have believed it of her, never for one minute have imagined Celia could become so feeble. The entire thing baffled me. How could her nature have undergone such a swift and total change because of a love affair with a man? That is what I have to call it, but I saw precious little love there. Lust, yes, I saw that. Andrew Bayliss knew perfectly well that Celia was a virgin, inexperienced and shy, and he determined to have her. She responded to his attentions like a flower to the sun, she opened out, glowed, smiled so much more and it was lovely to see. But only for a while, then the new vitality began to wane. She lost weight, became tense and brittle and started to keep away from us. Instead of dropping in every other day, it became once a week and then there were sudden phone calls cancelling Sunday lunch, which was a sacred date in our family calendar. I told myself to be glad about it. Had I not longed for Celia to have such a hectic social life that, like Rosemary, she could no longer fit us in? Had I not yearned for her to have a life of her own? But those were two illusions: she had no social life at all, but instead was virtually walled into her flat by Andrew Bayliss, who permitted her no freedom. I was astonished when I called round one day, to see if Celia was well, to find him opening the door and appearing to bar my way. 'Celia's in bed,' he said, 'she doesn't want to be disturbed. Can I give her a message?' I simply stared at him, huge and broad, filling the doorway, and said nothing. 'It's just that she's tired,' he added, scratching his cheek which was half covered in shaving cream. He was in pyjamas and a dressing gown. I finally found my voice, a very faint one, and said I was sorry to have disturbed them, perhaps I could telephone later. When I did telephone, after a day of agonizing, I got him again: Celia was in the bath, was there anything in particular I wanted?

It was all so sudden. Up till then, Andrew Bayliss had been careful to be well-mannered. Then he just stopped. He looked at me as though he had never seen me in his life before and was barely civil. I could not understand it. Why did he think I was an enemy? How could he think of me as wanting to hold Celia back from anything she really wanted to do, including take him for a lover? And the worst thing of all was that Celia herself, when I saw her, had become remote. She had transferred her allegiance to Andrew. I tried so hard to take an interest in Andrew (not then knowing a thing about his background), but every question was regarded with suspicion. Why did I want to know his age, where he grew up, where exactly he worked and what exactly he did. *What for?* All those questions seemed normal to me, but Celia resented them. I suppose she knew by then that Andrew had been married twice and did not want to tell me. It spoiled her happiness to present to us a twice divorced man. She did not like any questions about their living arrangements, either, though I had no desire to be censorious. She knew I had never objected to Rosemary's adventures so why should I have been likely to disapprove of hers? But I tried, for several months, to abide by the new rules. I did not call round, nor did I telephone. I waited patiently for her to come to us and when she did I was scrupulous about not making resentful remarks or cross-examining her about her recent movements. I always tried to be glad and welcoming and uncomplaining, though it was very hard not to complain about one important point, which was that she never came alone. Andrew Bayliss accompanied her at all times, his hand literally grasping her elbow in a most proprietorial manner. It made all conversation stilted. I found myself having to invent things to do, while they were there, to cover up the awkwardness. Celia's eyes never seemed to meet mine, she fidgeted, looked this way and that, and was clearly relieved when Andrew announced they had to be going.

This unhappy state of affairs went on for, oh, I forget how long, months, almost a year, and, though the hurt continued, I had practised accepting the virtual loss of another daughter with such ruthlessness that I was half-way to being reconciled. I do not deny that I was bitter: other women seemed to have daughters who, when they became attached to men, widened the family circle instead of dropping out of it. I had always believed that, as a parent, you received back what you put in. I thought I had instilled warmth and mutual support, but it seemed, then, quite otherwise. I was cut off. Even visiting me had become not a pleasure but a duty. If I had not still had Emily at home, I expect I would have toppled over into a real depression. But Emily kept me sane. She was as brisk in her judgements as Rosemary had been, but kinder. 'Don't fret so, Mum,' she would keep telling me and then she'd hug me and I would feel greatly comforted for a while. Emily's commonsense and open affection helped me to keep at bay the awful fear that I had founded my life on quicksand. My family did not want to be a family. Soon, I would be left as I had begun, a woman without a family.

I see now, of course I do, how very silly I was. At nearly seventy, I can look back and feel sorry for my middle-aged self. But that is what life looks like at that age to widowed ladies to whom family has always been all. It is a female predicament. The trouble is that one is so busy marking the passing of time in one's children's lives that one fails to relate it to the passing of time in one's own. I grieved that my daughters were not the same to me, without stopping to consider that I was not the same to them. I took their problems into myself and brooded and made myself unhappy over them, and that is what grown-up children absolutely cannot bear. They want you to get on with your own life and not upset yourself over theirs, because then you become a burden to them and, if they are burdened already, that is the last straw. Such wisdom now, such a lack of it then. In many ways, that was the worst period in my life, until Celia herself precipitated a crisis.

She rang me one morning, early, sounding very secretive and said would I like to meet her in the park, Regent's Park, and have a walk before she started work. I leapt at the chance, naturally. At eight o'clock I met her in Queen Mary's rose garden. She was in her dreadful, ugly overalls. We climbed a little mound behind the waterfall and sat on the seat there. There was no noise at all. Celia explained that the hedges round both the Inner and Outer Circle roads deadened the traffic. I admired the roses. She told me there were 20,000 rose bushes, at least, and that there was only a staff of fourteen to look after them. She said black spot had been very bad this year, and mildew, but red spider hadn't been such a nuisance . . . A duck, or what I took to be a duck, flew overhead. Celia said it was a mallard. She said she would show me where the mallards nested in hollow trees and in the cornices of Bedford College. I said how interesting. There was a further bit of chit-chat and then she said she was sorry she had not seen much of Emily and me lately and I interrupted too quickly, in my haste to be agreeable, and said that was all right, I quite understood, and she said no, I did not, that was the point. I did *not* understand about Andrew. He was, she said, very possessive, he could not help it, it was just how he was. It made him nervous, if she kept coming to us all the time, it made him think he was not enough for her and that made him feel a failure. Then she told me he had been married twice before and each marriage had gone wrong because he discovered he was not enough for his wife. The trouble, really, was that he had had no family life himself and had no concept of what belonging to a family meant, that it was not a threat to other personal relationships. Andrew thought it was. She had told him that I was an orphan, an abandoned baby, brought up in an institution, as he had been, but it did not seem to make any difference. He still mistrusted me and the whole family scene. So, and here she stopped and turned to look at me with such real pain in her eyes, so she had promised him not to see us for six months or so. We would telephone each other but not meet. She knew it was stupid and ridiculous but he got upset about it and she could not bear it.

I tried to smile and shrug and be casual and reassuring but I do not claim to have succeeded. All the time I was thinking how dare he, how *dare* he, and how can she agree. It sounded mad. It was the most preposterous request I had ever heard. I felt shamed by having to listen to it. What kind of man was this who could be so childish, who could make the person he loved so wretched? At the forefront of my mind was the thought that the whole situation was dangerous. I managed to keep relatively calm and asked her only if she was sure she knew what she was doing. She said she did. She said at the end of the six months Andrew wanted to marry her and then everything would change. All he needed was confidence. She told me how each of his wives had deserted him. Fortunately, there had been no children. Now, at thirty-nine, he was ready to try again and this time he knew it would work. Celia said she knew, too. She loved him. She knew he was odd, but then, she said, so was she. Andrew was the first person whom she had ever felt to be like her.

What I felt, as I listened to this halting account in the cold morning air, was disbelief. I did not, for a start, believe a single word about the reason for those marriages breaking up. I did not believe Andrew was going to marry her, either. I did not even believe he had been an orphan. Instead, I had this fixed and unshakable conviction that

Andrew Bayliss, policeman or not, was a liar and a cheat who had duped my innocent daughter. There and then, even while she was still talking, I resolved what I was going to do. As soon as I got home I began to put my plan into operation: I rang a local solicitor and asked him how I could hire a detective. He told me. I hired one. I told this detective to find out for me as much as possible about Police Sergeant Andrew Bayliss, aged thirty-nine: the dates of his marriages, the grounds of divorce, his background and upbringing. Within a few weeks, I was sent copies of birth and marriage certificates and of divorce proceedings. As I had sensed, Andrew Bayliss was a fraud.

The degree to which he had lied was not really very great, but it was revealing. The only serious factual lie was that his wives had not left him, he had left them. It was true that, until recently, there had been no children. It was also true that, although not brought up in an institution, as he claimed, Andrew Bayliss had been fostered from the age of ten and had clearly had a rough time being passed from one family to another. I suppose I might have begun to feel sorry for him, if it had not been for the most interesting revelation of all: he had married for a third time two years before he met Celia. No divorce had been applied for. And, according to my detective, he was still in touch with this third wife. Occasionally he spent weekends with her. Worst of all, she had a baby of about eight months.

I had all this information for a week before I did anything about it. I read it over and over again, trying hard to be rational and logical. I saw that, as one would expect of a policeman, Andrew Bayliss was certainly not engaged in any illegal activity. There was nothing legally wrong in living most of the time with another woman, while still seeing one's wife and child. There was only Celia's word for it that marriage was indeed in the offing. So what could I do?

Going to see Andrew Bayliss was one of the most terrible things I have ever had to do in my whole life. I tried to convince myself that a letter would do just as well – indeed, I wrote several drafts of such a letter – but I always knew it would not. It would be both dangerous and cowardly. I was tempted to consult Rosemary and Emily, but resisted the urge. It would have been wrong to implicate them in what had to be my decision. So, greatly daring, I went to the police station where Andrew Bayliss worked, at a time when I thought him most likely to be there, and I asked the duty officer if he would be so good as to ask Police Sergeant Bayliss if I could see him on an official matter. I gave my maiden name. In no time at all, a puzzled Sergeant Bayliss presented himself and stopped short when he saw me. He was ready to refuse to speak to me, but the Duty Officer was there and he could not risk a scene. He said, abruptly, that he was busy and could not spare me any time. I said, if he preferred, I could say what I had to say there and then, it would not take a minute. I was careful to speak calmly, though my heart raced and the hands clutching the counter in front of me did not feel like mine but like shaking gloves I had to control. The duty officer looked at me curiously. I was, I hope, dignified and, that word much loved by policemen, 'respectable'. Andrew Bayliss was well aware of the excellent impression I was giving. He opened a door into a small room leading off the entrance hall, and gestured for me to go inside. There was a desk, which he immediately placed himself behind, and a chair which he did not invite me to use and of which I did not avail myself. I said I would come to the point immediately, that all I had come to say was that I knew he was married and had a child and that, if he did not immediately either leave my daughter alone or tell her at once about his circumstances, then I would do so myself. I said all that concerned me was that her choice to live with him should be a real one and that, at the moment, in possession of only half the facts about him, it was not. Then I walked out of his office. He said, 'Now look here,' but I had the door open and when I stood in the open doorway and turned back and said, 'Yes?' I suppose he did not dare say what he really wanted to say. I said goodbye to the policeman outside and left the police station. When I got home, I felt drained and exhausted. The humiliation of it all was hard to bear. It was not that I felt either ashamed or guilty, though I did feel apprehensive about how Celia would interpret my action. But I cannot say, even now, in spite of what happened afterwards, that I have ever regretted it —

*

Well, she should've regretted it. It was monstrous. How complacent and virtuous she sounds, and yet what she did was vile. Presenting herself as Celia's saviour, when she was trying to smash her love affair and not seeing that discovering the truth *herself* might have been

128

salutary for Celia. Playing God, that was what she was doing, yet without the Almighty's superior and much more comprehensive information. Maybe that third wife was a bitch, maybe Andrew always intended to tell Celia, maybe he *was* ill done by. Who could tell? Certainly not Mother. For an intelligent woman, she seems to have been remarkably silly. My God, if it had been me! But she wouldn't have tried it on with me. She'd given up trying to protect me. Celia, though, still belonged, still had things done for her sake, but really for the family's. No wonder Mother felt 'apprehensive'. She ought to have been bloody terrified.

What kind of world did Mother think she was living in? Victorian England? She never doubted for a moment that Andrew would confess and saintly Celia would recoil in horror and cast him off. Of course, Andrew did no such thing, not straight away. He bundled Celia off, sharpish. Mother rang me, when she could get no reply from Celia's flat, after telephoning non-stop all week. She'd been told by the Regent's Park supervisor that Miss Butler had taken a month's holiday. Mother seemed to have some crazy idea that Andrew had abducted her. I tried to calm her down. Why shouldn't they go on holiday? Was there a law against it, or another saying mothers had to be informed? Then Mother told me Mr Bayliss's True Circumstances (though not how she discovered them). I said I couldn't see it mattered, frankly. Mother kept bleating that I didn't seem to have taken in the fact that *there was a baby involved*. When the truant pair returned – no having-a-good-time postcards, I'm afraid – Celia went to see Mother. She said Andrew had told her on holiday about his existing wife and his child. She said she was sorry to hurt Mother but, in spite of the shock, her feelings for Andrew hadn't changed. She still loved him. If anything, she felt he needed her more than ever: he'd got into such a mess and it wasn't his fault. Mother apparently blocked her ears and said she wouldn't listen to such *cant*. I know all this because Emily told me. Emily and I were so amazed at old Celia making such a stand that we both tried to support her by ridiculing Mother and waving the flag. But Celia didn't want us. She was totally obsessed with reforming Andrew and showing him that the love of a good woman could redeem anyone. Well, it didn't. Andrew left her after a year, during which I think she must've gone through hell. Afterwards, of course, Mother took her to her bosom and consoled her, but Celia didn't need her in the same way any more. Mother said Andrew Bayliss only brought Celia 'heartache and misery', but she was quite wrong.

And now the gardeners are coming in and I must stop.

May 21st

Hadn't even thought of doing another Exhibition, not so soon, but Rosemary came to take me to the first day of the Summer Exhibition at the Royal Academy. Ought to have suspected something straight away – she hates the Summer Exhibition, sneers every year at my pleasure in it. Only fifteen people waiting to go in. We were first into the galleries. Such lovely pictures. No 314 was so sweet, an elderly woman, in a red hat, sitting in a most comfortable, old chair and looking at a photograph album. To her right, a chest out of which spilled toys; to her left a bookshelf of children's books. Rosemary said it was a perfect example of what gave this exhibition a bad name. *She* was ecstatic over something called *Convolution* by Sandra Blow, a pointless (to me) big square of white, with blue stuck on it in a vague flower-like shape. The sculptures were lovely. A darling, fat, little girl in Gallery 9 and a duck which Celia would love. Rosemary liked something called *Sphinx*, a female figure with a bird head and claws. Ugh. Rosemary went ahead, stood waiting at the bottom of the last gallery. I thought she was bored, so I hurried. No 1752 was an etching of a bridge in Bath, pretty. No 1756 an aquatint of an acacia tree. I like things like that. Did wish Rosemary was not so impatient, that she didn't make me so self-conscious. Then my eye caught the title of the last etching, No 1758. *Daniel in Uniform*, it said. I looked at it. I looked back at the catalogue. My heart started to thud. No 1758, *Daniel in Uniform* by Rosemary Butler. Rosemary turned, smiling, quizzical. She said what a joke. My daughter, with a picture hung in the Royal Academy. Tears in my eyes. Rosemary laughing and scoffing, me clutching her: how foolish we must have looked. Rosemary said it was a very small etching, a nothing, and, as for being hung in the Royal Academy, the Summer Exhibition didn't count, it was an embarrassment not an honour. But she couldn't spoil my elation. It was not just having the etching there, the honour, I insist the honour, but doing it and entering it, because she could only have done it for me, couldn't she? To please me. To think she even *wants* to please me pleases me. Maybe it should not. Maybe it is an ominous sign. But I refuse to interpret it as such. No 1758, *Daniel in Uniform* by Rosemary Butler. That is something.

*

Wasn't that sweet? I'm glad I left that diary entry for this time. Quite uplifting. What a nice daughter I am after all.

Mother is in hospital, having the most minor of operations, though from the fuss Celia is making you'd think it was a heart transplant. She's having a wisdom tooth out. I'd have thought, at her age, that she'd be past such horrors. I suppose most old folk have artificial choppers, so the problem never arises. Anyway, Mother's having this tooth whipped out and she's in the Royal Free, for a day and night, so for once there's no hurry. I can stay as long as I want and read as much as I like. The trouble is, my enthusiasm is waning. I want to jump ahead to see what Mother says about Emily and Daniel but I know that's a long way off still. I know I really ought to finish off Celia because Mother's going to get all that *so* wrong it's my positive duty to correct her version. Wow, how easy it is to be as pompous as Mother.

*

— typically, *announced* she was giving her inheritance away. There was no warning, no discussion. Celia simply made these tremendous changes in her life and then informed me. She was selling her lovely flat and moving into a bed-sitting room. She was giving the money she would make to Shelter, the charity housing association.

It was, I think, cruel not to prepare me, especially when, as Celia perfectly well knew, I was feeling so happy about her future at long last. Andrew Bayliss was forgotten and she had given up gardening to start training as a social worker. I was *delighted*. Nothing had pleased me more for years. Rosemary made sarcastic comments about Celia being one of nature's social workers, why train her, but she could not spoil my pleasure. It seemed to me that Celia might now begin to fulfil herself. Then she came out with this extraordinary piece of news and I was angry.

'You'll only sneer,' she said when I asked for an explanation. She blushed as she said it. Celia blushes easily. When she was a child, it used to be rather charming but now her red face makes her look choleric, i a most unattractive way. I asked her how she could imagine I would ever sneer at my own daughter. 'Then you will laugh,' she said. 'You will mock me, as you always do, you and Rosemary.' I said surely she was confusing affectionate teasing with unkind mockery. She said she was not, but that, even if I called it teasing, she still did not want to have to put up with it. I saw she was close to tears and was moved, in spite of my furious disapproval. I tried to be gentle and understanding, begging her to *try* to explain, promising I would not deride anything she said. What she did say, in a halting and emotional voice quite unlike her normal phlegmatic tones, was that she could not go on having so much when others had so little. She did not need her flat. It was I who had wished it upon her. She was not a homemaker like me and Emily, her domestic surroundings were unimportant to her. All she needed was one big room and decent cooking facilities. She said she was acquainted with the truly homeless, that she had met them in the parks, the people who had nowhere else to go and were not tramps or derelicts. It made sense to her to give the proceeds from the sale of her flat to Shelter. She was relieved to be moving to one room in a poorer area. I suggested, cunningly, that she would miss a garden but she said she could make do with mine, if I had no objection.

'No objection'. All I objected to was the unnecessary silliness of her extravagant gesture. I could not stop her. I have never stopped any of them from carrying out these foolish decisions. 'I don't want much,' Celia said and I replied, 'Then you ought to.' Afterwards —

*

All these fine phrases – phoney. Mother's back in the 1930s, in a melodrama. Celia's as bad, if she really did talk like that. She should've said sod off, Mother, it's my money, so cut the crap. Something like that, short and sharp.

Of course, I agree with Mother, who wouldn't. Bloody stupid thing to do, so uncreative, not even fun. And she carried it through, sold her gorgeous flat and rented a bed-sitter with kitchen in Notting Hill Gate, which in those days was one of the most run-down areas in London. It was worse than any place I ever had and it shocked Mother who cried woe is me for years. But Celia loved it. Living where she did meant she was never off duty as a social worker, once she qualified and got a job. At last, she was in her element. I went to see her occasionally, just for a laugh. I liked to see her in action, endlessly besieged by scroungers who'd got her measure and were exploiting her kindness. They took the piss shamelessly, I thought, hardly bothering to pretend otherwise. At one time, Celia had three unmarried mothers all sleeping on her floor, dear God. She spent hours filling in people's forms and writing official letters for them, all without complaint. I was deeply sceptical. Someone, I knew, would come along sooner or later and really fuck her up. She was such a pushover.

Frank was an ex-prisoner, ex-alcoholic, ex-everything you could think of. He was a total wreck and worst of all *older than Mother*. Celia said he came from a family of fourteen, from County Mayo, and that He Had Never Had a Chance. (Mother's face set mutinously at that.) Once she'd met Frank, who moved in permanently with Celia towards the end of 1969, Mother went so far as to say it was past her understanding. God knew why she'd taken him in, God only knew where it would all end . . . She was only prevented from turning the arrival of Frank into a major catastrophe by the distraction of Emily's illness. But I presume she will go back and begin at the beginning with Emily.

*

— everyone had thought I would be ecstatic. Mark Perrit was such a nice boy, so steady, so strong, so cheerful. Not a black mark against him. He came from such a pleasant family, so respectable, so caring. He was clever and diligent. He had such a good future before him. What more could a mother have wanted, especially for a daughter whose aim had always been to marry and have children? But I did want more. I wanted Emily to have some freedom first. Eighteen was obscenely young to marry, straight from school, no life in between. When I said so, Emily frowned and reminded me I had been only eighteen myself. She was going to marry not die, what did I mean she would not have any life? Were not wives alive? Were not mothers alive? Emily said she could not wait. She wanted to marry and be a wife and have children at once. It was no good going to University or College, it did not appeal to her, the very idea of studying as a way of life was ludicrous. She would rather be a dancer but she could still dance, for fun, and set up house and have babies. I wasted my breath in arguments. Yes, Emily said, she knew she was consigning herself to domestic drudgery, to being a man's slave and she was *glad*. That was what she wanted to do.

I thought Mark ought to have persuaded her otherwise, if I could not. He was, as everyone said, a truly nice boy. A little gauche, a little solemn, but certainly indisputably nice. He met Emily just before 'A' Levels. His subject was maths (he was training to be an accountant). Though he had done well, he did not want to go to University but already had a job in the City. Like Emily, he had some money left to him by an uncle, which he had come into at eighteen. This, he explained to me at tedious length when he asked for Emily's hand, was sufficient to buy a small house in Surrey, somewhere about forty miles from London. I need not worry about Emily lacking security. It was supposed to please me, I expect, this quaint request for Emily's hand. I could almost hear her telling Mark to do it properly, take some flowers, put a suit on, Mother will love it. Mother did not love it. I heard him out and then I said no, my permission would not be forthcoming. Legally, they did not need it but, if they thought my agreement was therefore a formality, I was afraid they were going to be disappointed. I did not want Emily to marry yet and that was that. Mark was upset rather than angry. He looked at me with those rather too narrow, blue eyes and said, 'Don't you like me?' It was impossible to reply that, although I liked him well enough, I did not think him a suitable match for Emily. I could not tell him I thought he was dull and boring, whereas she was lively and fun-loving. I could not add that I thought his proposed way of life even duller and more boring. So I said that, of course, I liked him, that did not come into it. All I wanted was for them to wait. I asked him if he could not *see* what would happen to Emily, if she became a housewife in Surrey at the age of eighteen and had, as she intended, four children as soon as possible. He said he thought she would be very happy and what was so awful about it? He would have thought I, of all people, would approve. It was not as though he was suggesting living-in-sin or anything. I stared at his aggrieved face and thought my dear boy you are never going to know about anything as exciting as sin, you will condemn my daughter to the most sin-free existence possible, and she will drown in virtue.

There were no scenes. Emily acted as though I had not said what I had said. She was so happy, nothing was going to be allowed to mar her happiness. She sang around the flat, beamed and smiled, went on being

135

as cheerful as ever and merely mocked my gloom. The wedding plans went on without me and, of course, I could not keep up my hostility. If Emily was determined to marry, and she was, she must be married from home. She told me that, if I really did not want anything to do with it, she (giving me a kiss) would do it all herself and I (giving me another kiss) could sit at home and talk to myself like the old grump I was. Not even my tears, which I never intended and of which I was ashamed, moved her. She wiped them away, and told me firmly to stop getting in a state. She was quite, quite sure she wanted to marry Mark. It was her life and I must let her live it her own way.

I detested Mark's parents. His father, Lionel Perrit, was a small, thin, precise, pernickety man with an unexpectedly loud voice. I was surprised he was not in any way opposed to his only son's marriage at such a tender age, that he did not turn out to be my ally. But no, he appeared delighted, he was emphatically in favour of the marriage (or 'the love-match' as he so odiously called it). All he wanted for Mark*ie* was that he should 'settle down quickly' in every way, which was just what he had done himself. His father had been a shopkeeper, owning a chain of grocery shops, and Lionel at sixteen had gone to work in one of them, rising quickly to the heady heights of manager at the age Mark now was. He was delighted that Mark was going to be an accountant. He had no further aspirations for him, nor had Freda, his gushing wife. She was absolutely awful: silly, vacuous, giggly, and noisy. What a mother-in-law for Emily to have to endure. When I first went to their house in Pinner I could hardly tolerate being in the same room. I felt stifled, not just by the excessive heat from the imitation coal fire on top of central heating, but by the atmosphere of self-congratulation. Freda could not stop boasting: Mark was a lovely boy, lovely manners, so clever, so hard working, so domesticated, so lucky to have a little nest egg from his Uncle George, who had been so fond of him because he was always a lovely boy with lovely manners, so clever . . . I wanted to scream. And there was nothing I could say to offset this gushing. I know I came across as stiff and frigid and aloof, that I was distant and off-putting. All the time, as we crouched in front of the hideous fire belting out unnecessary extra heat, I was thinking that Emily had done no better than I had done. I had to take on Grandmother Butler, Emily the overpowering Perrits.

The Perrits were very religious, C of E, naturally. Lionel was a sidesman at the local church and Freda did the flowers every third Sunday. Mark had been a choir-boy until his voice broke. It was Lionel and Freda's dearest wish that Mark should marry in their church and, to their delight, Emily agreed. I was disgusted, accused her of blatant hypocrisy on top of everything else. She said that it harmed nobody and pleased Mark's parents. It was an easy thing to do to make them happy. I wanted to ask why it was more important to please Mark's parents than it was to respect *my* wishes but I held back from this complaint. I knew I was behaving badly enough already. I must stop. So I concentrated on the details of the wedding and, though I got no pleasure from this, it did console me to do the job efficiently. Although I rarely sew, I made Emily's dress myself. It was long and severe and simple. The material was exquisite, a thick, creamy satin, which seemed to give off light as she walked. She looked absolutely beautiful. The Perrit bridesmaids looked vulgar and loud in vile pink net dresses more suited to gaudy fairies on the top of a Christmas tree. There were two of them, both nieces of Lionel's, both ugly fat girls of around ten. I could hardly bear to see them anywhere near Emily. Oh, the whole charade was heartbreaking and the worst part of all was seeing Emily come down the aisle on the arm of her piano teacher. There was no one to give her away, no father, brother, cousin, uncle. Simon Birch, who might have obliged, was by then working in America. It was all too humiliating. That I could summon up no delighted man to perform this solemn duty seemed to me an indictment of my way of life. Emily suggested her piano teacher. He had taught her for ten years, brought her from Grade 1 to 8, and she had always adored him. He was a lovely, gentle, kind man and appeared genuinely moved at Emily's invitation to stand in for her father. But, as I watched Emily come towards me on the arm of this substitute, I felt such acute pain I had to turn away and hide my face. Never, *ever*, have I missed Oliver more. On either side I had Rosemary and Celia, who both nudged me as my sobs refused to be muffled, but I felt isolated and defenceless. Emily's wedding seemed the nadir of all my hopes and expectations. When the words of the marriage service were said out loud – 'till death do us part' – it was like the sound of doom in my ears. We *were* parted.

Nine months to the day after her wedding Emily had a son, Daniel Oliver. I have never seen anyone so happy: to look at Emily on that day was to see happiness defined. I went down a week before the baby was due to the little semi-detached house near Cobham where they had lived since their marriage. I had been there often, of course, but never to stay, although I had been invited. I thought Emily and Mark needed their privacy and was extremely sensitive to any hint that I was being indulged or worse still patronized. So I had stayed resolutely at home until then and had never experienced what it was like living as Emily now lived. It was an entirely different world from Primrose Hill, where she had been born and brought up. Everything was duplicated. Not just the rows and rows of identical houses, nor the gardens, all the same length and width and in the same state of maturity, nor the cars, all parked in neat driveways in front of much prized garages: it was the way of life, too. The people coming out of the houses looked the same. The men really did all leave at the same time to catch the same train and they wore suits differing only minutely in cut and colour. The wives stayed at home, crisp and smart, driving their own cars to shop or to take extremely clean, orderly-looking children to school.

I was uneasy in Emily's house. I am uneasy in anyone's house, but it was sad for me to find I could not feel at home in my daughter's. The feeling had nothing to do with any lack of welcome from either Emily or Mark, but more with the actual house. I detested that house, it gave me claustrophobia. Emily had lavished great care and attention on No 32 Haven Road but this cosseting somehow made her house seem even more pathetic. Everything was freshly painted, walls all white 'to make the rooms look bigger' (impossible task), carpets self-coloured cord, the same light grey throughout 'to give a feeling of space' (no chance of this). There was evidence everywhere of Mark's handiwork, shelves put up, cupboards made under sinks and in alcoves. The furniture was all new, and both practical and pretty. But I felt stifled and restless and completely out of my depth. I could not bear to see what Emily did every day, though it was no different from the sort of thing other young wives did happily all day long.

The birth (at home) was straightforward and relatively short. Emily was ecstatic. Mark's pleasure, beside hers, seemed flat. He was far more tired than she was, but then he had been far more anxious. Emily's love affair with her son excluded Mark from the first. Her passion for Daniel was a consuming business and it absorbed her completely. I remember that one afternoon, as she sat up in bed breastfeeding him, while I sat beside the window sewing, aware of the touching tableau the room made, she suddenly said, 'Poor Mother, you never had a son. It wasn't fair. I should have been your son.' I smiled and felt quite calm, as I told her that, yes, of course, I had wanted her to be a boy, especially because her father was dead, but that it had been astonishing how soon that had stopped mattering. I had not craved a son for years and now I had a son-in-law and a grandson and was very well off. 'It isn't the same,' Emily said, a look of great pride on her face. She bent her head over her baby son and then looked back at me and then at him again, quite suffused with adoration. I felt alarmed and just slightly irritated: there was something too intense about Emily's affection. All she wanted to do all day was feed, bath, clothe, walk and cradle Daniel.

The next year Emily had a miscarriage and the year after a still-born baby, another son. I went to look after her each time and observed with distress how she doted on Daniel even more as he grew older. It was natural, of course. Each time she lost a baby it was easy to understand why she clung to Daniel. Everyone, including me, told her she was young and healthy and had plenty of time to have a dozen children, but she had lost faith and was terrified she would only have one. 'One isn't a family,' she wept after her still-born son had been taken away. I tried to convince her one *could* be a family, but she shook her head.

Vanessa was born the following year, when Daniel was three. It was quite obvious from the beginning that she did not love her daughter as she had done, and still did, her son. Emily now conceded that she had a family and might call a halt to producing more babies for a while. Mark, I think, would have made a stand in any case. They had their house, their car, their boy, their girl. All was well, all firmly on a par with the neighbours. Emily had made her bed and I must leave her to lie on it. I had to stop wishing I could have prevented her marrying so —

*

What a farce Emily's wedding was. I really don't know how Em put up with it. I'm sure Mother's passionate objections pushed Em into it, or made her more determined. And Mother's snobbery came to the fore with a vengeance. If dear Lionel and Freda had been anything but lower middle-class shopkeepers with a few bob, Mother would have reacted differently but, as it was, she saw Emily not only throwing away her education and a career but also her social advantages. I swear she hated *what* Mark Perrit was, more than *who* he was. He was terrified of her. Emily told me he was so nervous, when Mother spoke to him, that he developed a stutter and to be left alone in the same room as her scared him rigid. Because Mother had become formidable. All that reserve, all the quiet dignity she had always had when she was younger, had metamorphosed into a coldness which belied what she really was. Her restraint, instead of being charming, was off-putting. Her diffidence had hardened into abruptness.

Emily's marriage was a watershed for all of us. Mother was no longer the strong centre point. There wasn't one. And this, I suppose, was the testing time for all her passionately held theories about the Family. I think she knew that none of us, for a mixture of motives, would ever say goodbye-mother-now-I-am-pissing-off-on-my-own, but I do think she feared a growing indifference between the three of us.

I found myself thinking about her a lot, after Emily got married. It was lucky she'd sold that big family house some years back and had been settled in her flat for a good few years, or it would have been pitiful to think of her rattling around. She couldn't rattle much in three rooms and a garden, so there was no special poignancy in Emily moving out from that point of view. But I thought about her in the late afternoon, not having anyone coming in, and knew how she would mind. What she needed was to be coming in herself, from a job. Mother had walled herself up in her precious family, and now look where it had got her. I would fret a little each time I left her, feel guilty, then think, oh damn her, I can't bear it, and become involved once more in my own concerns, which, God knows, were complicated enough. At Mother's lowest trough of inactivity, I was at my own peak of action. I was living so hectically, there didn't seem a spare five minutes in a day. The tiny firm I had joined blossomed in the design-conscious climate of the Sixties and, against all expectations, especially my own, I had become a partner in an enormously expanding and lucrative business. I headed the graphic department, where we employed a staff of thirty. Every day brought new orders, new ideas, new excitements. And I loved it. No two days were the same, that was the great joy, and I was able not only to decide what I wanted to design but also to carry out the designs. Oh, happy days. I was the whirlwind of the family.

Mother did once say to me, on my thirtieth birthday, in 1965, just when our firm was really beginning to expand, 'How different your life at thirty is from mine at thirty.' I said, 'Thank Christ,' but it turned out she wasn't getting at me for having no husband, no children. I would have expected her to think of me with sorrow, as a poor misguided creature to whom the delights of mother love were unknown. But not a bit of it – Mother appeared to approve of my career. She was eager to share in every detail of our developing firm's progress, liked to hear of my trips here, there and everywhere. It was Emily, happily married suburban Emily, with her own sweet family, who came in for Mother's wrath. Emily was wasting herself, that was Mother's opinion, though she never actually said so to me. (She was always so careful not to talk to each of us about the others in any critical way. Pass on news, yes, but offer criticism, no.) Mother used to tell me frequently how well I was doing, how pleased she was. She was not so pleased, of course, with my personal life. I didn't hide my lovers from her. Sometimes, even in the few meetings she had with them over Sunday lunches or suchlike, she would take a particular fancy to one of my men friends. Then hope would spring eternal and she would be disappointed when the favoured one disappeared. Not that I was by any normal standards promiscuous: my liaisons lasted a year, two years, long stretches of time, I thought. I never again got myself in a Tony situation. All my affairs were with men who were much better for me than Tony, but not one of them meant as much to me.

When I was thirty-five, I began to think I would like to have a child. What an extraordinary thing! I actually found myself looking at children longingly and wishing I could have some close to me. It was nonsense, pernicious nonsense. I had never, like Emily, drooled over babies. On the contrary, I had gone out of my way, perhaps falsely to mock them, to say they were disgusting smelly things, knowing that this was how I was meant to react, that it was in keeping with the image people had of me. But it wasn't true, even then. Watching Emily or Mother playing with Daniel and Vanessa, I covertly examined the Infant Phenomenon and was fascinated. The usual stuff, how tiny the fingernails, how perfect the feet, that kind of thing. What I never did was handle them, babies I mean, yet I often wanted to. Babies seemed to cleave to Emily and Mother, to fit so easily into the contours of their bodies, and I was afraid they would not find my body so accommodating. With small children, it was different. Once they could talk, I got on well with them, and rather prided myself on doing this without any of that icksy-bicksy baby talk. I loved Daniel and Vanessa. There, Mother, I often felt like saying, you haven't failed: here is your sense of family, not much in common with each other, but a great deal with the next generation. I was delighted that Vanessa looked exactly like me and that I could see that she did – how amazing, all those genes stepping smartly sideways. Naturally, I was made her godmother, Emily still being into pleasing her dear (then) husband's family with christenings. Emily called her daughter Vanessa Rosemary Celia, which both Celia and I took as an enormous compliment. Em, amenable in all matters like that, would have been perfectly willing to make Mother happy by using her name but, strangely enough, Mother said no. She preferred Emily to use one of her sister's names and so Em bunged us both in.

The christening was, if anything, even more ghastly than the wedding had been, but Mother behaved better and, as she was in charge of Daniel, she had something to occupy her. She had by then let go quite a lot, let go of Emily I mean, even if in a pretty fatalistic way. She didn't approve of Emily's life, any more than of Celia's or mine, but she accepted now that there was nothing she could do. And, of course, she was no longer sitting at home polishing the silver and other silly things. Mother had got a job. Not only had she got a job, she'd got a Friend, definitely a matter for a capital letter. *What* will she have to say about *him*?

*

— saw an advertisement, it was as simple as that. I cannot remember the exact wording, and I am surprised to find I have not kept the cutting, but it was something like 'Mature lady with family experience required to assist in setting up of Centre for Adoptive Parents. No professional training necessary but nursing, teaching or other skills to do with caring for children an advantage. The work will be mainly of a counselling nature.' Something like that. I read it several times, feeling pessimistic. I was fifty-one, was that too mature or not mature enough? I had had no nursing experience for over thirty years. I was sure I was unsuitable, that I did not stand a chance, and yet I wrote off immediately. Naturally, the letter took all day. There seemed so little to write about myself. What had I to say, beyond the bare fact that I was a widow with three grown-up daughters? I did not know whether to make much of the fact that I had been an orphan myself and that I had had an adopted child. What happened to Jess would hardly be considered to my credit. But I decided truth was of the essence and wrote briefly about it. I did not tell any of my children. It seemed too pathetic, I was too proud and embarrassed.

I received a reply almost by return post, which surprised me. It was a simple acknowledgement, from the GLC, of my application. Then there was a wait of some three weeks before I was asked to come to County Hall for an interview the following week. More hesitations and agonizing. Was I wiser to try to look efficient and smart or homely and motherly? I could not imagine. My best clothes, the dress and jacket I had worn for Emily's wedding, seemed far too frivolous and I remember thinking I would have to buy something new. But I controlled myself, choosing an ordinary dress I was fond of, even though it was well worn. I did buy a hat though. I have always liked hats, wished often they were not so unfashionable. I felt transformed when I put on a new hat, it gave me a lift as nothing else could. I went for that interview, which was most alarming, and then a week later for another, before a board, which was even more frightening. The job in question seemed too humble to require such a powerful selection body, but I know now that this was just the usual government bureaucracy. The questions themselves were harmless enough, it was the people asking them who appeared intimidating. I remember the final question was 'Tell me, Mrs Butler, why do you think you're suitable for this job?' I said I did not know if I was suitable, that all I knew was that I thought there was nothing more important than the family unit and nothing in which I was more interested, or felt more sympathy for, than the problems of the adoptive family. I got the job. I was euphoric —

*

Here it comes, there's nothing like a convert when it comes to proselytizing. It really was rather wearing to have Mother constantly extolling the joys of a career, as if they were her own personal discovery. That's what is so bloody annoying about her – all this insistence on analyzing what doesn't need analysis. So OK, she started work and liked it and that's fine, that's great, now can we get some sleep. But no, it all had to be exclaimed over, as though she'd discovered penicillin or something. Christ knows what she did at that phoney-sounding centre, anyway. It didn't sound as if it added up to much, but, if I tried to get down to brass tacks, she went all mysterious and self-important, as though she was working for MI5. Everything was 'confidential'. She bustled off to this dreary place, somewhere near County Hall, and there, so far as I could make out, she sat all day talking to people who wanted to adopt kids. It was just an office job really, not that I want to knock it. I was grateful it had come along and only hoped it lasted. But what was maddening was the way Mother jumped to quite unwarranted conclusions. She always did that, always, about everything. She assumed, after working five minutes, that careers, jobs, anything outside the domestic bit, went *on* being exhilarating. She assumed being 'a different person', which was her own banal description, was something one went on wanting to be. Well, I for one was tired of it. Work made me feel different, too, but by 1970, when I was thirty-five, I was played out. I wanted that other scene, the one Mother had already had. When I said to her, 'Mother, I think I'm going to start a baby soon,' she almost had a heart attack. Scarlet face, puffed out cheeks, great gasps for breath – it was a pantomime performance. 'What *do* you mean?' she asked. I said, funnily enough, I meant what I said, I wanted to have a baby, and she said *why* and what, without a man. Not quite, Mother. With a man, yes, I said nastily, no hybrids for me. With a man, but not a man I'm either married to or necessarily living with. It's the baby I want, not the man.

Her response was so disappointing. I suppose I had always looked to my mother to rise to the occasion and not act like other mothers. The one thing I'd always been proud of was her ability to treat pieces of startling news calmly, without hysterics. Think of the infamous abortion: not a flicker, whatever I now know she felt. But, when I gave her this bit of news, she let me down. She didn't, as I had imagined, begin to discuss the pros and cons (I knew it was asking too much to expect to get away without that), but instead was instantly scandalized. She said she didn't know how I could, why I wanted to, what on earth I thought I was doing, at my age, throwing away a wonderful career for the sake of some sentimental whim. I had never liked babies, never had anything to do with them, wouldn't be good with them. And, as for deliberately choosing a man to father a child and then denying him the rights of a father, it was monstrous, it was *unnatural*. For a while I countered this with all the standard arguments. What, I argued, was unnatural about it? All nature decreed was that a man was necessary to fertilize the ovum; after that nature left it to the mother to house the unborn child, bear it and feed it. Nature had nothing programmed for the father, after that one second's involvement. Society imposed the paternal connection. Mother interjected with the usual stuff, about how could I support a child, and I said very easily, no problem, my insolvent days were long since over. And what, Mother shrilled, about when I went back to work, was I going to shove my child into a nursery or find a babyminder? What kind of life was that? A fine one, I said, but I was only being facetious. I tired very quickly of arguing with Mother and I was angry with her, too. She'd made us worship at the family shrine all our lives and now, when I showed the first sign of true conversion, she didn't like it. She calmed down eventually, of course. Even apologized. Said it was just that she didn't think I quite realized what I would be taking on, how lonely and hard it was bringing up a child alone. I think that was supposed to be a poignant reminder. At least she didn't ask what people would think. She didn't care what they thought, only what she thought. Her next tack was to say I ought to go and stay with Emily for a week and that would change my mind. Emily, Mother said, was drowning in motherhood and it wasn't a pretty sight.

Despite the casualness of our relationship, I had been to see Emily quite often since Vanessa's birth, though never to stay. A day was long enough, not because of the children, but because of Mark, or rather Emily and Mark. There was nothing wrong with Mark, really. He was a nice man, a good husband and father. Mother hasn't done him justice and I don't suppose I'm going to, either. It was the way he planned his life that I couldn't stand. It was all worked out and he liked it that way, he said he got the best out of every day by organizing it properly. I remember, one day when I was there, Emily sent me to get some soap powder from the utility room. There wasn't any left, just a box of Persil with about a spoonful in the bottom. I put my coat on and shouted that there wasn't any soap powder left, that I'd go and get some. Mark suddenly appeared. He looked at his watch and said, 'Of course there's no soap powder. It's April 30th. It arrives today.' I was mystified until he smugly explained that he had worked out how much soap powder – and cat food, cereal, paper nappies and God knows what – was used in a month, and every month a new load was delivered from a bulk-buying firm. Even as he was talking, a van drew up outside the house and there was the bloody soap powder and everything else. He was triumphant. But he was lovely with his children, playing with them, taking them out, always very affectionate. I felt quite jealous watching Daniel entwined in his arms while Mark read him a story. I even pretended I could remember sitting like that with my father (which I couldn't). He was good in the house, too, automatically sharing all the chores, without pointing it out. But what he wasn't so good at was being a husband, he wasn't so good for Emily, I mean. He worked hard, earned a good bit of money, was obviously going to be a junior partner at some amazingly young age, but all this made him so *dull*. It was what Emily had admired and I could quite see why. All three of us were probably looking for the inevitable father figure, lacking in our lives. Mother had been nothing if not dependable; we didn't look to men for dependability but for some other more impressive evidence of absolute strength and confidence. Mark seemed to have it, and indeed he proved he had. Emily could lean on him as much as she liked and he would never crumble. But he lacked imagination and what I can only call verve, and, increasingly, that was what Emily began to want. She *did* love Mark and she was passionate about her children, but as time went on she felt constrained by them. There was no possibility of change, she told me fretfully. In five years Mark said they would buy a bigger and better house, in a more attractive place, but that was as far as any upheaval would go. It was no help saying, look, you were told you ought to live a bit before you married and had kids. She knew that. She didn't regret marriage and children, it was all the rest that she didn't want. Why, because they had children, did Mark expect them to live as they did? Why couldn't they go and live on a boat, or tour round America or do something *different*? What Emily was discontented with was Mark's preconceived notions as to how life would be. And *that* worried him.

God knows why I had this need to go around telling everyone I was going to choose to become a mother, but I did have it, and I told Emily and Mark. Mark was even more outraged than Mother. It was the first and last time I ever saw him furious and I must say it was almost a relief to find him capable of shouting. He said it was both wicked and irresponsible. Children were not self-indulgences, something you treated yourself to, like a new dress, and then discarded just as easily. They were a sacred trust and every child had the right to be given the best start possible, which mine could never have. Why not? Because I was going to handicap them deliberately from birth. I laughed in his face at first. I said I could think of quite a few children whose biggest handicap in life had been their father and quite a few women who had managed very successfully to be both mother and father, mentioning no names. Mark said that was not the point. My mother couldn't help being widowed, nobody could help accidents, and certainly she and all the others like her had coped magnificently, but those were false circumstances, quite unpreventable. What I was doing was cold-bloodedly robbing my child of its father. Not *cold*-bloodedly, Mark, I said, it won't be *cold*, it will be very hot blood indeed. He said, if I was reducing the discussion to such a level, there was no point in continuing. I said there was no point, anyway. There *was* no discussion. I would do what I wanted to do and my conscience was quite clear. I wasn't feckless. If I thought I did not have an even chance of giving my child as good a life as he gave his, then I wouldn't go ahead. His final shot was that I had no respect for the family, to which I riposted that he needed to examine his definition of what a family was. We parted quite good friends after an awkward hour or so – Mark was far too kind a man to be dictatorial. I think I'd just caught him, as I had caught my mother, completely and totally unawares. They just could not believe I seriously wanted a child and so, I suppose, I sounded flip and casual, which antagonized and offended them. But, of course, their resistance to the idea had the effect you would expect: it stiffened my resolution. I began to wonder who to choose as my child's father.

*

— work was more important. But John was significant, too. To describe his background would tell you very little about him. He was that rare thing, a man with a real sense of community. He was unmarried but did not live, as I did, in a little world of his own. On the contrary, as well as his job as a probation officer he had always been an indefatigable worker for community welfare, belonging to a score of different organizations all concerned with making people feel that what mattered to one was of concern to another and that they did not live in isolation. He had run all sorts of clubs and associations, was a local councillor and a governor of two schools. I was never entirely clear as to why he had taken the Centre job, but he was apparently instrumental in setting it up and was on the board which interviewed me. He was my immediate superior.

John was an immediately attractive man, but not because he was handsome – he was not. He was tall, far too thin, and had a scholarly stoop. He had been wounded in the leg in the war but I never asked how. His left leg dragged a little when he walked. Sometimes, when he was in pain from this leg, he would look ashen but mostly he had a good colour, from being out of doors as much as he could. That, originally, was our great link: neither of us could bear to be inside a moment longer than we needed. On my first day at the Centre, when I went out for air, I ended up on the same seat as John, in the forecourt of the building where we worked.

John and I had an intellectual companionship. There is a tendency to think that two people in their fifties would have no other sort, but it is equally surprising how often people mistook our relationship. We were often regarded as a married couple, by those who did not know, and even those who did read more into it than was in any way justified. It is not that I minded this confusion – I would not have been ashamed or indignant or embarrassed about being thought of as John's wife or mistress – but just that it ought to be cleared up. I think even my daughters imagined things. They did not realize that what drew John and me towards each other, apart from work, was conversation. We liked to talk to each other. Each of us was, to some extent, starved of conversation and needed a confidant. Mind you, unlike me, John had many friends, friends stretching right back to his childhood in Gloucestershire, where his father had been a vicar. He was one of five sons but the other four, all of them, had been killed in the war. The burden of his parents' sorrow had rested heavily on him ever since. His mother was dead but his father, at the great age of ninety, was then still alive. John went to see him every weekend at a Home, near the village where he had been vicar for so long. That was our first conversation, really, about parents. He felt miserable and permanently guilty that he did not have a home to which he could welcome his ailing and aged father. My comforting words as to how well he looked after his father's welfare nevertheless irritated him, and we began to discuss the vital difference between love and duty, or rather between acts performed for one's family out of love and those carried out to fulfil an onerous sense of duty.

John very quickly knew all about my past and present life and I knew about his. It was not possible that such an attractive man could have reached fifty-four without having some romantic attachment and I was prepared for the discovery that first John's fiancée had been killed many years ago, when he was still a young man, and secondly that he had had a long affair lasting nearly ten years, with a woman who was already married and whose husband would not give her a divorce. I didn't ask why this affair had ended and I was not told. So John had had, in one way or another, a good deal of heartbreak in his life. Maybe he would have been compassionate, anyway, but his experiences had made him more so. Whereas I was quick with my judgements about the people we dealt with, and often severe, John was slower and kinder. He always looked for the good motives, always gave people the benefit of the doubt, whereas I was much more suspicious. And his idea of family was much wider and more all-embracing than mine. In our interviews we were supposed, among other things, to assess the quality of the family life being offered by our clients. There were all kinds of trick questions we became skilled at asking and from which we had been trained to extract the most. John was always gently pointing out to me that I was looking for a degree of perfection, perfection according to my own very stringent rules, which not only could not be offered by many people, but which it was not necessary for them to have.

The reasons given for wanting to adopt children were an odd mixture. I realized that, if the Centre had existed when I was abandoned and if through it I had been adopted, I might have found myself with some very unexpected parents indeed. Not all the people who came to us were consumed by a passion to be mothers or fathers, though you might think they would have to be. Some of them saw adopting children as a way of making a contribution to society, not at all the same thing. I was against such applicants but John was not, not necessarily. He argued that such a feeling was good, that we needed more of those feelings in our society, anyway. Our social structure was too rigid, with its tight little family units, which might be strong in themselves but which were an encouragement to exclude everyone who did not belong. What we needed to encourage, John said, was a wider sense of family. He met my scepticism calmly, said he knew it sounded far too idealistic but that he believed in it. He said his own particular family unit had been smashed by the war and that he had never reconstructed one to replace it, but felt he belonged to all sorts of different families, all the same, and that these were just as satisfying. He rhymed off all sorts of such 'families' and would not accept that they could not be thought of as I thought of mine, would not concede that blood was the vital factor. And he said that he now had another family, the Centre, and that I was part of it.

This made me uncomfortable. I respected, admired and liked all the people with whom I worked, especially John. I certainly felt solidarity with them. Within a very short time, I knew all about their problems and felt involved with them: any of them could (and did) ask for my advice or help and were given it. We shared treats together and celebrated each other's good news. When any of us was sick or depressed, the rest rushed to succour them. But did that make us a family, as John alleged? I thought not. There was no common background, no common base, never mind a blood connection. With my daughters, I had a sense of total familiarity, which never in a million years would I ever have with my colleagues at the Centre. Family means more than being together. Family means a common ancestry, which in turn presupposes a common stock. Family is more than being a group, it is being a group *without choice* and that is at one and the same time inhibiting and relaxing. It can be a curse or a glory, but it exists.

Naturally, I discussed my family with John, especially Celia. I told John about Frank, about Celia devoting herself to this fifty-five year old, broken-down Irishman, with no prospects whatsoever. He scolded me for judging my daughter by my own standards. Celia was obviously happy, that was all that mattered. I said it was not, that the future mattered, too, and Frank could offer Celia none. He would never get a proper job, never marry her – indeed I would not want him to – never give her all the things she needed. '*You* need. Not Celia,' John said. I was quite shocked. He exasperated me. Then he surprised me by confessing that marriage with all it entailed was important to him as well as to me. He had always wanted to marry and felt himself incomplete without a wife. He asked me if, during all the years my husband had been dead, I had not been tempted to marry again.

We were sitting at the time beside the river, on the south bank. It was a brilliantly sunny day. We sat side by side on a bench and John had his arm running along its back, holding the wooden paling I was resting against. I was encompassed by his arm without being touched by it. I remember very vividly, not so much the rest of our conversation – how can I, at this distance of time – but being aware that John could quite easily move his arm a millimetre or two and drop it onto my shoulders. I was so afraid he would do this that I sprang up and brushed some imaginary crumbs off my dress (we had been having a sandwich together). I said it was time to go. He looked at me curiously, smiling in a contained sort of way, and I knew he knew what I had been thinking. I cursed myself for bringing up the subject of marriage in relation to Celia or anyone else. I wanted to be honest with him but I could not. I wanted to tell him that, yes, I had had dreams. When I jumped to my feet it may have been through fear —

*

Fear? Mother was shit scared. John Grey was in love with her, it was obvious to anyone with half an eye. Mother didn't invite any of us to meet him formally – she wouldn't have been able to bear what we might think that implied – but, inevitably, we all met him. He was the biggest thing in her life for years. She allowed him to 'drop her off' at our respective residences and there was a good deal of casual oh-by-the-way-this-is-my-boss stuff. Didn't fool anybody. I invited him in the second time it happened, which she didn't like but couldn't do much about, because he accepted with such alacrity, and she was indebted to him, anyway, because nobody in their right mind could have believed someone who lived in Camden Town was dropping off another person going to Fulham, without going hellishly out of their way. I quite like him. That's grudging, I like him a lot. He has a nice, dry wit and makes gentle jokes at Mother's expense while clearly admiring her. He is one of those people who are interested in everyone, he asks genuinely inquisitive questions, not just polite ones. When we first met, I could see he was appraising me in the light of what Mother had doubtless told him. It struck me as distinctly odd that, all these years when we had been growing up and Mother had been in her prime, we might reasonably have been expected to face this situation, but we had never been called upon to do so. Never. We'd never had to face up to a man who found our mother attractive and to whom she was attracted. I gave John every encouragement I could, without being indecently pushy. So did Celia. She met him the same way and was equally taken. He was so *suitable*. Neither of us could decide, though, whether he loved her. I wasn't sure. Did he want to go to bed with her? I wasn't sure about that, either. But he did want to be her friend, and she was afraid to find out whether that was all he wanted. I think. Mother didn't want to be put to the test, that was for sure. It was all right bringing *us* to decision point but not herself. Avoidance was her technique, one denied to us. *We* had to 'face up' to things. We were brought up by her to believe we were in charge of our own destinies but Mother apparently wasn't. She was different.

June 1st

Walked in St James's Park with Celia. She misses that silly gardening
job so much, especially watching the birds. She talked all the time
about birds. She doesn't chat, she lectures, but she can't help it. She
lectured me on the tufted duck and the nesting habits of the pochard.
Tried so hard to take an intelligent interest. Expressed concern that in
1963 many pochards died due to the excessively cold spring. Wondered all the time what a pochard actually looked like. Thank God, I
can recognize a pelican. Celia says the pelicans have been there since at
least the seventeenth century and that in 1930 one pelican actually
started to eat young tufted ducks. No wonder Daniel loved going to the
park with Celia – his mind responded as mine could not. While Celia
related some story about a mute swan cob, I was wondering why she
dressed as she did. Covertly, I glanced at her dreadful skirt. Tweed, in
June and *gathered*, with her enormous hips. Doesn't she see what
gathered skirts make her look like? And corduroy shirts, straining
across such a bosom? She should have her hair cut. It is too long.
Beautiful hair, but nothing made of it. Looks incongruous at her age.
I've bought her clothes, in which she would look good, but she wears
them once, politely, then never again. She can't even be comfortable in
tweed, in corduroy. She looks constrained. When we rested near the
drinking fountain, she told me she had once seen a pied flycatcher there
and a wheatear bobbing on the grass. Autumn mornings, just after
dawn, used to be the best times, she said. I thought she spoke
nostalgically. Couldn't help asking her if she missed her old job as a
gardener. She said yes, she did. As ever, she gave no reasons. Was it
being out in the fresh air, I asked? She said not. Suddenly, she blurted
out that in gardening there was 'no agony'. It never worried her. Social
work did, it was all worry, she would never be really good at her job
because she could not cut off. She had to deal with so many people who
had never had a chance and never would, and there was no real help to
give them. I knew she was thinking of, and remembering, Frank and

153

found myself squirming on the bench with irritation. Celia's simplistic assumptions *do* irritate me. For someone so clever she is stupid about the ways of the world. And I disliked the realization that her job was, to her, a kind of penance, a hairshirt she put on every day. Quite illogically, I found myself wishing with passion that Celia had not given up the oboe. She might have joined an orchestra and met —

*

Some droopy young bore who played the violin or 'cello, a Nigel or Julian, who was looking for a nice steady girl, like our Celia. It was one of Mother's recurrent fantasies, hence her eagerness to encourage both Celia and Emily musically. My daughter the oboeist, my daughter the pianist: Mother hungered after socially acceptable roles. It's weird when you remember that she didn't want them to impress her friends or relatives, as show-offs usually do – who did Mother have to impress? – but merely to hug to herself, to give herself pleasure. She started on it very early, always prodding Celia, in particular, towards stardom. When Celia did get a place in the National Youth Orchestra, for one brief tour, Mother was ecstatic. It was like that when Emily got a distinction in Grade 8: we all had to be euphoric to match Mother's mood. It made us all furious, Emily especially. I remember telling Mother not to make so much of these little musical triumphs, but I think she just thought I was jealous. She couldn't help it. All success was progress to her and the only success she recognized was that which led up existing, well marked-out ladders. Nothing else. What she didn't appreciate was that music meant very little to either Celia or Emily. They practised, they were diligent, they quite enjoyed it and were certainly accomplished, but neither of them was musical in the sense Mother assumed that they must be, simply because they did so well. Celia was always leaning over the banisters to see how many more minutes she had to do, when she was practising – the only decent clock that kept good time was on the landing wall – and I remember thinking that if, as Mother claimed, she was 'devoted' to her oboe she wouldn' even notice the time passing.

But bird, especially ducks, were a real passion. All the parks wher Celia worked all those years had ducks on the ponds and she was reall mesmerized by them. In her room she had a huge chart she'd mad herself, with every single duck that existed in the British Isles on it. Sh had books and pamphlets and all kinds of material to do with the breeding and habits of ducks, and her main occupation in her spare time, before she took in Frank, was going out with her very snazzy, expensive binoculars to watch ducks. It took her out of London, too. She joined some kind of naturalist club and went off to rivers, where special sorts of ducks bred – oh, there was no end to the good ducky times. And I don't meant to mock, they *were* good times. Any genuine enthusiasm leads to good times. In Celia's case it also led to a little romance, all among the Suffolk reeds, that Mother never knew about. Another duck fancier, of course. A young farmer Celia met while duck-spotting some rare species, a crested mallard that had come from Scandinavia. These ducks, two I think, settled on this fellow's pond and Celia went backwards and forwards several weekends to lie in the field and observe it. The farmer invited her for a cup of tea and a warm at his fire, and in the end warmed rather more than her wet feet. How vulgar of me. It lasted a few months. Mother would have been sure it was going to lead somewhere, if she had known. I don't know how it ended. I only knew it was happening because Celia used me as an alibi to explain her absence from several of the dreaded Sunday lunches. I'm surprised Mother was taken in. If she had stopped and thought about it, she would have realized Celia and I would *never* spend a day together, but she always liked the notion of sisterly affection, so allowed herself to be duped. Celia managed this affair very well, anyway. She didn't get depressed or upset, she seemed quite calm about it and certainly had a good summer out of it. She'd grown up, really.

Frank was a further growing-up stage. How bloody patronizing that sounds, like Mother at her most insufferable. What I mean is that those two years Celia lived with Frank (or the other way round I should say) were not the wretched ones Mother infers. Oh, it's as true that Frank was pathetic as it is that Andrew was a pig, but the point Mother never grasped was that he made Celia happy. Not only did she love him, she admired him. She used to say he had done so much in his life. This implied some startling list of achievements – brain surgeon, astronaut, nuclear physicist – yet all Frank had ever done, so far as we could tell, was bugger himself up. Mother hated him. At least Andrew had a career, at least he was handsome and terribly, terribly manly and strong, but Frank was nothing and had nothing. She was repelled physically by him, though I thought he wasn't that hideous. In fact, old

Frank wasn't unattractive in a Brendan Behan sort of way. Battered, bruised and generally knocked about by life (or Life as I'm sure Celia would like me to put it), but not unattractive. If I could've understood a bloody word he said, I'm sure I'd have found him witty. About all I ever did make out was something that made me burst out laughing, unfortunately. 'Hasn't your sister the face of the Blessed Virgin Mother herself now?' Frank said. He was so hurt at my vulgar cackle. It wasn't that I was thinking surely he didn't imagine Celia was a virgin but that I was trying to imagine him making her a Mother. No chance. Frank, I'm sure, couldn't get it up by then. He was a sick man, needed all his energy to get backwards and forwards to the lavatory.

Their set-up was bizarre. Frank was encouraged by Celia to look after himself, to rest in bed as much as he could. He was delighted to oblige. Celia took him breakfast in bed before she left for work, plumped up his pillows and left everything he might need within reach. Frank lolled there, hawking and spitting his guts out all morning, puffing away on the fags Celia 'hadn't the heart' to deprive him of, then he staggered up and consumed the delicious lunch Celia had left for him on a tray. She left him 'a little something' for his tea too. When I once witnessed these tempting dishes being prepared I asked her who the hell she thought she was – Mother Teresa? She blushed that awful mottled purple she goes and said she hadn't asked me to come. No, she hadn't. I went out of curiosity, like I do most things. I wanted to see this weird creature, *older than Mother* (Emily always whispered this).

What particularly enraged Mother was that Frank did not deserve Celia's attentions. He had brought his own condition on himself. Too true. What effort had Frank made? He'd joined the army, deserted, turned to labouring, boozed, stolen to get the booze, been put in prison for petty theft, come out, gone on the dole, boozed: it was a dismal record. But Frank was not worthless. He must've had something because otherwise Celia could never have had such a deep relationship with him. And she had. Of that, I'm quite certain. Once, on one of my rare, fleeting visits, I came upon Celia and Frank unawares. They lived at the top of a four-storey house, a rooming house I suppose you'd call it, and though they had a separate front door to their room and kitchen it had no lock on it, only the actual front door of the whole house had a proper Yale lock. They did have a bell but it never worked. Frank was much too delicate to tackle exhausting jobs like fitting a new battery, or whatever. It was quite common to have to disturb the woman on the ground floor in order to gain access. Anyway, this particular evening I was let in by her and when I reached Celia's room the door was slightly ajar so I didn't bother knocking. For a split second before they saw me, I saw them. They were playing a game, some crappy board game. Frank was in bed with Celia sitting beside him, her arm round his shoulders. What was so startling to me was the atmosphere which rose off them like steam – there was an immediate sense of warmth, cosiness, real intimacy. They were not only physically close, huddled up on the bed like that, but emotionally so. They were languid, relaxed, both smiling, rather dreamy. There was nothing erotic about the scene, it wasn't that I'd interrupted any passionate embrace. On the contrary. There was an innocence about the pair of them, a wonderful naivety, that stopped me in my tracks. It was no bloody good my trying to fathom *why* I envied them. All I knew was that nobody had ever been in any danger of arriving unexpectedly and feeling like that about me and any of my lovers. Whatever else Mother could say about Frank, she couldn't say he didn't appreciate Celia. He did. Their devotion was reciprocal.

But it couldn't save Frank. Once he got stronger, as he soon did under Celia's tender care, he began to wander. Not far, at first. But soon the lure of the pub on the corner got too much and he was well away, pissed whenever she came home. It's too familiar a pattern to need to repeat. Celia struggled, he struggled, but his liver obviously hadn't the energy to be bothered. She didn't manage to nurse him at home right up to the end. When he died, Mother said Celia was 'free to start again'.

*

— orchestra and met someone. But she didn't join an orchestra and lucks led nowhere. At thirty-one, after Frank died, she was as solitary as she had been at twenty. I never asked her if she had made any new friends, because I knew she hadn't, nor could I express my anxiety to her. How *can* a mother commiserate with a thirty-one year old daughter because she has not found a mate? It would be offensive. I never let Celia, or Rosemary either, see how much I regretted that they were not married, though —

Oh, for Christ's sake, she never let us see anything else. We were a *disgrace* as far as that went. She minded passionately and made us mind too. We felt failures –

I'll start again. Mother ostensibly saw nothing wrong in not being married but, on the other hand, everything wrong in not creating another family group for oneself. This meant she permanently contradicted herself. Celia and I got caught in the crossfire and grew so tired of it. Quite apart from our own personal happiness, we felt we were robbing Mother of hers. She wanted grandchildren and sons-in-law, she wanted to see us at the head of our own little units and she made us feel terrible failures because we weren't. It was ironic when one looked at Emily, of course. Emily had a family, yet what happiness did that bring Mother? Precious little. She adored Daniel and Vanessa and saw lots of them, but she didn't get on with Emily. In fact, from being the closest to her, Emily suddenly sank to the bottom of the popularity poll. Mother didn't approve of how Emily was running her life. She realized long before anyone else did that Emily's marriage, that wonderful love-match, was in trouble, and she blamed Emily. If Mother couldn't bear for Celia and me not to be married and have a family, she found the fact that Emily might put her family life in jeopardy even more agonizing. To fail in marriage, to fail one's family, was a much more heinous crime than not to have one. But will she say so? I want to see what she has to say about Emily almost as much as I want to see what she says about me.

— ectopic pregnancy and nearly died. Throughout my life I had had those sort of morbid dreams all mothers have, though they are not so much dreams as self-induced daydreams, masochistic in nature. Quite often, when my children were small, I would be standing in the kitchen doing something comfortingly ordinary like washing the dishes, gazing vacantly out onto a garden full of cheerful japonica and forsythia, and there would come to me this vision of one of my girls pale and wan on a hospital bed, and, above the noise of the birds through the open window, I would hear a doctor's voice telling me he was very sorry but he was afraid . . . I was ashamed of these dreadful images, could no understand why or how they happened. I never wholly cured myself. After Jess's death, strangely enough, they seemed to stop for a while, only to be renewed, at double strength and frequency, when one by one the girls left home. It was always when I was particularly happy that I was tormented in this fashion. I was never plagued by these fears when I was miserable.

But of course when these things do happen, as everyone to whom they have happened knows, there is no previous apprehension. They come out of clear, blue skies to catch the contented unawares. Mark rang me up, at work, and no alarm bells sounded, even though he had never done such a thing in his life before. I thought, in so far as I thought at all, that he was ringing about the arrangements for me to have Vanessa that weekend. 'I'm afraid I've got some worrying news,' he began, and then he told me Emily was in hospital and that she had had an ectopic pregnancy. My mind flew to textbook diagrams, as Mark described coming home and finding Emily on the floor, haemorrhaging, with Vanessa sitting beside her crying. Then the rush to the hospital. All the stuff of my imagination told matter-of-factly now made very little impression upon me. He said she was on the danger list, could I come. I went by taxi, all the way to the general hospital where Emily lay, perhaps dying. I did not feel numb nor did I shake or cry. I felt perfectly calm and rational, now that my worst fears were actually realized. All I wanted to do was to *get* there. My energies were concentrated on the journey. I sat on the edge of the seat, bolt upright, glaring at the traffic clogging up those dreadful South London high streets. Every red light was a personal insult, every hundred yards of open road a triumph. What finally released my emotions, so that at last I began to tremble and sweat and feel faint, was not the sight of Emily, still and white in her standard hospital bed, but the sight of Mark and the children, who had never featured in these dreams at all.

Mark looked appalling. Normally so neat and fresh, he now looked wild and dishevelled. His hair, which I had never seen unbrushed, was all over the place, his usually immaculate clothes looked crumpled and stained, and his open and placid face had tightened into a thin set of lines. He had a sleepy Vanessa on his lap, and Daniel was beside him, playing with a toy car which whooshed backwards and forwards across the leather seat. My first thought, my very first thought, was concern for the children. I took the damp and sticky Vanessa from him at once. Mark was absolutely certain Emily was going to die. His fear was so great that it threw round him an invisible cordon only his children could breach. It was a relief when a doctor came to talk to us. He left us in no doubt as to the severity of Emily's condition. Emily was in deep shock and had shown no signs of recovering from it. He thought it might help if Mark sat beside her for a while and talked to her, even if she did not appear to respond. But Mark, poor boy, chose that moment to collapse. The doctor went away to get a nurse to bring him a tranquillizer. I sat with Mark's head on my shoulder, as he sobbed and shuddered, and the children stared in fascination. My arms would not hold all three of them. When the nurse came, I asked her if she would tell me where I could make a phone call and then, as she took Vanessa from me, I left the sagging body of my son-in-law, took my grandson by the hand and went to the telephone and phoned the family, first Celia and then Rosemary. Come, I said —

*

Our heroine. I don't mean that to sound sarcastic. There's no doubt in anyone's mind that Mother saved Emily, perhaps not in the technical sense, but she made it possible at a crucial stage for others to do so. Mark found it hard to forgive her. I don't think he could bear the sight of her, indeed of any Butler, for months after it all. Not that he didn't want his wife saved, but he wanted to do it himself. Nobody blamed him or thought less of him because of his breakdown while Emily hovered between life and death, but, naturally, he blamed himself. His shame was awful. And there was his mother-in-law who, as everyone knew, had surmounted similar tragedies and never wept a tear in public. There was nothing at all that could be done about it – the facts were indisputable: Mother masterminded everything, the Butler family had closed in, just as she had always envisaged it doing. In a crisis, send for the family troops, yes sir. In we zoomed, me there in half an hour Celia in an hour. And how we took over. Off Celia went, back home with Daniel and Vanessa, instructed by Mother as to what to give them to eat, what to buy for a treat on the way home, where their bloody pyjamas were, what the bedtime ritual was, the lot. I was detailed to support Mark who, by the time I got there, had stopped weeping and was sitting, with his head between his knees, trying to stop being sick

Mother, at her most tactful, told me to comfort him as best I could. Meanwhile, *she* went in to Emily.

Mother sat with Emily all that night and most of the next day. She held her hand and stroked it, and, whenever Em flickered open her eyes, she was there, bending over her and smiling. She talked and talked and talked, quietly, so none of us coming and going past the observation window could hear a word. The nurses and doctors adored her. 'What a wonderful woman,' they said, as they came and went. I don't know what she said all that time. When I asked her, she shrugged and said it was nothing much, memories, stories, just chat. Em certainly couldn't remember later, though she *could* remember Mother being there. She said she thought she was a child again and had had a nightmare and Mother was tucking her in and reassuring her and she felt happy and sleepy. By the next evening it was thumbs up. Emily came off the danger list and Mark began to pull himself together. I hadn't done much supporting or amusing. I just sat and smoked defiantly, right under the 'No Smoking' sign. Mark seemed to sleep most of the time, moaning every now and again. I got him coffee and he drank it, eyes tight shut, hidden within himself. Once he came to with a start, when he'd been genuinely nodding off, and said, 'Is she dead?' When I said no, she was holding her own, he began to cry again. I sat and thought how curious, how extraordinary to have somebody actually caring so much about you that, in the face of your imminent death, they were themselves destroyed. When we were told, in that quaint hospital imagery, that Em had 'turned the corner', Mark's first words were, 'It was just that I love her so much – I couldn't help it,' said with great resentful force.

He took over from Mother. Thereafter, he was her equal. He coped brilliantly with the recovering Emily, with her grief over losing the longed-for third baby, with her depression, with her apathy. Mother told him he did the hardest part, but he never believed her. And even a fool could have seen that the damage was done: in his own eyes, Mark had failed his wife. All the next weary six years, before they were divorced, the night Mother stood in for him left a residue of bitterness which soured his marriage. I always felt that, if only he could have said damn your fucking family Emily, he would have got over it, but such hate was never part of his make-up. At the time, they seemed to get over their little drama quite well, but I don't think they did. Mother didn't make any comment, but then, of course, I was to distract her soon from concentrating on what was going wrong with Emily and Mark. With my baby.

*

— seemed to fix upon her age to focus my anger. It was so dangerous, so very unwise both for herself and her baby. She assured me she had had the appropriate tests and that these had established that the baby was normal and also, by the way, that it was a boy. This seemed to please her hugely. 'I didn't want a girl,' she told me, and that annoyed me, too. I would have thought a single woman on her own would prefer a girl but, no, girls apparently were 'a nuisance'. She wanted a son. He was to be born at Christmas – 'perhaps your birthday, Mother' – and Rosemary told me in August. She was greatly pleased with herself and well aware of the element of shock, because, since floating the idea some years before, she had never again referred to it. I well remember, of course, her coming to tell me. She walked into my garden looking extremely tanned and well, she had just returned from a holiday in Greece. She was wearing some sort of loose white dress and did not look in the least pregnant. We sat in the sun and she talked about her holiday and about Colin, the man with whom she had been on holiday. He had been in her life, off and on, for several years, so I knew about him. He was a freelance film editor, and had been married a long time before, when in his twenties. I liked him. He was quiet but determined, it had always seemed to me, quite capable of dealing with Rosemary's headstrong nature. At any rate, I asked about Colin's next job and she said he was going to America. Then it came out. 'I'm quite glad, really,' she said. 'I don't want him around the next few months.' Then she smiled and actually took my hand and said, 'Take a deep breath, Mother. I'm going to have a baby, at last, and I want you to be glad.' The warmth of her hand resting in mine bothered me. I squeezed it and patted it and said inane things. hope I *sounded* glad. She began to tell me that Colin was the father, o course, and that he was thrilled but that she had made it clear it wa to be *her* baby. She'd made it clear right from the beginning of thei attempt to have one, and Colin had understood and been agreeable He did not want to get married again, ever, and she herself had nev complicated things by wanting to either. She finished by saying, 'So there you are, Mother, another member of your family on the way *and* a boy, so the family name won't die out. In fact, I'm going to call him Oliver, not because of Dad, really, I just like the name, Oliver James Butler.

I felt incredibly distressed. It was hard to conceal. It was not for a minute any outmoded, outraged notions of propriety: that did not upset me, I did not care what people thought. What moved me was the pathos of it all. This baby, born to what? Not a family. And Rosemary, a mother on her own, when the road ahead was so hard. Did she realize how hard? Rosemary knew what I wanted for her, knew why I could not 'be glad' in the way she wanted. But then, with her hand still in mine, and her smiling, happy face so close to me, I could only hug her and try to hold back my fierce grief. After she had gone, I had held it back too long to let go. I remember how drained and exhausted I felt, how sad and helpless. Gradually, however, I overcame my depression and began to push myself into a more positive attitude. Rosemary would be a good mother. It was her choice to have this child. She was a mature woman and knew what she was doing. Her wild oats had been long since sown. She was economically secure, with no need of that inheritance she had so frivolously spent. She would manage on her own very well, and, as for her son, he would never know anything else. There was no reason for me to imagine that he would turn round and accuse his mother of wilfully cheating him out of a father, and, if he did, Rosemary would be well able to deal with it. I thought of Emily and her increasingly unhappy marriage and I could not truthfully say her regular, ordinary family was necessarily better than anything Rosemary had in mind.

Rosemary's pregnancy was a happy time. She had been made a director of the design firm for which she worked and she drew a substantial income from it. Now she used that money to buy herself a house, which to my great pleasure was not far from me. It was part of a new development, town cottages they were called, built in a gap where a bomb had demolished the existing terrace. Rosemary intended to let half of it to somebody who would look after her son, when needed. She had it all very well thought out. I expressed astonishment that she should leave Fulham but she said firmly that her son would need a park to be walked in and that he might as well be near his only

163

grandparent. Such idyllic days, we had, walking on Primrose Hill, Rosemary stately in a blue cloak, which suited her beautifully. We walked, even in the coldest weather, well wrapped up, and Rosemary would come home with me and put her feet up and I would make tea. She seemed serene and calm, and, though she grew enormously large, not at all discomforted. I felt somehow humble in her presence, in the presence of maternity, and shy. There was such power in her. I was so aware of the life she held inside her and there was a strange excitement in thinking about it. My own body, not then old but not young, seemed a poor, dried-up thing, tame and quiescent.

Colin came once. He was back, briefly, from America. He came to tea with her one bright December day. When I saw them together I felt a return of that emotion I had experienced, when I was told the news, and once more had to struggle to be sensible. They looked right together. I had not thought Rosemary on her own did *not* look right but suddenly, seeing Colin at her elbow, solicitous, even proud, I knew I had been deceiving myself as to the success with which I had accepted my daughter's independence. I would have given anything to see Colin and Rosemary, if not married, then *settled* together. When he left I felt bereft and I could have sworn that Rosemary did, too. Over the next few weeks she was quiet and reflective, not quite so happy or at ease. She was irritated by my most general queries as to where Colin had gone, and told me she knew what I was thinking and I had better stop. It took a while for us to re-adjust. By the time her baby was due to be born, Rosemary was herself again but I noted that she talked less often of Colin who, up until that visit, had featured often in her conversation, as though she had been determined to show me she was fond of him but could do without him.

The baby was not born on my birthday. December came and went and still Rosemary had not been delivered of her child. We had a quiet Christmas. By the end of the first week in January, I was becoming concerned. Rosemary was not. She was against an induced birth and would put no pressure on the hospital, but on January 9th, when she was ten days overdue, they took her into UCH. Right up to the moment they took her into the delivery room she was relaxed and cheerful – nobody could have been a better patient, nobody. All the doctors and nurses said –

A lot of crap, that was what Mother's revered doctors and nurses came out with, quite unbelievable shit. It could have happened to anyone, don't think about it, try not to dwell on what's over, you've all your life ahead of you, sssh, sssh, have a good cry, there, there, you'll feel better soon, here's something to make you sleep, these things happen, nothing anyone could have done, sssh, sssh, sleep, sleep . . . I was treated like an idiot. There wasn't one single person who came near me, all that terrible week, who could even begin to cope with me. Except Mother, of course. Mother knew. She didn't say a word for the first two days. I screamed and yelled at her, said awful things, hurled insults at her and she just sat there, inscrutable. I called her smug and self-righteous, asked her why she didn't say I told you so, why she didn't say it was a judgement on me, even accused her of being glad, because unmarried mothers shouldn't have babies, they don't belong to *proper* families. I emptied all the evil bile in my own head out over hers. I hated her, too. I shrieked at her to get the fuck out, that I never wanted to see her again but, even when they wanted to, she wouldn't let them sedate me against my wishes. As for saying the doctors and nurses thought nobody could have been a better patient . . . They thought I was a pig. The praise stopped when they saw how I treated Mother. Oh, they told me I was a good girl for being so brave during the birth, but they didn't rate that for long. It was Mother who was the heroine, putting up with me and never complaining or turning on me. Though she did, eventually. The day before I was discharged she said to me, 'If you're going to love your own pain, then carry on as you have been doing and I'll go home.' I swore at her, and then that was the end.

God knows what happened. I didn't want the details at the time and I don't want them now, though I expect Mother is going to tell us. What bad luck we Butler girls had in childbirth, yet Mother sailed through her three deliveries. There's Em with her miscarriages and stillbirths and ectopic pregnancies and there's me with my pathetic whatever it was, some hideous-sounding complication that meant a late Caesarean, too late. One in a thousand, but naturally. Maybe it was even in a million, but why boast. All I remember is coming round from the anaesthetic, or maybe only half round, and seeing this character at the end of my bed saying, 'My dear my dear my dear,' like a stuck record and the face swirling and swirling in front of me. The words, 'your baby is dead I'm so sorry', were gentle and echoey and I think I smiled, it sounded like a lullaby. I think of it often, that moment, pleasantly. I clutch onto it sometimes and replay it, so soothing before the raw awakening that followed. I could have seen the dead baby, if I had wanted to, but I didn't. Probably I should have done. There was nothing wrong with him, I know that. Mother saw him. She said he was beautiful, quite perfect. I hit her when she said that, slapped her, hard, right across the mouth, and screamed that of course he wasn't fucking perfect when his fucking heart wouldn't work.

Mother did say, timidly, some weeks later, 'You could adopt a baby, Rosemary. I mean if . . . ' Lucky she left the rest unsaid. I wanted my own baby, I wanted to make it and have it and nothing else would have been any good. I didn't need motherhood, like Mother and Em did, it wasn't the mothering part that I'd wanted. An adopted child would have been no use, it would have been a graft that did not take. I could do without mothering, if I could not biologically be a mother. Which was just as well. At forty, I was in no position to try again and I don't think I could have endured it. After all, at least I had been pregnant, I had had that first stage of being a mother, and I'd loved it. I wanted nothing to spoil the memory, no sickly second pregnancy to cloud the blissful reality of the first. I made my peace with all this, but an essential part of it was preserving those nine months intact. I thought about them often, quite gloatingly. I don't think it was unhealthy, why should it have been? It helped me stabilize myself. I sold the house, went back, not to Fulham, but to Chelsea proper. It suited me better. Being near parks and grandmothers was too absurd. I thought about going abroad but I didn't go. I thought, if I was going to be a childless middle-aged woman, I had better start adapting straight away. And I returned to hospital, six months after I had given birth, to be sterilized. I wanted any lingering romantic fantasies that might arise dealt with ruthlessly. It didn't upset me. I remember coming out of that place and thinking, well done, that was wise, now let's get on with life. I didn't tell Mother of course. She would have approved in theory, but I think it would also have upset her. She didn't need to know. I can't say I found myself mooning over babies or anything like that, but then I never had done and I didn't feel any resentment towards Emily's children. In fact, loved them more, not less, which was just as well, because at that tim they were in need of as much love as they could get. Daniel was very much like the boy I would have wanted Oliver to have been, and I found it hurt less to admit this than to pretend I did not feel it. So. It was away with one phase of my life. I put on my cork jacket and became buoyant again.

June 4th

Spent a long time in Cole's choosing wallpaper for the sitting room. Remembered how I used to think that when I had time I would love choosing wallpaper, love taking the trouble to get something exactly right for the room. But I don't love it. It seems a worthless, trivial occupation. After an hour I felt ashamed, yet why should I? Chose a Victorian trellis pattern. Rosemary is sure to hate it. To redress the balance, walked from Mortimer Street to the National Gallery. Had seen somewhere that their new acquisition was called *Mme André Wormser and her Children*. It was in Room 46. The painting was done in 1926/7 in the Wormsers' Paris home, 27 Rue Scheffer. It showed Mme Wormser standing in the middle of a rather grand sitting room, while one of her daughters played the piano. A boy watched and two other girls sat on a sofa. A family scene. The walls in the room were dark green, the chairs were covered in green brocade, the carpet was green patterned. Everything was stiff and formal. The mother looked quite removed from her children as she stood there, complacent, with a fussy little dog at her feet. She was called Olga. The children were Oliver, Diane, Sabine and Dominique. The dog was called Pouf des Landes. I stared and stared. They were not real to me, those people. If I had had my portrait painted, Mme Butler and Her Children, I would not have chosen to stand elegantly in the middle of the room. I would have wanted to sit on that sofa with my children close. What Olga wanted was to use her children as showpieces. I saw that the picture, by Edouard Vuillard, had been presented to the Gallery by an officer of de Gaulle's Free French Army 'as a grateful remembrance of the years 1940–1945'. Was M. Wormser killed in the war? No, surely not. Room 45 is so much nicer. Van Gogh's *Sunflowers*, Seurat's *Une Baignade*. Much prefer them to what I am doubtless going to see in Florence. I worry about going there. It is kind of Rosemary to take me but will she regret it? Why is she taking me? Pity? Duty? She can't be *choosing* me as her travelling companion. Why does she not go on her own? It isn't as though I suggested myself, the idea would never have occurred to me. I know my place.

*

Knows her place? I could get side-tracked on that one with the greatest of ease. But I must get on, get through this. I've rung the Royal Free, Mother's fine, tooth's out and no problems. I could go to see her this evening, but I can't stand hospitals and Celia will be quite enough for her. I want to make the most of this most perfect of opportunities. A drink, a fag, and I'll be ready for Daniel. As yet it's Emily. Emily, every time I turn a page.

*

— once read in a newspaper article written as one of the many that celebrated the Queen Mother's eightieth birthday, that the greatest pain of her life had been the divorce of Princess Margaret and Antony Armstrong-Jones. If that is true, I know how she felt. Nothing hurt me quite so profoundly, apart from those family deaths I have described (which belong to another order entirely) as Emily's and Mark's divorce in 1976. Emily once said to me that, if it had not been for knowing how I would be hurt, she would have been divorced long before. She said this resentfully, as though thinking of it had been a nuisance, as though I had wilfully exerted an unpleasant power over her. I don't believe I was the contributory factor she likes to allege. I think the only thing that held her back from divorce was the deep love of her children for their father and his for them.

The reasons for divorce were cited as 'irretrievable breakdown', the usual meaningless words that covered ignorance of the real reasons. Neither of them really knew what had gone wrong, it seemed to me. So far as Mark was concerned, there was no real desire to break with Emily. It was she, from the start, who pushed for divorce. She became obsessed with the need to be rid of him. I would not say she hated him, but she no longer loved him and he annoyed her intensely. Everything he did annoyed her. She jeered at his respectability, his tastes, even his success, because Mark had more than fulfilled his promise and was by that time an established accountant whose services were in great demand. Boring, said Emily. They had moved, as Mark had planned that they would (everything in their lives had gone as Mark planned, except for his wife's response to his achievement) nearer to town, to a house in Dulwich. It was most attractively situated, on a hillside, with tree-filled gardens all around, and the merest tantalizing glimpse of the river through them in the distance. Boring, said Emily, even worse than Surrey, which once she had found so delightful. It is true I had no sympathy for her and, yet, it is also true I grieved deeply for her. She was a lost soul, restless and angry but without direction: she was not really furious with anyone or anything, except herself. Her resentment was fierce but unfocused. She had none of Rosemary's analytical powers. Emily could not stand outside herself and examine her own condition. I wasted countless hours stupidly trying to remember if she had always been like that. All I could see, in my mind's eye, was her round, beaming, cheerful face as a child. I tortured myself with memories of her exceptional happiness when she was a child – there had never been any problems with Em. And now there she was, miserable and drawn, hardly ever smiling, working herself daily into a frenzy of regrets. She never said I should not have allowed her to marry, because she knew how strongly I had voiced my objections at the time, but there was, all the same, an unspoken impression that I had somehow contributed to her mistake. It seemed Emily had been 'taken in', as she put it, by the false picture I had painted of the glories of marriage and motherhood. I should have been realistic. I should not have enlarged upon my own privileged experience of matrimony, nor extolled the delights of children. It was all nonsense, of course, and Emily knew that it was, but in her unhappiness she was vicious and she lashed out in all kinds of ways at innocent targets. She desperately needed someone to blame and I was a handy and even willing target, willing because of the eternal guilt I, like most mothers, can feel at the slightest provocation. How Emily's predicament could have been avoided by me, I do not know, but I searched continually for an answer. What had I done? What had I not done? How much was the failure of my youngest daughter's marriage my fault?

Emily had no idea what she intended to do, once this divorce had taken place. All she wanted was 'space'. She said that when she had left Mark she would then, and only then, be able to sort herself out. I called her selfish. I said she was putting herself first. She agreed, said she certainly was, that she should have done so a long time ago, that it had never occurred to her that, in taking on the duties of a wife and mother, she would submerge her identity. When I asked her what identity, she pounced on my innocent question and said triumphantly that this was precisely the point: she did indeed *have* no identity now, other than Mark's wife and Daniel's and Vanessa's mother. She needed to find herself. I cringed. To hear any child of mine coming out with such a cliché offended me. I had thought better of her.

Emily had not proved to be a good mother, not once her children were out of infancy. Over the years, I watched with anxiety as Emily's possessiveness increased. She could not let her children alone. Everything they did she had to do with them, which at first was wonderful for them – they were greatly envied in the neighbourhood for their young and energetic mother – but then, later, it became a burden for them to carry. Their friends were Emily's friends and it led to absurdities. Yet she loved her children dearly and they adored her, even when she was too much for them. They were so proud of her youth and prettiness and her enthusiasms, especially for dancing. With them, she maintained all the contact she had lost with Mark. She spoke to them, but not to him. The worst thing she did was to voice to them her boredom with their father, unforgivable. Daniel, aged thirteen at the time of the divorce, was completely devastated by his mother's disloyalty. He had no defence against it. Vanessa was less sensitive and better able to rally.

I had my grandchildren a great deal then. I had retired from my job (it seems now such a brief period in my life) and had once more plenty of time. It was a strange feeling having them in my flat. I was aware of quite different feelings towards them than those I had had towards my own children. It was true that the distance of a generation leant an enchantment to the relationship, which meant it was blessed from the beginning – until the divorce. Until then I enjoyed my grandchildren without reservation. My lack of true responsibility for them was a great liberating force. I was an indulgent grandmother but also one heavily and gladly involved in whatever stage they were at.

But then, in 1976 when the divorce happened, my easy times with my grandchildren stopped. Emily, naturally, had told them what was happening. She would have liked Mark to have been with her to break the news, but he refused. He said he did not want a divorce, that he was simply worn down by her insistence, and that he would be unable to prevent himself contesting the things she was bound to say, which would be an additional, unnecessary ordeal for the children. Emily could tell them and then he would talk to them himself. So Emily told them. What exactly she told them I do not know. I only heard what Daniel and Vanessa made of it. Daniel told me he supposed I knew Mum was leaving Dad and that they were going to be divorced. I said, yes, I did. My distress at the sight of his solemn little face, eyes watching me carefully, was great, but I knew I must not show it. Yes, I said, I did know and I was sad. He asked me a funny thing: 'Gran,' he said, 'will they hate each other always?' I said quickly that, so far as I knew, they did not hate each other now and never would, they just found it hard to live together. Daniel said he knew that, about not liking living together any more, but that, if that was not because they hated each other, what other reason could there be. I said he would have to ask his parents. 'I don't like to ask them anything,' he said. 'I don't want to hear the answers.' He was too old to take on my knee but not too old, not quite, to embrace. I put my arms round him and told him he must not take his parents' problems on his own shoulders, that it would not help anyone. I said I was not going to pretend it was not a terrible blow, because it was, but that it was not as bad as it seemed, he must just make the best of it. Cruel words to a thirteen year old. He unnerved me again by asking 'Whose side are you on, Gran? Is Mum right or is Dad?' And I disappointed him by giving the predictable answer. But afterwards, when Emily had found a flat, I saw Daniel withdrawing visibly from the family life with which he had seemed so happy. It was harder for me to reach him. Of course, things would have changed anyway as he —

*

This is sickening. And sickly. I don't believe it. 'Whose side are you on, Gran?' – never. Daniel would never have said that, absolutely impossible. Mother has put those words into his mouth. That's what she would have liked him to say.

My memory is that Daniel made no comment about his parents' divorce, ever. He would have found it deeply embarrassing to do so, it would have been against his code, and, even when he was very young, he had his own code. Mother might say he would talk to her when he would not talk to me, but I doubt it. Daniel liked to make people happy. He was expert at realizing the role people wanted him to play, and he tried to oblige, so long as what was required of him did not actually offend him. He knew Mother wanted him to confide in her, that she saw herself as a cosy white-haired Gran against whose ample lavender-scented bosom he could press his curly head, while he unburdened himself. She would set up those questions and the answers, and Daniel, being smart, would spot them. He would give her what she wanted, more or less, so that now she's convinced herself he spoke like that of his own volition. But he wouldn't have done, I swear.

*

— approached puberty. I would not have expected to retain the same place in his life as a fount of wisdom and comfort. But the divorce accelerated the growing-away process and I felt curiously ashamed of how I had failed him. Later, when he was a young adult, we did re-establish some real contact, but many years had been lost when I might have been of use in helping him understand. To leave him to tussle with Emily alone, as he tried to understand and bear with her, was cowardly. I could have been a refuge and was not.

For Vanessa I was, but then that was different. When her parents divorced she cried bitterly but it was easy to hug and kiss and coax her out of her tears. Mark rang her every single day and visited her at least three times a week. He had both his children every weekend and was not the sort of father to fill time by taking them to the pictures, or suchlike. His own house became a true home to them and they slotted in and out with a remarkable lack of fuss. I suppose Mark had lady friends but, if so, they never impinged on the children's lives and he did not marry again until last year. I admired him tremendously after the divorce. He came with the children to see me very regularly indeed and we struck up a new and surprising friendship, which quite startled Emily who —

*

Who hated it. Mother had never had any time for Mark and now there she was, becoming his best friend. Em resented it bitterly. As she explained to me, it wasn't that she wanted Mother to take sides, or anything so crass, but, on the other hand, she didn't want her to go out of her way to woo Mark, and that was what she seemed to do. Em said she felt disapproved of. Mark's behaviour was constantly praised and she got tired of this. When Mother told her all the time how well she thought Mark was coping, Em flared up and said what on earth was so

173

praiseworthy about that? He was just behaving as he had always behaved, being diligent and methodical and organized. It was no effort for him. Everything ticked over and he could hardly claim credit for a way of life that was second nature to him. She, on the other hand, had a tough time.

Emily had always wanted to be a dancer, right from a little kid. She went through all the ballet-classes-in-dusty-church-halls stuff but it wasn't that kind of dancing she liked. It would've been easier if she had: Mother would've adored a daughter who had got into the Royal Ballet School or Sadler's Wells, or wherever it is that the great ballerinas start off. But Emily didn't want that. She liked *modern* dancing. She kept telling Mother this but Mother didn't know what the hell she was talking about – 'You mean quicksteps, tangos, that kind of thing?' she asked. No, Em did not. She meant jazz dancing, all loud music and flashy clothes. Her ambition, at sixteen, was to dance in *West Side Story*. Fat chance once she'd got married and stuck herself in Surrey. All her ambition drained away into motherhood, or seemed to. She kept dancing but I always thought there was something unbearably pathetic about Emily trying to keep up her former passion in those circumstances. She didn't even have a room where she could move more than four steps.

Well, at thirty-two, after she'd divorced Mark, Emily certainly wasn't going to find a big future as a dancer. She had no training, she was much too old, and she hadn't danced in any performance since school. Mother was always reminiscing about Emily's Last Great Performance and how 'utterly charming' it had been. She was right, it was. She and three others made up this dance sequence, with them all dressed in Charlie Chaplin type gear – oh, how lovely Em looked, spotlit, twirling her stick, stepping so lightly through the intricate little routine she'd devised. But she'd missed that particular boat a long time ago. No more spotlights ever since, nor ever likely to be. The only option open to her, which she was sensible enough to realize, was teaching.

She was lucky, for once. The great boom in dance and exercises was just beginning here and Em was able to offer what people wanted. It didn't happen without effort. Em spent hours and hours working out what she was going to teach. At first, she came to my flat because I had a large studio room. She practised assiduously. I thought she might not like me to watch but, on the contrary, she craved any audience. I watched at first with a smirk, but ended up applauding and amazed. How could anyone with no training at all look so bloody professional? She looked so good, so supple and fit. Christ, what an old slag I felt sitting on my arse all slumped and unhealthy. She had on bright yellow cotton pants and white leg warmers and a glittery silver strapless top, and her hair was caught up in a red-spotted chiffon scarf. She looked glowing and terribly impressive. I couldn't think where all the energy came from (she said 'From healthy eating and exercise.' My God.).

I still didn't see all this as any more than playing. I couldn't imagine how Em could move on to earning a living. But, of course, I'd forgotten one vital factor: Emily, alone of the three of us, still had her inheritance. It was salted away. Good, virtuous Mark had refused to touch a penny of it. He said it was her independence – wonderfully ironic – and wouldn't let her put it into their joint account, as she wished to do. After the divorce, Em was able to buy a small flat and still have something left. Mark had seen to it that her original ten thousand was wisely invested, so it had trebled. It was enough to make anyone sick. When the bright lights called, Em rented a studio. She gave something called Funky Disco Exercises twice a week. I was staggered at her nerve. How come Mother didn't admire it?

Mother found Emily's brilliant new career 'embarrassing'. She thought Em was too old for such childish things, that it wasn't 'appropriate'. The more successful Emily became, the more disapproving Mother seemed to be. After two years of this, by which time Em was well established and had moved into Covent Garden, I took Mother along to watch her. Emily thought Mother might be won over when she saw how hard she was working. She ought to have known better. Mother has always been susceptible to atmosphere – the desire to have everything 'nice' is deeply imbedded in her character – and the atmosphere of the Pineapple Studios in Covent Garden was abhorrent to her. She was flinching from the minute we turned into Langley Street and heard the raucous music coming out of the warehouse windows. As far as Mother was concerned, we could've been walking into a den of vice. She was wretchedly uncomfortable as we fought our way through crowds of dancers to find Emily's studio. I felt pretty awkward myself. It was like going into a club where you know you don't belong, and never will. The people thronging the narrow corridors and staircases placed such emphasis on *bodies*, the look of them, the feel o them, the functioning of them. I shrank into my loose, dark, bagg clothes and shuddered as much as Mother did, encased in her well-cu navy blue suit. We couldn't stop ourselves recoiling from all thos beautiful bare limbs, glistening with sweat, and from the joyous animal vitality unleashed all around us. It took us so long to find th right studio that Em had started her class and didn't notice us peerin through the glass panel of the door. Probably as well. We only stayed five minutes. Mother watched Em going through her routine withou comment. Her eyes ran over the room, over its bare wooden floor, ove the wall of mirrors, and found nothing to please them. Em danced ii front of the mirrors and her class copied her. All their movement seemed designed to alarm: contortions, exaggerated and ugly, rathe than steps. In short, neither Mother nor I could identify or appreciat any skill.

'All that matters,' I said, as we walked back to the car, 'is that Em i happy doing that.' And I believed myself. Mother never said a word She was at her most infuriatingly sad.

June 17th

Only Emily for lunch. Weeks and weeks since she has deigned to come. Perhaps she knew Celia and Rosemary would not be here. Felt nervous. Fussed about all morning quite unnecessarily. When was I last at ease with Emily? I am afraid of her misery. Every word I say seems hearty or unfeeling. But at the same time I so desperately wanted to see her. Knew that what I wanted even more desperately was to see her happy, without problems, the *old* Emily. At least she looked a little brighter. She can never quite abandon interest in her own appearance, like Rosemary can, she can *never* not brush her hair. And she smiled hello, head up instead of down. At least she was trying. We talked about Vanessa. I praised her extravagantly, her warmth and vitality. Emily shrugged. She looked straight at me and said that I knew, didn't I, that sometimes children were just incompatible with a parent, it wasn't anyone's fault, fault didn't come into it. She and Vanessa were incompatible. I lowered my head, gazed steadfastly at the tablecloth. It was so cruel. Sweet, kind, happy Vanessa, discarded as incompatible. What did I say? Already I do not remember. Probably because I don't want to. Something evasive, some muttered banality. I was terrified of what she might say next. Jumped up, got the fruit salad, ate distractedly. Emily said, 'Why does the truth always upset you?' I said because it wasn't necessarily the truth, and, even if it was, that didn't prevent it from being upsetting. It's no good having children and then saying one is incompatible with them. Emily said Vanessa was grown up, not a child, that facts had to be faced: she and Vanessa did not get on. But it isn't like a friend, like falling out with a friend, like not getting on with a neighbour – 'getting on' should not come into it. I couldn't argue with Emily. I couldn't ask her how she had come to hold these extraordinary ideas. She was not brought up with them.

*

I am *exhausted*. But I'm also nearly at the end. Only an inch or so of

177

paper left. I'm tempted to read all night and have done with it but I don't think I can. There's too much to digest. And I want to read about Daniel calmly. I can finish this off in the morning, bright and early, before Mother gets home.

*

— how Daniel became a soldier is more than a mystery to me, it is an insoluble puzzle. No child could have been less soldier-like or more removed from military influences. Nor will it do to say that perhaps he was reacting against his own nature and that this forced him into that very profession – I suppose one has to call it a profession – because when he did start soldiering, it was with dedication. I suppose his school had something to do with it. Mark sent him to Dulwich College, to my extreme distress and also of course to Emily's. It was one of the few subjects on which Emily and I were in complete agreement. It was not only the political implications of this decision, but also that Dulwich College was quite wrong for Daniel. He needed less discipline, not more, and lower sights, not higher ones to strive for. He was always a highly motivated, over-conscientious boy, who took examinations and so forth far too seriously. The lighter aspects of his personality were heavily overshadowed by this deeply ambitious streak in his make-up. He needed a school that would make him more at ease, looser, less not more competitive. Dulwich College, said Mark, would stretch him and, indeed, for once that educational platitude was accurate. It did stretch him, as tight and taut as an electric wire. He did well right from the beginning, to Mark's immense gratification, and from the beginning there was confident talk of Open Scholarships to anywhere he should deign to try. I ought to have been proud – as Emily bitterly remarked, scholastic achievement was what I had wanted for her – but I only felt sad. Daniel became greyer and older than his years every time I saw him. He did not need to work as desperately hard as he did, but there appeared to be nothing else in his life, and he went at his studies as though the hounds of hell were after him. When he stayed with me at the weekend he spent three, sometimes four hours an evening working. It seemed so pathetic to me for a fifteen year old boy, and not all the A grades at 'O' Level in the world were worth this single-minded, narrow commitment.

At Dulwich, Daniel joined the Combined Cadet Force, an amazing thing in itself. So far as I know, it was an entirely independent decision. No one, neither parent nor teacher nor friend, suggested it. He did it by himself and was not a bit put out by the derision with which the news was greeted. Emily went wild when he first decked himself out in that awful uniform and began cleaning those absurd boots and making his buttons gleam. She screamed at him just to look at himself and *think* what he was doing. Mark did not like it either, being an intensely peace-loving man. And when Daniel said to me, 'You don't approve, Grandma, do you?' I was quick to say no and to give him reasons why. He listened carefully, as he always did in that disturbingly don-like way, and then he countered my objections calmly. Daniel's arguments were all to do with Hobbes and Machiavelli and a host of other political philosophers whom I have never read. He sat there, hands clasped over his uniform belt, looking like a parody of The Young Soldier, and earnestly defended his position. How his dead grand-father, a reluctant soldier himself, would have enjoyed standing up to him (his living one was the only member of the family who was proud of Daniel's military inclinations). In fact, he brought Oliver into his rationale, saying he felt men like Oliver had died to preserve a certain way of life, and that he felt the same, and knew – because apparently history showed it – that pacifism was not the practical method of dealing with aggression when it occurred. An army must be ready to meet such aggressions. What about the bomb, I asked, but that was a mistake. Daniel was off, at once, on an even longer and more learned lecture about nuclear deterrents.

But he was only a boy, a young boy, and finally I stopped mocking his passion for the Cadet Corps. At least it was a passion for something other than swotting, and I reflected cynically that it was a terribly healthy outdoor one, what with all the marching and those blessed camps. He talked a great deal about it. It was touching to see him coming up against the Fascist spirit, which certain members of the corps so clearly manifested: the rights and wrongs of behaviour were fascinating to him. He found the shouting and bullying objectionable and had to learn to accept both as an essential part of army life. He also had to accept that he was an odd man out. The swots at Dulwich very decidedly did not flock into the CCF. On the whole, it was the athletic, hearty sporting types or else the dimwits, not that anyone at that school

179

could possibly be called dim, but everything is relative. Daniel did not enjoy being associated with those at the bottom of the form or those renowned for how many heads they had broken in rugby matches. I often wondered how he stood up to it at all. He was physically immature until he was seventeen, small, slight, in no way, I should have thought, able to defend himself. Nor would I have thought he could get by as a popular fellow. Would Daniel have been popular? I doubt it. He was quiet and shy and his own man. Yet he never made any reference to suffering ill treatment of any kind and I am sure evidence of it, if it had existed, would have surfaced in some way. Perhaps he earned an affectionate place in school and in the CCF for his brains. He wore his learning lightly, never flaunted it, and had a certain dry wit which may have endeared him to the rest. At any rate, he seems to have been accepted.

I remember when Daniel was very young, five or six, the worries of the world at large began to sit heavily upon his shoulders. He would pick up references to every sort of disaster – famines, pestilence, air crashes, wars in obscure parts of the world – and ask about them. Anything that appeared on television, before or after some children's programme he was allowed to watch, would enthrall him, if it showed clips of weary survivors from some catastrophe or victims of another. He would cry for them, literally, until we all took to watching vigilantly for such news flashes, when we would censor them. In the street, cripples and deformed people were the object of his interest and compassion (if that is not too ridiculous an emotion to attribute to a child). 'Will they get better?' he would ask me and when I said no, as often I was bound to, it was useless to add 'but they are not in pain'. The pain was irrelevant. What mattered was the existence of visible suffering of another sort. Once we were served in a shop by a pretty girl with only one arm and three little stumps of fingers coming from her other shoulder, instead of another arm. Daniel stood and sobbed and the girl, who at first had smiled, began to become upset herself. I rushed him out of the shop, cuddled him and carried him home with me, trying to explain to him about Thalidomide and that crying like that made it hard for those he was crying for. I told him he made himself a burden to them: the thought of a small boy crying at the sight of her deformity was what had upset that girl, not her deformity. But he was only five or six and I dreaded becoming too sophisticated in my arguments. 'But it's so sad,' he kept wailing. I had never come across anything like it. Then there was poverty. Daniel grew up knowing nothing about it. He lived then, remember, in pretty Surrey-with-a-fringe-on-top. Everything was green grass and affluence. Poverty belonged to India and was foreign and not much was seen on television at children's viewing times. But as he grew up his naturally sensitive eyes were opened. He travelled across London often to me or to his aunts, and he was observant. Heaven knows, the streets of London, the London which Daniel became familiar with, are hardly Dickensian. There is no real squalor, no shivering barefooted children clad in rags or the like. But there are the meths drinkers under Charing Cross Bridge and there are occasional tramps, and that was enough. The reality of any kind of poverty was another worry. He would look, too, at the blocks of council flats and the dreary back streets through which his bus often trundled on the way to and from the more salubrious areas to which he was accustomed, and he fantasized living there and got depressed. Emily once called him a little prig in one exasperated moment, but it was not priggishness. Daniel cared. When more spectacularly terrible conditions were revealed to him, like the atrocities at Soweto, he did not sleep for weeks. And once he was at Dulwich the contrast between his world and the world of others became doubly hideous to him.

Yet this was the boy who joined the army. Insanity. He would not even take an army scholarship to University first and then be moulded into shape at Sandhurst. No, it was to be the proper army, in the ranks, at once, as soon as he was eighteen and his 'A' Levels were over. He joined up *for nine years* in September 1981. God knows what that signing-on Sergeant or whoever he was thought: barely eighteen, Dulwich College, astronomical examination results, sensitive type and dying to get into the army. No lust for battle, no bully-boy tendencies, just a quiet, clever lad, very polite and very, very determined. I would like to have seen what kind of report was written, if one was. Did they think he was a masochist? Did some army psychiatrist get trotted out to check he was not unbalanced? Or do the army experience this all the time? Perhaps my Daniel was more run-of-the-mill than I realized. But it is all irrelevant now. He went off for training in October 1981. At least, said his suffering parents (united for once in their disappointment at the waste), there is no war on, it is not as if he will have to fight. We all thought Daniel would become disillusioned and leave the army quite soon, before his contract became binding, or else we thought he would become the head of an army training unit or something like that. He was brilliant at languages and I thought myself that they would certainly discover this and make use of it. Perhaps it would not be too bad having Daniel as an army interpreter. We all trained ourselves to think like this and stop minding so much. Daniel was not his mother, I reminded myself. He knew what he was about. Give him time and he would sort himself out.

But of course time was exactly what he did not have. As soon as he finished his training Daniel was attached to the 2nd Battalion, the Scots Guards. He reported there for duty at the end of March 1982. Before he did so, he came home and I had him all to myself for one day during this visit. He had grown again. He hardly grew at all until he was seventeen, then he put on a tremendous spurt and in a year shot from five foot seven to six foot. And in the army he had grown broader and heavier and squarer in the face, so that altogether he was transformed. I feasted my eyes on him and openly admired him and felt quite shy of this *man*, my grandson. I thought he was cheerful and more relaxed. Certainly he smiled more. He talked a lot, about his daily routine and his friends – he seemed to have made several good ones straight away, which surprised me – and about his superiors. He told me how hard the training had been but also how revealing it was about his own abilities. He said the army was not at all how I imagined it and I said I was glad to hear it. Vanessa came to collect him and hung on his arm and said wasn't he handsome. I refrained from grandmotherly banalities about the possibilities of some girl snapping him up as a prize, but I could not help thinking this. As he left, I felt happier about him than I had done for years. However much I loathed his being a soldier, it seemed to agree with him, and that was the important thing. I knew from my own children that such contentment cannot be faked and should be valued above all else. Daniel was content and I did not cavil at that contentment.

When the Falkland crisis first began to rear its monstrously misshapen head, I hardly noticed. I have always, to my shame, been a lazy reader of the hard news in newspapers. My eye runs lightly over the front page and I always turn to the features and reviews. So I knew nothing of what was happening, and even less of the significance for

Daniel, until the middle of April, when the seriousness of the situation first impinged upon my consciousness. That was when I read somewhere that Mrs Thatcher was calling a War Cabinet meeting. *War*, I thought and wondered where I could have been living not to know we were on the point of war. I began, like most people, to sit up and take notice. It seemed scarcely credible to me that we had sent a ship laden with troops to defend islands which were eight thousand miles away. I could not believe it and yet it was happening. I had a dreadful argument with Mark over it – he was exceedingly jingoistic in spite of his essentially pacifist outlook – and only stopped attacking him when he suddenly made some reference to hoping Daniel would not be involved. I lost interest at once in the rights and wrongs of this ludicrous war. 'What do you mean?' I demanded, in a bad-tempered way I expect, impatient as ever when I thought people were being stupid. Mark shrugged and said war was war, war required soldiers, Daniel was a soldier. I felt an awful weakness at the base of my spine. 'But he is only eighteen,' I said. 'Don't be so absurd, they wouldn't send an eighteen year old, just trained. They don't even send eighteen year olds to Ireland, even I know that.' Mark hoped I was right.

After he left, I remember feeling that, if I believed in premonitions, then I was experiencing one. But I did not and I do not. All I was experiencing was the normal fear and dread everyone recognizes, when someone they love might be in danger. The fear was real, that was all. I struggled all that week to keep at bay that kind of mawkish thinking of which I had always been ashamed – visions of Daniel on a troop ship, Daniel under fire, Daniel dead, Emily weeping, funerals . . . *Stop it at once*, I ordered myself. When Emily arrived in a state nearing hysteria, I was harsh with her because her outward condition reflected my own inner one. She rang me at the beginning of May to say Daniel's regiment was being sent to the Falklands. I clung to straws: because the Scots Guards were going, it did not mean that Daniel was necessarily going, especially as he was only eighteen. What a fool I was. This, it seemed, was real war and needed young blood. Daniel was in the contingent of Scots Guards who departed from Southampton on the QE2 on May 12th 1982. He was not even allowed to come and say goodbye, fortunately, I now think. He rang us up, his mother, his father and me. I could hardly speak and was at my brisk and impersonal worst. I repeatedly said, 'Take care,' in my haste not to say bitter things, like now he would see what the army was really about. Platitudes were safer. I told him to keep a diary and said I would write to him, which seemed to please him, though he said he would probably be home before my letters got there. As soon as he put the telephone down I began a letter to him, feverishly, impetuously, as I had once done to Oliver. In the morning I tore it up and sat in the sunshine, and wrote another much more suitable one. I was unable to persuade Emily to do the same. Instead, all thoughts of dancing quite forgotten, Emily spent every day devouring the newspapers and sitting transfixed in front of the television. It was the worst possible thing to do. She tortured herself with accounts of the terrible conditions our soldiers were enduring. She read of the freezing cold, of the exposure cases, of the torrential rain, the snow flurries, the nights and days spent lying motionless in sodden sleeping bags, the hours spent slogging over the bleak, rocky hillsides laden with equipment and weapons. She read, she watched and she wept. In vain, I pointed out that Daniel was still living in luxury on the QE2, but she shook her head and gripped her handkerchief tighter and would not be comforted. She said I could not possibly know how she, a mother with a son at war, felt. I, she said, had never known such suffering. From May 27th, after Mrs Thatcher had announced in the Commons that the British Forces had begun their assault, Emily never left my flat.

At the beginning of June, I forget the exact date, HMS *Sir Galahad* was bombed at Fitzroy, soon after the Scots Guards landed there. Emily was hysterical. When, some two days afterwards, pictures of the *Sir Galahad* survivors appeared on the television screen, she started screaming and drumming her heels on the floor in a frenzy of distress. As they showed a survivor being rushed away on a stretcher, with his bloody stump of a leg stuck horribly and pathetically in the air, Emily started shouting Daniel's name over and over again. We were all there, all the family, gathered together in a ritual of fear in my sitting room, all the family sitting stupidly in front of that hateful screen. Rosemary jumped up and turned the television off, but instantly Emily leapt up and turned it back on. 'You're a masochist – don't be so cruel! Rosemary shouted, but Emily ignored her. She sat with tears streaming down her face, only an inch or two from the screen upon which flashed a relentless sequence of images of tired and wounded soldiers. Emily could not possibly have recognized anyone. All she could have seen was a jumble of light and shade. After that, she would sleep only on the floor in front of this television set. I placed food in front of her, as if she were a sick dog. I went about my normal day, suffused with pain, and Emily passed hers moaning and shivering on the floor, saying over and over again that she could not bear it.

On June 12th, the 5th Brigade, Daniel's brigade, moved into position. On the 13th, they fought a battle, the battle of Tumbledown. On the 14th, Argentina surrendered at Port Stanley. But for the Butler family it was too late. Daniel was killed on Wireless Ridge, the day before his nineteenth birthday. Our family was devastated. I cannot —

*

Yes, they were. *We* were. As usual, when Mother has real tragedy to record, she does not exaggerate nor does she display, thank God, any ghoulish tendencies. She doesn't go on to describe at all the hell of Daniel's death, just that stark announcement, for which I am grateful. And her rage was our rage, rage more than grief for a long, long time. Blind fury with the government, personal hatred for Mrs Thatcher with her own dear son safely piddling about in civvies, terrible anger towards every flag flying anywhere in patriotic support of Our Boys in the Falklands. I actually went to a debate in the House of Commons and had to be forcibly ejected from the Strangers' Gallery for screaming abuse during a speech about these 'regrettable deaths' being necessary. It was a relief, my screaming I mean. The release was wonderful. I enjoyed being manhandled and kicking and yelling all the way down the stairs, enjoyed the hard grip of the three men it took to get me out. I didn't in the least want them to be understanding afterwards, which they were. I would have liked them to despise me, not pity me. They offered me tea, but I rushed onto the pavement outside and sat and cried in the middle of the traffic. It didn't do any good, it was no release in the long run. Nor did it help to go to St Paul's in July, the day of the Thanksgiving Service – how *dared* they give thanks – and stand outside catcalling all the dignitaries who went in. It took me ages to reach the stage of acceptance. Mother got there first. Emily said it wasn't surprising, she was 'only' Daniel's grandmother, but then I was 'only' his aunt and I was in pieces. I think Emily was so obsessed with her own suffering that she acknowledged no other. She had the pitiful arrogance of those whose pain is so great they cannot conceive anyone else can know what they mean. Emily was at the centre of a maelstrom of sorrow whose ripples spread out to touch every facet of her life – nothing else existed. She shut herself up, in a dark room, and the smell of despair curdled my stomach when I walked in. Mother said to leave her. It was necessary, she said, that Emily should embrace her grief like this, there was no other way, nobody could help her. In the end, she would achieve her own personal catharsis. She spouted some poem at me about 'Tired out we are, my heart and I', and said that was Emily, tired out emotionally. Mother was wise, but she was wrong about Emily. Em didn't achieve anything as poetic as catharsis. She simply exhausted herself, that was all. Then she crawled out, bitter and crippled, and found herself an unfortunate survivor. The only thing that helped, marginally, the only thing that restored her to any kind of sanity, was going on that awful trip the guilty government arranged for the relatives of the dead, to the Falklands I mean.

Why the hell I went with her I do not know. The mere thought of it appalled me, it was a horrible, revolting idea. I'm not sure how it all began, but I think Em and Mark got a letter from some army official saying that they would be entitled to go, if they wished. They definitely got a letter asking if they'd like Daniel's body brought back. Whether the two were connected, or even whether it was an either/or situation, terrible thought, I can't recall. But Em latched onto the trip at once. Mark would have nothing to do with it. I think he was disgusted by Emily wanting even to consider it, but then he was pretty disgusted with her disintegration, anyway, especially because of the way it affected poor Vanessa. As far as he was concerned, Mark would have settled for a decent burial and monument. He wouldn't have been satisfied with nothing of this kind, or if his son's body was left to rot on some hillside, but then that wasn't likely to happen. The army wanted some ceremony too, so Mark would not in any circumstances have gone, with or without Em, and the only other serious candidate for the depressing post as Em's companion was Mother. If Em had asked her she would have gone, hating every minute and violently opposed to it but she would have gone. Luckily she wasn't put to the test. Em didn' ask her, or Celia, the obvious choice surely, she asked me. I thought hadn't heard aright. I only just stopped myself in time from saying sh must be crazy, why me, I wouldn't even consider it and neither shoul she. The enormity of her request so paralyzed me that I found mysel nodding acquiescence like a dumb idiot. And that was that. It was by far the weirdest trip of my life, positively macabre. There were 535 of us, flown out in two British Airways jets. Most of us were women, a lot of them dressed like Em in a collection of black, fiercely funereal garments. Em even had a black veil – she said she didn't want to look at the others or to be looked at by them. It was extremely embarrassing and also hideously funny, in its own terrible way. There were a surprising number of children, even babies, on the trip and naturally to them, or at least to the younger ones, it was all exciting and thrilling. They couldn't contain their own high spirits and, anyway, why should they have done so? We played games on board the Cunard liner (to which we transferred after our appalling seventeen-hour flight to Montevideo in Uruguay). There was a sort of Bank Holiday atmosphere as children ran shrieking round the decks, enjoying it all. Emily hated them. Other people smiled sadly but indulgently. Not Emily. She shut herself up in our cabin and only came out when the Falklands came into sight.

They were a surprise, the islands. Like everyone else, I had this image of them being bleak and grim, with a barren and intimidating coastline. I imagined the islands as colourless, but with black rocks, like landing on the other side of the moon. But they were not like that at all, not then. It happened to be a pleasant, sunny day – it was early April – and, as I hung over the rail with most of the others, my first glimpse of this battleground I had learned to hate was beguiling. The coastline that arose from the calmest of blue seas was soft and even pretty, a blurred impression of greenery and gentle blue hills. As we drew closer, everyone fell silent. The little whitewashed, red-roofed houses clustered round the bays looked so friendly. Fear and hate were dispelled. The islands, at that distance, had a charm that was almost shocking. It didn't last, of course, but I remained grateful for that first impression. It helped me cope with what followed, with the shabbiness of it all. Port Stanley was a dump, squalid. Someone had thought up this insane scheme which involved us in lunch with 150 local families who wanted to show their gratitude. My God. Emily was not the only one who stalked away in disgust, from the handing out of commemorative plates and posing in front of Union Jacks in Falkland tee-shirts.

The war memorial, to which we made our pilgrimage in due course, was on a treeless hillside above Blue Beach. We climbed up the hillside, some carrying wreaths of poppies and lilies, to the cemetery. This was a circular corral, about fifty feet across, enclosed by a wall. The sun lit the honey-coloured stone tenderly. Inside, there were 14 gravestones set in four neat rows. I was disappointed that these monuments were made of granite, glinting wickedly above the violently orange marigolds planted all around. Granite. Solid, enduring, hard and cold inside the warm, pretty sandstone wall. I stepped forward when my turn came and read the inscriptions. Daniel Butler 1963–1982. Dear Christ, so short a life. Then, I cried too. I don't think Emily noticed. I don't think she noticed anything at all. Later, when I mentioned how crudely cheerful the marigolds had seemed, she looked at me in amazement and said, 'Marigolds?' as though I was deranged. I don't think she heard the wailing tune of 'Praise My Soul the King of Heaven'. Just as well. Nor did she hear any of the prayers. 'Be with them in their sorrow, support these families in their suffering, oh Lord.' Emily didn't hear a word. The Last Post, which echoed plaintively round the bare hills beside us, rising above the distant throb of helicopter engines, went unnoticed by my sister. Her suffering was so terribly evident I think it first frightened, then angered, others who were suffering, too. They avoided her. In any of the shuffling gatherings in which we found ourselves, as we were politely herded to this place and that, Emily and I had an empty circle around us. Even the wild geese – oh, where was Celia? – even the geese flying overhead seemed to avoid us.

We shared a cabin, naturally. It was pretty spartan and cramped, but that was irrelevant. We had to spend quite a lot of time in it while we were there. Em wouldn't eat or sit with the others, and though this made me cross, I felt there wasn't much point in having come with her in the first place, if I wasn't going to be with her literally, so I stuck it out. It was the first time in our whole lives that I had ever spent any length of time alone with Emily. We were not strangers to each other, not even figuratively speaking, but we were certainly not intimates. But intimacy was what she seemed to fear, which was why she'd asked me, I suppose. Celia or Mother would've driven her crazy with their fussing. I was quite surprised when another mourner – no other way of referring to them – said how alike we were, even before she had been told we were sisters. I couldn't see it myself, and pointed out that I was dark and Em fair, I was tall and Em smallish, I had brown eyes and straight nose and she had blue and a decidedly snub nose, and so on

'Oh,' this woman said, 'I didn't mean the actual features, it's more the expression, you've got the same expression, the same way of holding your heads and looking at people.' Considering Em was shrouded in a veil worthy of Greta Garbo, I thought this uncomplimentary to me, to say the least, but maybe there was something in it. I knew I *did* feel some connection with Em, as I didn't with Celia, but that connection was Mother, Mother in us both. Where Em reminded me of Mother I felt connected to her. I felt no kinship to her other than that. And when we spent that time together, time that seemed an eternity because of the peculiar circumstances, I discovered there was not as much of Mother in her as I had always thought (and been envious of). It was not simply that Em's wallowing in grief was the antithesis of Mother, but the much more complex matter of the way that Em related every damn thing to herself. I suppose I am trying to say it was her supreme selfishness which distanced her most from Mother and made her almost intolerable to me. I tried not to quarrel but I did, regrettably, have one outburst on our second day.

We had been round the battlefield – so called, though by then hard to imagine as one – for the third time and then we returned to our quarters, where we were asked if we would like some hot soup or coffee. Em said no, she wanted nothing, she was going straight to bed. I said could they send some soup to me. When we reached our cabin and Em lay down as usual on top of the bed and closed her red-rimmed eyes, I asked her why she had refused the soup so curtly. She in turn asked me how I could bear to think about soup, about any sort of food at all. She, Em, would never be hungry again. I tried at first to keep my temper. I said I was tired, that I felt depressed and low and needed something to put some life into me. Em laughed, an awful, hard, false little laugh, and said that was how she liked to feel, low. It was what she was, what she would now always be. The idea of *soup* – the stupid laugh again – *soup* making her feel she had some life in *her*, just showed the difference between us. Then I burst out. I said she was fucking right it did. I said what it showed was that she was utterly and completely self-centred and that she was proud of it. I told her not to give me any shit about my not understanding, that I understood only too well what she was doing. She was making Daniel's death into a cast-iron excuse for giving up on other people. I told her Daniel would have absolutely rejected her way of grieving, that he would have wanted to see some of the bravery and compassion Mother had showed in her time. Then Em sprang at me, she jumped off the bed and rushed to where I was sitting in the chair, and shrieked that Mother could not have even begun to experience what her love for Daniel had been like, that, if Mother had felt that way for our father or Jess, she could not have carried on as she had done. She said she didn't *choose* to be like this, that she couldn't be anything else, that she felt totally empty, that her life was now meaningless. I told her to think of Vanessa, who needed her so much. And then, I know unforgivably, I said she was exaggerating her love for Daniel, that like all children he had grown away from her and died a kind of death a long time ago, and that what she was mourning was her own failure and disillusionment and general unhappiness: Daniel's death had just brought all this to a head and the sooner she faced up to it the better. She said, 'I will never speak to you again'. And she didn't, not directly. Not until Florence. Extraordinary, but true. Even when I instantly and sincerely apologized and pleaded with her, she would not relent. But I had definitely achieved something. Em returned from the Falklands in a new mood entirely. It was not a matter, either, of anything fanciful like having laid a ghost to rest. On the contrary, she clung to Daniel's memory fiercely and still does, but at the same time she did what people always tell you others will if you upset them sufficiently: she pulled herself together. What she pulled herself into may have been a shell, but it was preferable to the jellyfish mess she had been up to then. 'Emily seems very composed,' Mother said, with satisfaction when we returned. She had no idea then how composed.

*

— Mark married again soon after Daniel was killed. The wedding was in August and Vanessa came home with me afterwards. It was, of course, a very quiet wedding indeed, in a register office, with only about twenty people at the luncheon afterwards. Daniel's recent death cast a pall over everything. Voices were subdued, smiles tentative. One's heart could not fail to go out to Caroline, Mark's new wife. She was a nice girl, shy and quiet and a little pathetic in her eagerness to please. She was only twenty-five to Mark's thirty-eight, but somehow that seemed fitting. I have forgotten how they met but it was through work: Caroline was an aspiring accountant, just over her intermediate examination. They seemed eminently suited. It touched me that Mark had introduced me to Caroline originally as 'my friend, Penelope Butler' and not as his ex-mother-in-law or his children's grandmother. He also touched me by asking me to tell Emily he was going to marry again. They hardly ever met. She would very probably be appalled that Mark could contemplate marriage when his son had 'just' died. In her twisted way, she would see it as a kind of treason. So I told Emily that Mark was to marry again and to whom and where and when, and I told her Mark thought Vanessa should live with me while he went on a long honeymoon. If she came to me, she would have company and a change of scene and it might stop her becoming depressed. 'Depressed?' shrieked Emily. 'Don't be silly, Vanessa doesn't know what depression is, she hasn't a clue, but, yes, take her, I don't care, whatever Mark thinks, what does it matter, anything.' I suppose I looked as pitying as I felt, because then she shouted at me not to look at her like that.

Emily did not come to the wedding, not that she had been expected to. Not many first wives would do such a thing, in any case, so it was in no way abnormal. But Emily's spirit as well as Daniel's hung in the air. Mark's mother and I exchanged glances at one point and we knew we were both thinking of Emily, so beautiful in her white satin dress, so utterly and completely radiant in her love for Mark. Caroline could not compare with that. She was an insubstantial moth to the remembered glory of Emily as a bride. And Mark, who on that day twenty years before had looked distressingly young, was not to Caroline the trembling lover he had been to Emily. He was a tired, even bowed figure, brave and worn, full of affection for the girl at his side, clasping her hand fiercely, but without passion. Or so it seemed. Only Vanessa lifted the heart, standing not behind the couple being married but, at her father's insistence, upon his other side. She wore red, the colour Rosemary had always looked best in, and, though she was slightly embarrassed, her smile was the one purely happy sight in that dull room. She liked Caroline. She was glad about the wedding, glad too to have the chance to be glad about something. At the luncheon she was exuberant and carefree, the only one drinking her champagne with zest. And Mark was so proud of her. His little speech, quite moving enough because of his brief and restrained reference to Daniel, became unbearably so when he turned to his daughter and said she was, quite simply, the joy of his life. We all stood and toasted Vanessa who blushed and beamed and kissed her father and there was no more loving picture in the world —

*

Pause for special effects. Some soppy music please and dim the lights. 'No more loving picture in the world . . . ' Oh dear. It just sounds so good and it wasn't. Everyone was so tense, so jumpy. Nobody really knew how to behave or relate to each other. Mother goes on and on about Vanessa adoring her father and how wonderful he was to her, but it isn't like that. Certainly, they love each other, but Mother implies, without actually saying so, that there were no problems, and there were and are. Vanessa and Mark are not easy together. They are not spontaneous together. At the wedding they were both shying off each other like startled deer. Their embraces, their kisses, which Mother so loved seeing, were in reality acutely painful to witness. They were neither natural nor convincing. They were a performance. Not that I want to throw doubt on their love for each other, but it's not an enviable sort of love. It was that raw, agonizing type of which so much family love is made and if that's Mother's idea of a loving picture she can keep it.

*

— Vanessa came home with me and Rosemary and Celia. We flopped in the garden and wondered aloud how many weddings we had been to. Our particular family contingent was always so small, I remember complaining, and Rosemary mocked me for wanting to be flanked by seven sons and their seven brides and their forty-nine offspring. 'You're never going to make it, Mother,' she teased me and I said ruefully that I would settle for the few I had —

*

I did *not* say anything of the kind – '*teased* me' indeed. She makes me sound so vacuous. I don't tease Mother, the very idea is monstrous. How can she employ such a word to describe my attitude? All I did was make a plain statement of fact. I thanked God our family was small. That's all, and it is different entirely. Why put in all that totally invented inane remark about seven sons and so forth? Why on earth

…es she barley-sugar everything? But I can't correct every single silly …mark she makes.

*

… the wrong thing to have said. The atmosphere changed, I …member, and none of us asked what the others were thinking …cause we all knew. And just as we began to rally and to realize that …e must not upset Vanessa, Emily arrived. We could not believe it: …e had been so adamant that she wanted nothing to do with any of … that day. But now she stood there at my door, defiant and …bellious, saying she *supposed* it was all right if she came in, she …asn't banned or anything? As soon as she was seated with a drink in …r hand, she began her bitter remarks, one after the other, addressed … all of us in general. She said what a fine family we looked, what a …edit to the Butlers, how smart, how colourful, my goodness me how …phisticated. She invited us not to spare her the details, to tell us how …e bride had looked and what the speeches were like and the flowers …d did Mark look his usual noble self? Had we eaten our fill, were …ere any nice people on Caroline's side, had the champagne flowed, …d Grandfather Perrit make a fool of himself as usual . . . do tell, she …id. Vanessa made a halting start to oblige, not fully realizing how …gry, how murderously angry, her mother was. And Emily turned …r big blue eyes upon her and parodied rapt attention and oh really-…l until the rest of us felt slightly sick. Then she asked us if we could …ess what she had done and, when nobody replied, because we all …ere afraid to, because we suspected it was a trap, she said brightly …at she had been to church. She had gone back to Pinner and sat in …e church where she had married Mark. She asked us if we didn't …ink that was a pretty touch, imaginative, sensitive and *neat*. …anessa said, 'Why, Mum?' and Emily mimicked her. 'Why, Mum, …hy, Mum? Ask your clever grandmother or aunts, *they* know why.' …said quickly that all I knew was that she was being melodramatic …d that I wished she would stop it. Rosemary chose that moment to …y she had to go. She kissed me and Vanessa and said goodbye to …lia and to Emily. Emily ignored her and Rosemary smiled with …hat looked like, but she assures me was not, enjoyment. Celia left …on after, as it began to get dark and, as she did so, the telephone …ng. It was her father for Vanessa.

Emily and I were left in the shadowy garden, hardly able to see each other's face. In the background, through the open window, we could hear Vanessa laughing. 'Don't pass your unhappiness on, Emily,' I dared to say, 'please'. She snapped at me not to be so stupid. I wanted badly to ask her why she had come at all but feared it would prove a fatal enquiry. Instead, I chose a less contentious question, the one she wanted me to ask, about why indeed she had gone to that church if, as she claimed, Mark now meant nothing to her. She was very pleased to have the chance to answer me. She had gone, she claimed, to try to remember herself, because she was unable to. Everything that had gone wrong had, she was convinced, begun at the altar. She had gone to sit there hoping that she would be able to call up some psychic power out of the air that would put her in touch with the person she had been. She wanted to understand her own former madness. I told her she had not been mad but perfectly sane which was perhaps not the case now. 'I'm a suitable case for treatment as they say, am I Mother?' I replied that she was quite capable of treating herself. She had the necessary mental equipment and should use it. She had to decide what she wanted from life and then she had to achieve her ambitions as far as was possible in an imperfect world. I pointed out that all her family were in a position to understand the meaning of disappointment and frustration and even despair, that she was no special case. I told her to think about us and to stop treating us as privileged creatures, with lives untouched by sorrow. I told her to draw strength from us, not beat us off. She said, 'As Rosemary would say, I don't know what the fuck you're talking about.' Then Vanessa came back.

During all the weeks Vanessa stayed with me, Emily only came to my home twice. Vanessa went to see her. I wondered, incredible as it seemed, if Emily was now 'not speaking' to me just as, absurdly, she was not speaking to Rosemary. My horror at this stage of affairs grew with each week's absence. It was not possible that any child of mine could descend to such depths. But, no, Emily had not cut me off, she was, said Vanessa, teaching dancing once more, five classes a week now, and just very, very busy. She would come soon, when things were easier. I sighed and schooled myself to bide my time. Maybe Emily needed to be cut off from us, as Rosemary had once. She was having delayed adolescence in so many ways, acting now as she had never done in her teens. I must be patient. But when I took the long view I felt troubled. Emily was thirty-eight. How could she rescue herself, how could her family help her? Like some gloomy biblical text, I found myself reciting, 'There *is* no help except in hope.' And faith. That was the worst part: I had lost my faith in Emily. I was deeply ashamed to confess this to myself, but I had to. For ten years now I had made excuses and I could not go on doing so, I could not accept that Emily was rotten at the centre. Every day I expected miraculous trans-formations in her. I really did fantasize her appearance on my doorstep sunny-natured and warm and happy, as of old. I could not get used to this disgruntled, hard, miserable creature who wailed about her misfortunes continually. It was *not* my child. Somebody had substi-tuted another woman for the one I knew to be my daughter. Emily had changed. It was perhaps as simple as that. None of us can guard against change, inexplicable and fundamental. Adult children are not small children grown to adulthood, they are an entirely different species. What I had to do was start all over again, from a different vantage point, and make my way by infinitely tedious degrees towards Emily now. If I could do it, if I had the heart as well as the mental and emotional strength. Because if I did not attempt it, Emily was dead to me and I would never know her again. Emily needed her family. We had to —

*

I used to spend many an idle hour wondering if I gave a damn about Emily, or about Mother and Emily. Could I say, I don't give a shit if I never see my darling little sister again? Probably. On the other hand I would never *not* want to know about her, should someone wish to tell me what she was doing, nor would I deny her support or help, should she ask for it. Big of me. Family solidarity goes that far, at least, which should please Mother. But Emily was more than a bore, she has been a menace these last few years. She has caused such misery and I grew tired of taking into account what might be called extenuating circumstances. Mother, just because she was her mother, writes about it being her duty to 'move towards' Emily again, and so forth, but I feel no such sense of duty. There *is* no sisterly duty. It doesn't exist. If there is no natural sibling affection, then, as far as I'm concerned, there is no responsibility. Parents, children – possibly. But I'm not going to be addled with the blood is thicker than water shit right across the board.

And what also comes into it is that I know nobody in the family needs to feel any guilt about our Em having had a raw deal. Sometimes you look at a family and you think, well, poor little bastard, fancy being number two in *that* hierarchy, what pissing awful luck. You look at two handsome, clever brothers and then at the third pathetic, stupid, ugly bugger and you think how cruel that he was the runt of the litter and the others had creamed off the best genes, and you think, well, I hope they have the decency to make it up to him. Or you get one member of a family being given some amazing opportunity denied to the others and it's so unfair that again you feel the need for some touch of justice. But it wasn't like that with Em. She wasn't in any way more disadvantaged than the rest of us and in many ways, which Mother has more than proved, she was actually the best off. Celia was the least advantaged, if anyone, though not by much. Mother shouldn't feel guilty about Emily, it should be the other way round. Yet that was the extraordinary part – Em appeared to feel no guilt at all, neither about Mark nor Mother nor Vanessa, all three of whom she has hurt so badly. Well, Mark found Caroline and seems happier now than he ever was with Emily, except during their first few years together, and Mother is strong, she can bear anything, but as for Vanessa, my God. The sweetest, happiest, nicest daughter anyone could have and Em ignores her. She seems angry with her all the time, just for being what she is, eighteen now, pretty, lively, popular. And Vanessa still loves her, as any fool except Em could see. She carries Em's misery around with her like an albatross slung round her neck, stinking to high heaven, which is why my greatest triumph has been to get her right away to educate herself in America.

I once gave Vanessa Philip Larkin's poems *High Windows* for a birthday present and I put a bookmark in the one that goes, 'They fuck you up, your mum and dad'. I hoped the last verse, about getting out as soon as you can, would provide a hint as to what she should do. Far from being impressed at my insight she was rather hurt and bewildered – it was far too sophisticated for her then. But after the last two years of her mother's unremitting hostility, I think she finally saw there was indeed a message there which made sense. She did get out. Mark has paid for her to do some drama course in California, and it sounds as if she is enjoying herself tremendously and the curse of Emily is lifting. When she comes back, she may be better able to cope. It would be

etter, really, if she thought of Mother as her mother and not as her
randmother, if she could somehow skip over Emily.

*

– to help her. And we tried. But even now I can make no sense of
mily's life. I have tracked it back to where she is now, I have followed
rst the straight, sure, untroubled road up to her wilful marriage and
very crooked turn during and after it, and I end up in a jungle of
ontradictions. Emily is lost, hidden somewhere under the dark, ugly,
reen plants of resentment that she planted herself, her feet trapped in
ne squelchy mud of apathy. But she took herself there, of that I am
ıre. Those 'tricks of fate', those blows of 'bad luck' that she blames,
ave really nothing to do with her plight now. It is wrong of her to act
s though she was plucked out of a rose garden and hurled into this
ark jungle. She was not. She cannot accuse 'fate', only herself. And
¬here did that self come from? From my own dark past? From my
1other or father, from genes we do not even know about? I do not
elieve it. Nothing angers me more than Emily's *bitterness*. And I do
ot know how it will end. The thought of her staying as she is for
nother thirty years or more makes me frantic. None of all the feelings I
ave written about here can match the horror I feel now at the prospect
f any of my children standing still, without taking charge of their own
ves and moulding them before age sets them irrevocably in a pattern
ney hate. Emily does not realize, as I do, where she is heading. Worse,
ne does not care. I, caring for her, am useless. I think she feels I am a
eparate entity and have been for many years, but I have only to see her,
owever briefly, and I know that all those feelings of distance could be
anished, if she willed it, in an instant.

June 26th

Rosemary dropped me off outside Buckingham Palace, after we had collected the tickets for Florence and had a quick lunch. Too nice to go home, a waste to be in the centre of London and not to do something. Walked round to the side of the Palace where the striped awning over the entrance to the Queen's Gallery made it look festive, as though a circus was there for a day. Lingered over the photographs lining the corridor leading to the pictures. Charming photograph of Queen Victoria with three of her daughters and two of her grandchildren. The Queen positively beaming at her family. Another, taken at Osborne, showed her at the centre of an enormous family group, forty at least, and there she was grim and forbidding. The smaller family unit is so much more congenial. Lovely photographs of Alexandra, Edward VII's wife, as a young mother with a child on her back – so carefree, a real mother. It gave me such pleasure to see her pleasure in her child. The paintings, when I reached them, very disappointing. Too many Georges. No really attractive family groups. On the stairs was Hendrik Gerritsz's painting of Charles I, Henrietta Maria and Charles, Prince of Wales. How pathetic it was, the Queen so far away from the King and the child unhappily balanced on the table. Why did he not stand with them? Why did she not hold the child? So solitary and nervous she looked. It was a relief to pass on to a painting of Caroline, Princess of Wales, cuddling Princess Charlotte. How affectionate she looked, her arms so fondly and protectively round her baby. She knew something about mothering. Surely. Came out into bright sunshine and crowds. Walked up the Mall smiling at all the tourist families walking towards the palace, all stepping out smartly to see the Queen. Such an air of optimism and buoyancy in that area of London whatever the state of the world. What I would really like to do is be there for a state occasion, a Royal Wedding say.

*

Wouldn't she just. Could Celia surprise us? I have my evil suspicions bu they're best kept from Mother – mention the merest hypothesis to her and she'll never let it go. Celia, I *think*, is getting heavily involved with somebody in the office, a widower with two children. That's all I know about him, except that his name is Leonard. She asked me to go with her last week to choose a dress because Leonard had invited her to a concert. I said I hadn't been in a dress shop for centuries and advised her to ask Emily, but she said Emily had told her she was too busy. Christ, as if I wasn't. I almost told her to ask Mother, then, but stopped myself just in time – how can any of us *ever* have thought Mother had any dress sense? I went with her to the only place I could think of that might suit, Wallis, in Oxford Street. I hate shops, new pristine clothes. Celia wanted a dreadful pale blue dress with a white collar so it was as well I went. I persuaded her into a black jersey number. I told her to think of herself as voluptuous, not fat. Now she needs her hair cut. Oh, what a caring sister I am. And where I showed it most was in Florence. If Mother turns out not to have appreciated this in these next pages, I'll be livid. At least there are some good photographs of us in Florence which I took myself with a timed exposure. I might do worse than make one of *them* the basis for this wretched painting I've promised her.

*

— should write about Florence in my diary, indeed, I have done so. It is too near in time to have any place in this, in this whatever it is. (Not, at any rate, what it was meant to be.) Yet already it seems a long time ago, the events of that holiday seem to have crystallized and stand glittering in my mind. I return again and again to those five short days and I see such significance in them. I cannot just abandon them to anything so slight and informal as a diary. I do not want the mists of time to obscure my memory. I want to test myself, when everything is sharp and not in doubt, when I have no need to feel, as I have felt so often during this account, that I am not being absolutely accurate.

But, all the same, where can I start? With the shock I suppose. I never expected to see Emily and Celia. They were waiting at the airport. I thought they had come to see us off. They were standing at the checking-in desk, looking defensive and awkward, and Rosemary said, 'Meet our travelling companions.' What did I say? A string of platitudes. They knew I was appalled. I knew they knew I was appalled. I could not think how it was going to work, how I was going to cope with the three of them together, how they would cope with each other. In the aeroplane we sat in twos, me with Rosemary and the others together. Even that seemed favouritism. I could not help whispering to Rosemary 'why' and 'how' and 'do you think it was a good idea?' and I think she was annoyed —

*

Annoyed? I was furious. Dear God, the organization that had gone on, the arse-licking persuading my sisters, especially Emily. And then Mother stood there, face frozen, and couldn't even applaud my little coup. I almost said fuck this, just go home, you two, you win, she doesn't like it, I must be getting senile and sentimental to imagine this would be the best present she could ever have.

*

— that I had not jumped up and down with joy. She snapped, irritably, that she'd thought it would be a lovely surprise, all the family together. I was so ashamed. I sat there feeling tense with a double anxiety: that this gathering would be a disaster and that my obvious horror had hurt everyone. Rosemary read a book. I stared out of the window. At Pisa airport we stood, Emily, Celia and I, and waited for Rosemary to hire a car. I tried to apologize to Celia and Emily, said I had been so taken aback, that I was thrilled, it was just that it took time for me to adjust. In the car I sat in the front with Rosemary, who was driving. I hardly dared breathe, sensing Emily's resentment (as ever) and Celia's discomfiture. It was a relief to have to concentrate on directions. We found the road and headed towards Florence. I tried some timid remarks about the countryside, the unexpected lushness of the scenery. I felt I was talking to myself. At Cisterna, we turned off the autostrada. Rosemary handed me another map showing the location of our hotel. I wound the window down as we climbed up a shady road. The scent of orange blossom flooded the car, releasing from all of us exclamations of delight. Our rooms had balconies and overlooked Florence. The city sweltered in a heat haze, the hills behind vague, like a smudged crayon drawing.

Rosemary took charge. We showered and changed (except Rosemary), then drove immediately to the Ponte Trinità, eager to begin sightseeing. Rosemary marshalled us, two by two, down the long

200

medieval streets to the Piazza Signoria where a band was playing. The arguments began. Rosemary wanted to go on with a quick preliminary tour, Emily to sit and eat icecream and listen to the band. I dreaded being asked to decide, but Celia nobly did this for me. She persuaded Emily to walk just a little further, pointed out that we could do a circular tour and return to the square and that she could eat icecream as we walked. (Celia has always been so good with Emily, as she was with Jess.) On we went, along the narrow streets, until the Duomo suddenly loomed above us, grey and white and pink, like a magnificently ornate wedding cake. Emily said she was hungry. She yawned, often and noisily, as Rosemary read aloud from her guidebook. Celia said, when there was a break in Rosemary's information that maybe we ought to eat before the restaurants got too crowded. This we did. Rosemary took us to a small restaurant in the Via dell'Acqua where we ate pasta, five separate courses of pasta, at a big communal table. How normal we must have looked: a mother and three grown-up daughters. Did anyone notice how furtively we looked at each other, all watching and waiting —

*

They would have had to be bloody fools, if they didn't. I was so grateful for that restaurant, that particular type of restaurant. What hell it would have been to be sitting, just the four of us, at one table. I don't think I could have stood it. Mother was rigid with apprehension. Emily didn't speak at all, lowered her head over her plate for most of the time or else sighed and looked at her nails. Celia kept making inane remarks, such as I wonder what the Italian for serin is – serin apparently being the name for a finch she'd noticed in the grounds of the hotel. What a good time we were not having. But it helped that everyone else, the other ten at our table, were certainly enjoying themselves. Of course, being Butlers, we didn't do anything so vulgar or natural as to talk to them, but our glacial indifference didn't inhibit our eating companions at all. Sod this lot, I thought, and replied with enthusiasm to the questions asked by the young American on my left. A nice boy. Back-packing his way round Europe, so what's new. Disappointed in Amsterdam, thrilled by Venice, next stop Greece. He'd been picked up at the station by his companion, a brash young American girl at some language school for a year. She was quite funny, told us how impressed her parents were when they came to visit and she said 'ciao' to someone in the street. They cheered me up. When it was time to shepherd my miserable little crew back to the car I was sorry.

*

— Sunday, we went to Fiesole. We walked round the outer streets looking for a viewpoint. There was the delicious smell of many dinners, cooking. Everywhere we saw gardens with roses and lavender, so English. We passed a nunnery, saw a nun robed in white as we stared through the closed iron gates. Emily stared, holding the bars tightly. She was furious when Rosemary unkindly said 'Oh my God, you're not — '

*

— feeling a sudden vocation, Emily, are you?' So? What the hell was wrong in saying that? It was a *joke*, all right? A sarcastic joke but still a joke. She looked so bloody ridiculous mooning over that nun. You could see what corny thoughts were going on in her little head. Herself in white, driven into a nunnery by grief over her dead son. What a pretty picture. How satisfactory. And Mother stood there, looking so anxious, it was ridiculous. Emily has this awful cloying quality. She irritates the hell out of me.

*

— lunch at Mario's, outside, in a large, paved garden, under an awning. Beside us was a child with long, black hair, one bright red carnation tucked behind her ear. Opposite her, clearly adoring her as he attacked an enormous hamshank of a bone, was her father. Again Rosemary read her guidebook aloud, describing the Etruscan settlement that had once been in Fiesole. Emily hummed steadily, a device Rosemary had herself used long ago. She and Rosemary still did not really talk to each other, everything was channelled through Celia or me, every remark oblique. Celia and I exchanged frequent glances of condolence. Such an ill-assorted trio of sisters, their only link being me. And I can no longer hold the balance, as I ought. I veer first towards Rosemary, then towards Celia, then to Emily. I approach and withdraw like the tide on a particularly rocky shore. I want them *one at a time*. I am worn out with them together. By the end of that lunch, of two hours of brittle non-conversation, I was drooping. Rosemary asked if I was tired, Celia if I was hot, Emily if I was bored . . . No, no, no, I said to all of them. How could I say I was exhausted with the effort of keeping them together? That I wanted to plead with them: we are a family so act like a family, *please*.

On the way back to our hotel, we got caught up in a procession in a street on the south side of the Arno. We parked the car, with difficulty, and stood on a corner watching. Hundreds of men marched past, all in magnificently colourful fifteenth-century costumes. They marched slowly to the sound of drums and trumpets, their step measured, their feet heavy in strange, clumsy shoes each with leaf-shaped patterns on the front, like the dancing shoes of a giant child. We stood entranced, our backs pressed against an ochre-coloured stone wall. Four English tourists lost in a tradition they knew nothing about. Four women watching the men go by and marvelling. Even Emily was spellbound. And when the last row of men had passed, for a fleeting instant we were as one and the first timid hope arose in me. We turned to each other and there was that flash of recognition —

*

Now wait a minute. All that happened was that this amazing procession – incongruously, it turned out to be after a football match – was enjoyed by us all. It shut us up, knocked us out, made us forget ourselves. What Mother so poetically calls a 'flash of recognition' was a simple reaction to what we had seen, that momentary pause, a sort of group relaxation that you can get in a theatre after a good play. It was a physical thing, meaningless, soon over. We caught each other's eyes but what Mother calls recognition was the exact opposite, none of us *saw* each other. We were dazed, smiling stupidly, a little drunk on the unexpected thrill. Why Mother says it made her hopeful, I cannot imagine. What did she hope? That we would get on better? I hoped no such thing. I knew we wouldn't, not ever, not so long as Emily fouled things up.

*

— which all families can have, when suddenly a mutual understanding passes between them. I did not expect it to last, and it did not, but that did not matter. I needed the reassurance that it was still there even though buried under layers and layers of mistrust.

On Monday July 2nd, we went to Siena, by car, a long, interesting drive through Tuscan countryside. Nobody spoke but by then I had grown used to the silence, it was not so oppressive, I did not feel the need to try so hard to break it. Siena was a revelation. When we came upon the great bowl-like piazza, we were literally stopped in our tracks and once more I felt that surge of unity. The colours made us reel, the purples, oranges, greens of the banners and flags draped over every wall to celebrate the Palio were so startling in that dull yellow setting, like icing on an already rich cake. We sat and drank coffee beside the boarded-off race-track, from which the dust rose in puffs of powder as it was prepared for the afternoon by the race officials. The boards round it were strengthened, the sand watered, and across the fan-shaped cobbles the crowds spread out, in search of seats for the great event. After an hour, Rosemary insisted we left, before the city grew too crowded. Emily said why did we always have to rush about, why couldn't we just go on sitting in the sun. Out came Rosemary's reasons, all excellent: we had no seats for the race, we would get hopelessly penned in and see nothing . . . Emily trailed behind us, sulking.

We lunched in Coll 'Alta, a fourteenth-century hill town we hit upon by accident. We sat in a courtyard and ate salami, thick and peppery, and warm bread and tomatoes. We drank a good deal. The sun, which previously had not found its way into the courtyard, suddenly blazed down from behind the high wall. We basked in its warmth, drank wine and ate peaches. I prayed that Rosemary would not move us on, that this harmony, a silent harmony, would come to a natural end. And it did. On the way back to the car, walking four abreast, I noticed Emily's arm lightly resting on Celia's waist. Celia's arm was linked through mine and my hand held the little basket with some peaches in it. Rosemary's hand was next to mine, helping me carry the basket. Flesh touched flesh —

*

Here we go again, romanticizing. It *was* a pleasant lunch which was lucky, considering it began as a mistake. My mistake of course, all mistakes on that trip were laid at my door. I was the organizer, the leader, there to take all the responsibility, to carry the can. We'd been heading for San Gimignano and took a wrong turning and, once we had done so, I damned well wasn't going back, not at one o'clock on a blazing hot day. I *made* them eat in that funny little place, so it was a miracle it turned out well. But not that well. Mother writes as if we pranced off into the sunset wrapped in each other's loving arms, all best-friends-and-jolly-good-company. Not so. There was a modicum of contact, where before there had been none. Nothing significant really happened till the next day.

*

— the Casa Guidi: 'I heard last night a little child go singing/'neath Casa Guidi windows . . . ' To me, the house where the Brownings had loved and lived was of great fascination. Not so to my daughters but they were prepared to indulge me. We had great trouble finding the place, though. We found the Piazza San Felice easily enough, but there was no sign to tell us which house, of the many identical houses, had been the Brownings' home. When we did locate it, the disappointment was acute. They left England for this? So bare, so bleak and forbidding. Where was all the light and sunshine, the beautiful view of my imagination? Not here. We went through a heavy double street door into a cold, stone hall and up echoing stairs into a dark hall on the second floor. No light, no sunshine. The apartment the Brownings had occupied was extremely dreary, the drawing room vast and ugly with its apple-green walls, the bedroom austere and grim. We were shown Pen's christening robe, unbelievably white and fresh and modern. 'She worshipped her son,' the custodian told us. Emily's eyes filled with tears. She was allowed to touch the robe and held it against her cheek. It was Emily, not I, who insisted on going to the cemetery once the custodian had mentioned it. She said that the English cemetery was —

*

It was a terrible mistake going there at all, that's what it was. One of Emily's morbid, mawkish fancies which ought not to have been given in to. Why did I ever agree? Because once Emily had got this stupid idea in her head, she would have gone anyway and Mother would have been too worried if she had gone on her own, so it was better to drive them and get it over with. The cemetery turned out to be a glorified traffic island, not at all the spooky, mysterious place Emily had doubtless longed to see. It was just an oval piece of land, round which scooters shrieked and cars screeched. There was a sort of wall round it, with an

205

iron railing fence and a gatehouse and double gates. The gates were locked. We shook the gates, as instructed by the custodian at Casa Guidi, and eventually the caretaker came out. As soon as I saw her, fat and squat, a memory came back to me of Grandmother Butler – she was the absolute image of her and just as terrifying. When she'd hobbled over to the gates she stood glaring at us, shaking her head and pointing to her right leg which was heavily bandaged. Money changed hands through the bars of the gates and then, with great reluctance, they were opened. We were in a hurry to get away from her but she insisted on taking us into the gatehouse and on flogging us a booklet, and even then she wouldn't let us go until she'd made it absolutely plain that we only had twenty minutes because she was closing.

The graves were horrible. No flowers, not much greenery, too much gravel and remnants of burnt-out candles. And all the time the hideous noise of the traffic. Elizabeth Barrett Browning's tombstone was ghastly, a great ugly lump of granite, dwarfing the more modest tribute to Holman Hunt's young wife. Quite without thinking, entirely naturally, surely, I said I thought this the least atmospheric cemetery I had ever been to. Imagine a poet being buried here, I said, the least romantic place in the world. Her sensitive soul must be turning in its grave. I prefer the place where Daniel is buried, I said, all windswept and wild and remote. Mother went white. She frowned and shook her head at me and pointed surreptitiously to Emily. I turned away, exasperated, so I did not see Emily collapse. When I turned back again, ready to urge them to go, she had her arm hanging over the little iron railing round the sarcophagus, her fingers straining to touch the nearest marble column upon which it rested. Her red skirt spread like a bloodstain over the plaque recording Elizabeth Barrett Browning's name. She was sobbing, her tears falling fast and furiously. I watched fascinated. By this time Celia was on her knees, awkward as ever, her arm round Emily's heaving shoulders and such a *silly* expression on her face. Oh, they made me tired, all that play-acting. To my immense relief I saw the caretaker waving at us, scowling, pointing at her wrist, upon which sat an incongruously large wristwatch. When none of us moved she began to walk up the path towards us, her sore leg dragging. Still Emily bawled. I knew I had a contemptuous expression on my face and struggled to get rid of it. The caretaker reached us. She stood looking down at Emily. It was impossible to decide what she was thinking. Finally, she shook her head and said something, which of course none of us could understand. But she patted Emily's shoulder with her heavily blotched hand and made clucking noises which passed for sympathy. Feeling this hand, Emily at last got up, her face destroyed. With Celia on one side and Mother on the other she trudged off towards the gate, with me following, fuming. What a performance Emily made of grief. She hadn't a shred of pride. Call herself a Butler? And it was too absurd, that level of grief so long after Daniel had been killed. To think that Pen Browning's christening robe had provoked such emotional extravagance. It angered me. I felt instinctively that it also angered and repelled Mother.

*

— was fascinating but it was not. Going there was a terrible mistake. I cannot bring myself, yet, to write about Emily's hysterics. What so shocked me was my own detachment. There was my child, giving herself over to the wildest abandoned grief, and there was I, repelled by the bathos of the scene. Instead of thinking my poor, poor Emily, oh my darling, oh my love, instead of cradling her in my arms, there was I, her mother, thinking only how *can* she be so absurd. I stood there, pawing at the ground with my shoe, a good yard or so away from her. Not wanting to touch her, only wanting her to stop. Why did I not empathize with this, my most unhappy of children? I had nothing to give her, I had long since become tired of giving. The mother-love, which once had seemed limitless, had run dry. I had reached a stage where I found myself judging as others judged. I stood there, stiff and useless, wishing someone would take the pathetic, shuddering *mess* away. To me, the one who had conceived and borne and succoured and reared her, the one who had known every crevice of her body, who had adored every fold of her skin and hung on every word she uttered, to me, she was, if not a stranger, strange. It had gone, all the intense closeness, all the 'love for love's sake'. My thoughts and feelings were no longer twined and budded about her as wild vines a tree —

*

Jesus Christ. I hate Mother when she's pretentious. She'd come out with yards of Elizabeth Barrett Browning's stuff in the car on the way to the cemetery and we'd all put up with it without complaint. It's rather like her so-called passion for Art Exhibitions, this passion for poetry. It doesn't convince me, I've never felt it came naturally. She can spout endless verses. The ones she recited in the car were the *Sonnets from the Portuguese*, with those lines about 'If thou must love me, let it be for nought except for love's sake only', and 'my thoughts do twine and bud about thee, as wild vines, about a tree', but her approach is purely sentimental. All she wants poetry for is what she wants art for: to see herself in. She ignores the important fact that maybe the poet or the artist had a little more on their mind than how useful they could be to one Penelope Butler. But, anyway. If it helped Mother, I suppose that is what matters. Did it help her? Not much, I shouldn't think. She was as shaken as Emily when we got back to the hotel. Both of them went straight to bed, even though it was only seven o'clock and light and sunny. Celia and I had a sandwich and some wine and sat moodily in the garden. 'I think I'm beginning to hate Emily,' I said. 'She puts Mother through hell.' Celia said Emily put herself through hell and Mother joined her. 'We haven't any children,' Celia said in that virtuous, pompous way she has always had. 'We don't know what it's like. We're not in a position to judge.' I told her to shut up. We were in the most perfect position to judge.

*

— but instead could find nothing to attach themselves to, except memories of what had once been. I had to leave Celia to attend to Emily. I went to bed and lay in the darkened room, first weeping and then thinking. Not really thinking, meandering over Emily's life. In the end, to my surprise, I slept and stayed asleep until eight the next morning.

I awoke feeling cheerful. Not even thinking of the day before robbed me of this cheerfulness. Nothing was resolved, but I felt as though it had been. It was our last day. Instead of dreading the thought of seeing Emily at breakfast, I welcomed it. She met my eyes, quite at ease herself. She told us, all of us, as she drank her coffee and ate her croissant, that she was sorry about embarrassing us the day before. It was not really the christening robe or the stone coffin or even thinking about Daniel, it was being suddenly overwhelmed by the thought of love getting wrecked all the time, of it never really lasting. She said it depressed her to think of it never being safe to build on any relationship: either it went wrong or it was taken away. If it had been late at night, we might have responded, but the busy dining room of a hotel at nine in the morning was not conducive to philosophical discussion. Emily's own tone had been matter-of-fact and we replied in the same vein. Yes, Rosemary said, life in that way was bloody silly but there were other things in it. Yes, said Celia, Emily was right, but on the other hand it was amazing how there not being any point did not stop one being happy sometimes all the same. And what did I say? I said, I think – it is much harder to listen accurately to oneself – I said —

*

Not much. That was the surprising thing. Just up Mother's street and she fluffed it. Deliberately? She looked very composed that morning, just how I like to see her, not all taut and anguished, as she so often can look. She wasn't stiff and distant either, another fault. No, she was in good form, smiling, reasonably relaxed, managing to keep that over-personal look out of her eyes. I'd dreaded her crawling into the dining room looking harrowed and soulful and fixing us with that plaintive, suffering expression she adopts at her worst. She was at her best. So was Emily. Her eyes bore clear evidence of the previous day's crying, but she wasn't sullen and she didn't look too droopy. I didn't feel I wanted to yell at her to straighten up. She even smiled. And she spoke directly to me for the first time in two years. What more could I ask?

Mother, then, said very little. After I'd come out with my platitude and Celia had come out with hers, Mother left a pause and said she didn't *quite* agree. Love – a little cough and fiddling with the teaspoons – love, of any kind, was worth having for its own sake, for its own length of time. She said it might always get wrecked, or come to an end in one way or another, but she didn't see that this wiped out what had existed. Then, there really wouldn't be any point, and now what were we going to do on our last day, mm?

*

— that I thought they were all being too greedy, actually expecting love, or loving relationships, not to be wrecked or ended, that they were forgetting what such love had been like. I hope I expressed myself better than that. For some reason, not just the location and general circumstances, I did not want the conversation to continue, so I changed the subject and asked what we were going to do on our last day.

We packed and drove into Florence and went straight to the Uffizi. Rosemary said there was not time to see it properly. She took us up in a creaky lift to the top galleries and marched us to Room 25. We stood in an obedient row and looked at Michelangelo's *Holy Family*. Emily shifted restlessly from foot to foot, Celia looked surreptitiously at her watch. After a long, long five minutes – does Rosemary never sense other people's boredom or does she not give in to it? – we were led off to see Botticelli's *Primavera* and *Birth of Venus*. The colours shone, the white almost effervescent. The galleries we passed along were cool and dark, windows opened to catch the morning breeze. Pleading fatigue, I was allowed to sit on a window seat and wait while the others plunged into more rooms. Emily soon joined me. She was dreamy that morning, as she used to be when she was a child. I was afraid to speak as we sat there on the wooden seat, with so little distance between us. I did not know what I wanted to show but I knew I wanted to show something.

In Pisa, where we returned the car, we climbed the leaning tower as all good tourists should. I had imagined something raw and concrete, besieged by the ugly flotsam of tripperish commerce, but the feeling was like that of a cathedral close. The grass was lush, the stone of the buildings white. I climbed, not intending to at my age, in bare feet. The indentations of the steps fitted smoothly. At the top, breathless, a little giddy, I felt exhilarated, as I lurched around the platform. The vast Tuscan plain was spread out below us and, all around, the hills enclosing it were blue and mellow. The sun blazed down hot on our backs as we stood, holding hands for balance and safety, staring down.

Home. They all came back with me, to my flat, before going their separate ways. I hoped, fervently, that none of them were going to their own homes thanking heaven their duty was done, the ordeal over. Rosemary was the last to leave. I found myself thinking, as I watched her drive away, that her life was the one I understood least. It should not have turned out as it has. But I am not sure why I think so —

*

Holy shit. If anything keeps me blaspheming in this vulgar childish way it is Mother coming out with things like that. So my life should not have turned out as it has. That kind of crass comment makes me so exasperated I want to scream. It would be no good tackling Mother head on, no good dragging her to that page and pointing a finger at those words and saying what the fuck does she mean? And really I ought to smile, not rage. Mother's never-ending desire to analyze, synthesize, is surely funny. She is nearly seventy. I am twenty years younger, but I know what she claims to know, but does not – that you can't take a life and organize it as you would like to. Life, all lives, defeat such strategy. Luck does exist, or fate, call it what you will, and it upsets all attempts to impose a pattern. Mother is stubborn, she won't acknowledge that. To her, luck is a dirty word, very similar to all those other four-letter words of mine she finds so objectionable. She persists in believing that it is how people deal with the things that happen to them that is important. So my father's death, Jess's death, they were not allowed to be bad luck. Mother would not let herself say, 'I have had bad luck, there was nothing I could do about it, my life was ruined.' To her all tragedies must be surmountable. She wants to move us around like counters on a board, up the ladders, avoiding the serpents. It can't be done.

What she means about my life not turning out as it should have done – as she would have ordered it – is that I never met what she would have regarded as 'the right man'. She has not, for a long time now, been so stupid as to envisage me floating down an aisle in white tulle, or even prancing up register office steps, but she is puzzled that I have been unable to make a deep and lasting relationship. She thinks it's my fault, just as she thinks Emily's misery her fault. She won't have it that it is just bad luck and nothing can be done about it. Nothing. Mother secretly believes I haven't tried hard enough, or that there is some fatal flaw in my make-up, to which I haven't been sufficiently attentive. But she's wrong. There isn't. There's no flaw, and I've tried as hard as I could. Mother saying this simply shows how empty her admiration for my very wonderful career is. She doesn't admire it at all. She sees me as 'unfulfilled', like Emily and Celia. We've all let her down.

If I had had children I wouldn't have been like Mother. Well, of course I wouldn't have, everything is different, I am, so are the times I live in, everything is – it doesn't need a genius to see that. But I wouldn't have been so determined to understand, I am sure. I think I would have accepted the inevitability of *not* understanding a very great deal. Mother has crucified herself in her efforts to understand us. There's been something quite manic about her desperation to know all. This information she boasts about possessing is in reality quite insubstantial. She knows very little. Here I am, at the end, so far as I can see, of her ramblings, and they've added sweet fuck all of any real value to my existing knowledge. I don't believe that if I had read them properly, every word instead of selected bits, I would be more enlightened. There *is* no enlightenment. Memories, accounts of things past, hardly illuminate the present at all. A stranger could take in any of us from the street and learn as much about us from meeting us in the here-and-now as Mother has done in all her solemn summaries. With *my* children, there would have been no charting of courses. I would have known I was flinging them into the sea by giving birth to them, and that where they were carried to could never be my concern. If you don't realize that, then you shouldn't have children. It isn't as simplistic as saying parents have to let go – they won't have much choice about that in the long run – it's that they have no hold in the first place, they only seem to have. If I were a parent that would be such a relief to me.

It's odd that she chose to *file* these 'private papers'. Odd, too, that she should call them Private Papers. She's always had an obsession with scribbling. One of my earliest memories is of her sitting, writing away, and, when I'd ask what she was doing, she would say, 'Just getting organized.' What a funny thing to say to a child. She's always kept a diary, of course, we all knew that. Once I asked if I could read what she had written on one particular day, and she let me. I was so embarrassed at how crashingly boring it was, I never asked to read it again. Her diaries are all in books, thick hardbacked diaries, terribly important-looking, and then there are her scrapbooks and commonplace books, stacks of them. But these papers are in a file, one of those box files, quite large and solid. They're unnumbered. They are not even in the correct order and the diary entries for this six months, the six months or so she was writing all this, are copied from her actual diary and put in the file. What do I make of that? Maybe Mother thinks that in the future her precious descendants – and Vanessa had better come up trumps soon, or there won't be any – will want to know what humdrum things she was doing while engaged on her magnum opus. All those pathetic accounts of trailing off to art exhibitions – God. She knows fuck all about art, not that I want to patronize her, or think you should only go and look at paintings if you're qualified to – I certainly don't think that – but I've always been deeply suspicious of her 'love' of exhibitions. It's always seemed false, to me. All these dreary accounts of trotting off to gaze at the Pre-Raphaelites, or whatever. Why? She doesn't really look at the paintings. She uses them as mirrors. What she wants to see is a reflection of herself, of her thoughts and life. Every damned exhibition is scrutinized for mothers and daughters, every painted portrait anxiously examined for fancied likenesses. It's pathetic. So is this ending. No more papers after those about Florence. She must've stopped writing about the end of last July. How bloody feeble. I feel cheated, frustrated. It isn't fucking fair of her to end with a whimper.

It occurs to me, all the same, that maybe she didn't see it that way, I mean, didn't stop because she was trailing off with nothing left to write. Maybe she came to some sort of conclusion (I *must* try to think this out coldly and calmly, to *think* instead of just reacting all the time). What Mother was doing, in the year 1984, was attempting to write an official family history. In the process, she was shredding everyone's evidence but her own. Her purpose, the one she began with, was to show what a very wonderful family life we Butler girls had had, yet we had failed to take advantage of it. She began to feel indignant, bitter and disappointed. Her teachings had gone wrong: she had taught us that anything said against the Family is obscene. Life, she taught us, has no meaning, no joy, if human beings do not nurture each other, with tenderness and care, and the Family is where they should and must start. That was how she began. I don't think it's how she ended.

I think that she stopped writing after Florence, because on that holiday she realized she'd got it wrong. According to her own definition we, the Butler family, are a striking example of that institution as a failure. We are not close or intimate. We stand alone, each of us, without that vast network of relationships she craved for us. We are three strong, assertive people to whom the Family is not sacrosanct. But what Mother came to appreciate was that perhaps this does not amount to failure on her or our part. We've only 'failed' according to her original image, the image I shall paint, to please her, when I tackle this painting I've promised her. Looked at from another point of view, we are successes, surely. So Mother became unsure of her own ground and wisely stopped. Her last lines were 'It should not have turned out as it has. *But I am not sure why I think so.*' Exactly.

Oh, fuck it. What the hell does it matter? Maybe she hasn't finished, anyway. Any day she could be resuming her narrative for all I know. Now what do I do? Tear it all up? All these papers, plus my contribution? Wipe out everything and, when the time comes, destroy the famous diaries, scrapbooks and so forth? But if I did that, I'd be as domineering as Mother, I'd be attempting to dictate history, too, I'd be acknowledging the power of the past, and I refuse to do so. And, if I did tear everything up, nothing's been gained. I want some profit, I want there to have been some point to all this. Really, I have no alternative. A confrontation with Mother would do no good, it would be simply too ridiculous. I'll leave her precious papers where I found them, but I'll leave my own too – it's only right that my perspective should count for as much as hers. Her papers are no longer private. I have made them my property, I have walked all over her memories, opinions and judgements, I have been a trespasser without mercy. And I have absolutely no regrets. In the unlikely event of Mother discovering and objecting to what I have done, I shall defend myself with pride. I shall say 'Mother, I am *your* daughter.' Then we'd see what the fuck she makes of that.